# North

Brian Martin was appointed MBE for Services to English Literature in 2002. His literary criticism has appeared in the *Spectator*, the *Times Literary Supplement*, the *Financial Times* and *Literary Review*. He lives in Oxford, where he spent most of his career as a teacher. *North* is his first novel.

# Brian Martin

# *North*

PAN BOOKS

First published 2006 by Macmillan New Writing
an imprint of Pan Macmillan Ltd
Pan Macmillan, 20 New Wharf Road, London N1 9RR
Basingstoke and Oxford
Associated companies throughout the world
www.panmacmillan.com

ISBN 978-0-330-45256-4

9 8 7 6 5 4 3 2 1

A CIP catalogue record for this book is available from
the British Library.

Typeset by Intype Libra Ltd
Printed and bound by Mackays of Chatham plc, Chatham, Kent

Visit www.panmacmillan.com to read more about all our books and to buy them. You
will also find features, author interviews and news of any author events, and you can
sign up for e-newsletters so that you're always first to hear about our new releases.

*Keep thy servant also free from presumptuous sins,
lest they get the dominion over me: so shall I be
undefiled, and innocent from the great offence.*

PSALM XIX

I FIRST MET HIM WITH HIS MOTHER, a short, neatly turned out woman, precise in the detail of her dress, but not obviously conscious of current fashion. She was an American, divorced, who lived and worked in England, her ex-husband living in the US. Hence North was Anglo-American, and, in contrast to his mother, was at one with the contemporary fashion of a certain reserved, refined youth cult. He was not ordinary, and that made him tantalizing. There is always something dangerous about the extraordinary: you do not forget Hitler's awful dictum, 'Extraordinary geniuses take no account of ordinary humanity'.

You might have described him as ahead of his years. There are few seventeen- or eighteen-year-olds who show poise, self-confidence, sophistication, an ability to converse with their seniors of twenty, thirty or forty years on apparently equal terms; but North possessed these qualities. He dressed with a dark elegance that matched his long, straight, jet-black hair: a dark blue button-down collar shirt, well-cut black trousers, no jacket but a long black loosely fitting gabardine coat, and laced black leather ankle boots, a modern equivalent of George boots which were worn in the Army with Number One Dress. His fashion tastes were expensive. His underwear, as his lovers were to tell later on, came from Emporio Armani or Donna Karan.

Yet his mother, for all her attention to detail of dress and the catch of perfume, *First* by Van Cleef and Arpels, did not convince you that she could afford his wardrobe. At once there was an anomaly, a mystery. Here was this young man, elegant,

1

athletic, good-looking, with high cheekbones and even teeth, finishing his career at a British school, but who was incongruous in relation to his mother. Perhaps the black emphasis should have forewarned those who knew him, his friends — acquaintances, admirers and lovers.

The term 'lover' I use advisedly, for when I got to know him it became clear that he had enjoyed these since he was about sixteen. First he was taken advantage of — that is to say, seduced — but quickly he assumed control in his relationships: his learning curve, as they say, was fast and steep.

Were he here now, he would weep at my telling you this, an invasion of his privacy, a revelation of his professional secrets; but then he would relent and see the point, smile and laugh with me. Subsequently, he would plot his revenge, and with superb adeptness and cool objectivity observe my discomfiture and downfall. Despite the intensity of his habitual warm accolades at greetings and partings, the disturbing heat of those kisses on both cheeks, the steely intent of his vengeance would be implacable. I have noted it well. He is not here: mine is the freedom. I use it not in revenge, but because I know we have to recognize his reincarnations.

He was exceptionally attractive. We all yearned for him, to be with him. He had a terrible magnetism: his presence, conversation, animation were seductive; most fell under his spell. I shall tell you about some of them. Some knew they were subject and enjoyed their slavery; others knew their obsession, hated it but could do nothing. Fortunately, my reading, my theology, gave me suspicions and put me on my guard. My experience told me to take care.

Evil exists in many guises. Sometimes it is outright and apparent, blatant and brutal: it has no ambiguity. You know it, and either succumb to it or fight it immediately. Sometimes it is subtle, deceptive and alluring: it is enjoyable, sweet and sensitive, and only with the passing of time does it turn sour, the nectar transform to venom. Eventually I came to think of Milton's Satan when I met North. I was always delighted to see him, as were all his other friends, but after a few minutes I would think of Lucifer driven out of Heaven to become Satan in Hell, yet still possessed of those ineradicable angelic qualities which made, and still make, him attractive and irresistible. It was necessary in any relationship with North to fear what you might be up against, and most people simply did not know his true nature: they were naïve, uneducated, ill-informed, lacking that clear view of the continuous war between good and evil. The 'immortal garland' of true virtue cannot be run for 'without dust and heat'. Milton warns that we must all learn to recognize vice. We have to be able to consider it 'and yet abstain, and yet distinguish, and yet prefer that which is truly better'. In the case of DH Lawrence the voice of his education constantly informed him. Mine warned me.

At the school which we both attended, North to learn, I to teach, there was a smart young girl who taught History. In fact, she ran the department. It had been to her intense surprise that she had been appointed two terms previously. It had been a put-up job, so to speak. She had not much experience. Aged twenty-seven, she had taught in Africa for a year, in Uganda, on one of those years out when the young must feel that they are doing good. The school was run by a charitable trust and educated children from miles around. Some children walked to school from the countryside for two hours in the morning and repeated the journey back home in the late afternoon. Such eagerness and devotion for learning she was not to come across in the young sophisticates of the UK. British youth, addicted to football, fashion and the club culture, attended school for the most part with patronizing resignation. In order to maintain a sort of street credibility with her students, she cultivated a knowing air of contemporary culture from which in age she was not too distant. Yet cults move quickly and disappear with extraordinary rapidity: her esoteric Cambridge education and remoteness from the Ministry of Sound created certain solecisms which betrayed her to the young. To her colleagues she seemed to be trying too hard to keep up with her charges.

She was good-looking. Tall, athletic, shapely in low-cut, tight-fitting tee-shirts, she painted herself with artificial tanning lotions (sometimes the imperfection of streaking was noticeable at the back of her legs and she carried a top-up bottle in her shoulder bag). The cosmetic ladies of some of Shakespeare's quips came to mind. She was attractive and lively: long blonde hair, pony-tailed or sometimes in bunched ringlets, a pleasant, agreeable, smiley face, firm and even teeth. It was no wonder that her male colleagues were infatuated with her, and her sixth-form students alternated between satirical censure and perfect adolescent love. How could such a bimbette run a history department? After all, her predecessor had been a scholar in his own right: a Leverhulme Award holder, author of a monograph on European romanticism; this girl might have been a primary school teacher. She was infinitely beddable, even to inexperienced minds. Their imaginations ran like x-rated feature movies.

Needless to say, North stood aloof from the sixth-form discussions and private group conversations that occupied his contemporaries. He watched coolly and quietly, did what he had to do, and, with an air of both reserve and confidence, produced his work. When he asked his teacher one day in bright sunshine if she would like to have lunch with him, he did it with finesse and he clearly meant it. Others thought it a joke to try and lead on their mentors. They would have made the suggestion satirically, expecting a refusal, the polite brush-off. There was no mistaking North's elegant seriousness. It could not be turned aside. His invitation had its own magnetism, its own mystery. How could it be refused? That was it: he was so unusual in his attitude; he had a dynamic ability to make you want to get to know him.

Bernie – her proper name was Bernadette, which she loathed and hence the preferred diminutive – at once accepted.

'I'd love to. I'm not sure I should, but it would be great. We can discuss the Vienna Settlement, and, in any case, I can find out more about you.'

'I shall need some help with the next essay, you're right. But that is not the main idea. I should like to know more about you too. I'm not sure that you are all that happy here.'

North spoke with an easy informality, with a prescience intriguingly beyond his years.

'Where shall we go?' asked Bernie. 'I don't know the eateries too well. I usually eat in town.'

The school was surrounded by bars, cafés and restaurants. Over the previous four years, two of the streets that radiated away from the roundabout which lay before the entrance to the old city had regenerated thriving small businesses. There was a tapas bar, a Mexican restaurant called Chico's, a fish restaurant, a Chinese takeaway and three Indian restaurants, including a Kashmiri halal in the backyard of which butchery took place (it was constantly being visited by Environmental inspectors and Health and Safety Executive agents).

What was this handing over of initiative to North? He was supposed to be under her tutelage, but she was inclined to hand over decisions to her junior. That was his nature: to prompt this type of submission in small matters and, later, as we shall see, in affairs of great importance. Even I found it difficult to resist North's control. You had to deal with him on a permanent intellectual plane. It was necessary to approach him as if he were an opponent in a game of chess or bridge: you needed to remember his moves or the cards he had already played. If you did not, then you were lost.

'We should, I think, go to Quod,' he said. 'It is far enough away and large enough for us to be *intime*.'

At the same time as wondering how many times he had been there, whether he was aware of her fears of impropriety and what sort of life he led away from school, she agreed. She noted his faintly provocative reference to intimacy and decided he was being gently ironical. Later, when she remembered his comment, it sent a tingle of excitement through her and created an intense expectancy which she could barely tolerate. She knew Quod, and it would do nicely.

'That would be good. When shall we say? Tomorrow? Or the next day? I can do either of those days this week.'

She recognized inside herself an eagerness to have this proposed lunch, this liaison. Why put it off? She knew it must be innocent, but there was something strange about it, about him, about her ambivalent feelings to his approach. It was unorthodox, bizarre even. It had never happened before. Still, she had not been teaching long: she did not understand that her inexperience put her in danger. Her knowledge of history and literature should have shown her vicariously that she was in mortal danger. Only that morning she had discussed Sir Thomas Wyatt's great poem 'They flee from me that sometime did me seek' and yet she failed to notice the warning in the lines '... they put themselves in danger/ To take bread at my hand'.

'Why not tomorrow?'

'I'll be there first,' she said. 'I'll be waiting. Let's say half past one.'

She hoped to put him at his ease in case he would find it awkward arriving at the restaurant to find her not there. After all, he was only seventeen, almost eighteen. He acknowledged her consideration with a slight incline of his head, but it was inconceivable that someone with such poise could ever find himself in company and at an embarrassing disadvantage. This gesture of hers was simply one of many misjudgments about him that she was to make. The idea of him being gauche in any adult situation was absurd. At the bar, or at a table in the restaurant, he would take his place and immediately look as though he was meant to be there by some sort of natural law. He could make conversation with anyone who was near him. Again, it was as though he had some extraordinary gift that set him aside from his classmates and put him on equal terms with his seniors. In any case, she should have remembered, he had made the first approach: he had asked her to lunch.

He raised his head, looked her straight in the eyes, fixed her shifting, downward gaze and held it with a surprising, shocking intensity.

'I look forward,' he said.

Disturbed, apprehensive, she walked towards the common room and her colleagues. Had they been watching, they might have thought that some aspect of his work was being discussed. She felt uneasy, excited. She could not explain to herself or anyone else why she felt that way. She felt a trace of blush appearing on her cheeks and checked herself: how absurd to be so affected by one so young. At the same time she knew that she could talk about her feelings to only one person: not to her closest friend, nor to her mother, certainly not to her father; she knew she could only sort out her feelings with the one person who had provoked them, and that was North. That in itself was confusing and, perhaps, shameful. The realization made her blush even more. How fortunate that the colour of her rising blood was hidden by her tan.

She went about her business preoccupied with thoughts of North, working on autopilot.

The following day it was fine and bright. I went for a walk, and round about midday I passed through the meadows and made my way towards the centre of town. Quod was on my route. Quite often I called in to read the *Financial Times* and take a coffee or a Campari and soda for refreshment. By the time I reached Quod it was twelve-thirty. I went in, ordered a Campari and sat against the bar, brooding over the *FT* with its bad news of the previous day's trading.

I had been there for a few minutes when the hotel manager, an old friend from another, smaller, establishment in the city, where he had also been manager, came in, noticed me and started chatting about this and that: the decline in the tourist trade, his luck in being able to employ students from a local catering school, his long working hours and the effect on his young family.

Quod was a smart place. It was mainly the ground floor of the Old Bank Hotel. Thus there was a dual operation: if you stayed at the hotel, you used Quod for meals, and Quod was open to the public. Alex, the manager, had overall responsibility for both. The entrepreneur who owned it, had converted the old Barclays Bank into a modern, luxury hotel, bar and restaurant. The rooms were very contemporary chic: lots of light-wood finish, brushed steel, glass and hard edges, a modern painting hung on every wall. Naturally there was television with satellite channels and computer terminals with broadband connection. The *en suite* bathrooms were Finnish-designed, lacking only a personal sauna. To use the current expression, the space was wired.

The restaurant was similarly designed, with huge wall pictures illuminated by the light coming in from tall windows at the front and back of the building. As in the hotel rooms, there was a hard-edge feel to the overall design. I wondered if, in the restaurant, the intention was to discourage you from staying too long. Yet it had its attraction, a clean, sharp, brisk atmosphere about it.

Alex was eventually called away by a receptionist and I studied the Lexus column, which mentioned a company in my portfolio. The news, though brief, was cheering: a contract had been secured to service and repair almost a million mobile phones for Nokia in the coming year. The shares had risen, against the trend, by three and a half pence to £1.21. As I digested this intelligence and thought idly of Dr Johnson's opinion that 'There are few ways in which a man can be more innocently employed than in getting money', I was aware of Bernie entering through the glass double-doors from the High. She looked gorgeous: very well turned out, nicely made up, her hair in tight tiny ringlets frizzed out, showering on to her shoulders. She had to be intent on making an impression. It crossed my mind that she must be meeting her bank manager, her wealthy godfather perhaps, her old college tutor, a future employer, or even her lover.

I remained unobserved by her, and I watched as she talked quietly to a waiter and was shown to a table. She clearly indicated that she would not order anything but wait for her lunch companion, whoever that might be.

It was not long, a few minutes, before a familiar, elegant, dark figure entered. It was North. Did he make an entrance? If so, it was not deliberate or obvious, but it was only natural, right, that he should be noticed. Heads came up from tables, eyes lifted to encounter this arresting youth who had just appeared. I knew him. One glance, indeed one sensory feeling that he was at the door, put me on my guard. I resisted mimicking the inquisitive or admiring regards of those lunchers who had noticed him and continued my scrutiny of the *FT*, but not before the quickest of glances had established eye contact with him. He acknowledged me with the slightest of nods and his eyes sparkled towards me for a moment. To tell the truth, it was disconcerting. He had no reserve or reticence. He did not care that I was witness to his assignation. It did not matter. If anything, I felt, it helped him to have me there. It made him perform better. I knew it: I felt his inspiration and his power.

He looked around the floor and saw Bernie, raised his hand in gesture of greeting and went up to the table where she was sitting. She rose and held out her hand. He held it, stepped inwards towards her, embraced her with his other arm and kissed her on both cheeks in the continental manner. There was no hesitation. This was his custom; it made no difference who it was, man or woman. The difference lay in how he performed the greeting: he could run the gamut from complete formality to implied passion.

I could see that Bernie was surprised, a little taken aback. She had not expected this familiarity, and North could make that accolade extremely intimate, charged with intent. It was like a text message that she could either respond to at once or disdain. She recovered herself and smiled with pleasure as he joined her at table. They sat sideways to my view. He did not point me out. He knew that he could make me part of a game, whereby he kept her in the dark about my presence and, more importantly, turn me into a voyeur. He enjoyed his power and he wanted to discover how I would respond.

We had great respect for each other. North knew I had no illusions about him, as I once had and as others in the restaurant now did. For him, I was Keats's sage Apollonius, a stern critic of his fabricated world '... do not all charms fly/ At the mere touch of cold philosophy?' But I lacked the power, or objective will to

10

destroy him. He recognized me as a neutralized force, a eunuch in his games of love, completely powerless, an impotent spectator. He relished his power – over me and over others. The people in the restaurant were captivated by this unusual, magnetic figure: he was constantly being looked at, when you might have expected Bernie to be the object of attention. He focused his casual charm on her. I could sense the grip he was exerting on her. I do not know what their conversation was about, but I can guess. He would have complimented her on her looks. Who instructed him in manners? Was it his American mother? Did he have some counsellor? How did he come by such charm? There is no answer to these questions except that his behaviour seemed to be innate. It was a natural part of him. There was no need for instruction, nor counsel. He would have asked her about her previous evening, where she had been, who she had seen. He would have discussed her colleagues and delivered perceptive judgments. He might, at her prompting, have touched on his academic work, but he would have glossed it and turned the talk back to more urbane and, for him, more urgent matters. He would not, for a moment, have betrayed a sense of urgency: nothing was allowed to ruffle the great composure he possessed.

I wondered how long I could go on watching this game of his. He was bewitching her, not obviously but subtly, and he, of course, knew it. It was intentional, calculated. I knew where he was heading. I almost felt that I should warn her.

In the end, I decided to continue my walk and make my way back to my study. I folded my paper and donated it to the bar. I could sense he knew I was leaving, but Bernie, deep in conversation and oblivious to all but North, did not notice me. I left at the back of the hotel, where the doors from its dining room give out on to decking which in the summer is covered with tables for *al fresco* meals. Through the car park, I made my way in to the mediaeval side street. Immediately, I felt a desire to go back. I wanted to be there with North and watch his manoeuvrings. At the same time, I knew that I should resist. Bernie was clearly trapped. The silk of North's web was beginning to stick to, and wrap around, his female prey. What was his design? What did he want? Was he just in need of diversion? I knew that the answer was not that simple. At this point, I did not know.

Back in my study, I brooded. I was supposed to be writing a lecture for a US visit to Cornell, where I had been invited to speak on CS Lewis. His concern with Milton's *Paradise Lost* has always fascinated me, and Lewis's conviction of the power of evil, an active force at large in the world, troubled me. Beware! The Prince of Darkness, the apostate angel. I had written the introduction, using Lewis's poem *On a Vulgar Error* as an anchor for my thoughts. It is a precise and shrewd poem, but at first sight a little enigmatic. In the end, what Lewis is saying shines brightly through: the poem is an elegant statement of what his life and work were all about. He researched the past, and all his writings are based on the accumulated wisdom of past ages, particularly as embraced by the Bible and Milton's *Paradise Lost*. 'So when our guides unanimously decry/ The backward glance …' they are wrong, even, perhaps, stupid. I intended to elaborate and illustrate this theme. Earlier in the day I had warmed to my task, but now could not see my way forward. My mind could not work out the sequence of what I wanted to say. Everything had become muddled. Naturally enough, thoughts of Bernie and North kept recurring. My mind flitted back to Quod and what might be happening there. A series of disturbing images haunted me.

I had watched North from a distance over a few years –

since he was about thirteen. He had been a dark-haired, silent boy who kept very much to himself. He exerted a certain sort of smooth charm even then, but his personality at that time was entirely passive: he kept from being noticed. It was in the sixth form that he emerged as an irresistible force, assuming very quickly a sophistication beyond his years.

The school organized art appreciation trips to galleries around the country, especially to those in London. We had close connections to two famous young artists, alumni of the school: one an installation artist who had trained at the Royal Academy, and the other, a pupil of Ken Howard, who now exhibits here and in the States. We had all gone off together to a show of the latter at Messums in Bond Street. North had been mesmerized by some dark landscapes.

When North was seventeen, Sam Burton, our art teacher, had set up a trip to Washington and New York. He found reasonably cheap hotels at which the party could stay. In DC he fixed special rates at a Holiday Inn but I preferred to stay at the Cosmos Club, which is in reciprocal agreement with my London club. I met up with the rest of the small party at the National Art Gallery, at the Phillips, at the Corcoran, and dined with them in the evenings in cheap restaurants.

On the last evening in Washington, the part-time art assistant, Sue, took most of the boys off to a cinema. Four of us did not want to go: Sam, North, Jenny, a delightful part-time drama teacher, and I decided we would eat out. In the end I invited them to join me for dinner at the Cosmos. Even then North was not out of place. Jenny was in her element. She was an extremely agreeable colleague, middle-aged, with a son and daughter of her own, separated from a well-off banker who travelled to the City each day. The idea of dining in the comparative luxury of the Cosmos, where she might meet some US senator, a movie producer, a famous academic who might be a

13

TV political commentator, some poet or novelist, appealed to her. Sam simply purred with pleasure: he was an affable, comfortable, well-padded, unflappable man, who enjoyed whatever turned up. He was a genial stoic: his motto, which he constantly repeated, was, 'I drink to you, and give you what you have already.' There was a hint of Juvenal about him but without the bitterness: his was a soft satire. North was quiet, unfazed. He had shunned the cinema visit to see some popular-vogue film with little plot and even less meaning. He was scathing about American films aimed at the mass market. Finding them cheap, culturally and morally, sensational and completely without value, he left them to others to enjoy. For him, the Cosmos offered a chance to observe, to watch the manners of a society he did not know, to absorb and learn. You could detect a purposeful concentration in his mind towards a part of his education. He accompanied us and conversed comfortably with us and was well satisfied with the evening. I warned him tactfully about drinking too much, linking the admonition with a joke at Jenny's expense. He understood, but clearly the warning shot was a waste of powder. His natural sense of place and occasion dictated how he should behave.

The evening was one of fragrances. Perfumes lingered in my senses long after we had parted. I recognized Jenny's heady perfume, Givenchy's *Fleur d'Interdit*, and I reckoned I could identify North's eau de toilette or aftershave as Balenciaga's *Cristobal*, which has a lasting, rich, musky miasma. Who gave it to him? Did he buy it himself? Everything about North provoked questions and, to satisfy your curiosity, you wanted to ask him about himself. Did his mother buy that perfume for him? Did he buy it himself? If so, how did he know what to buy? This polished, assured youth, who somehow knew how to behave in adult company, mystified those who were with him. He made you want to get to know him. It was easy to see how

Bernie could fall into his trap: the trap was honeyed. His victims fed on nectar gathered from the Elysian fields and were rarely able to look back. It was my theology that saved me. The godless found themselves in acute danger.

'Champagne?' I asked.

'Yes, please. What a treat and unexpected pleasure,' Jenny quipped.

'Sam. I know you are a beer man. Budweiser or champers? What do you think?'

Sam decided to have champagne. North was willing to float with the tide.

'I'll order Cristal if they have it.'

As it happened they did not, and we settled for some nicely cooled, refreshing Moët, which sparkled in our *flutes* like the glitter which occasionally shone in the eyes of North when some scheme was active in his mind. Jenny lifted her glass and toasted us.

'To us all! *Bon santé et bon chance, mes amis.* I love it here, and I am really enjoying myself.'

I was pleased for her. The last few weeks had been hard. Her son was finding it difficult to secure a career job having just finished at one of the new universities. He had studied catering management but was not keen on going into the trade. The trouble with vocational degrees is that they rarely fit you for anything different from their subject. I had told Jenny that I could probably recommend him to an acquaintance – my friend Alex, who at that time was running a small hotel in Oxford – but her son was not then interested. He lacked charm, kept his room at home in utter shambles, brought in no money, regularly emptied the fridge into his and his friends' stomachs, and was generally a boor. Poor Jenny liked her escape.

The first course came and went. We all had anchovy fillets

served with slices of avocado pear, two or three tiger prawns, some chicory leaves, a sprinkle of grated Parmesan and a garlic dressing. We had continued with champagne as the accompaniment to this course. The main course was much more traditionally American. Three of us ate steak cooked to varying degrees of rareness: North's was bloodily rare. Jenny ordered *poulet roti* with corn. I managed to find an excellent, mellow 1964 Chilean Syrah on the list which satisfied the demands of both the chicken and the steak. We talked about some of the paintings we had seen, the two *Repentant St Peter*s by Goya and El Greco, Cézanne's *Self Portrait*, Picasso's *The Blue Room*, the Singer Sargeants, the Whistlers, Renoirs, one or two of the American paintings. The one which had struck me was Winslow Homer's 1909 painting of a duck-shoot, *Right and Left*, the title alluding to the twin barrels of a shotgun. What a powerful painting: dominated by two birds, the one on the right, mortally stricken, plummeting towards the water, the other in frantic flight, leaving us to wonder if it is wounded or not. In the middle left of the picture there is a diminutive figure in the distance obscured by the smoke from the barrels of his gun, his boat emerging on the crest of a wave. The beautiful, marvellous ducks, one surviving, one doomed, are contrasted against the ominous background of dark sea waves. I made out a case for it as the best of modern American paintings. Sam agreed with me and talked about paintings which are on show in the small upstate New York town of Corning. Jenny had melted, by the end of our main course, into a resilient state of torpor, in which she found herself amiably agreeing with anything anyone said. North listened to Sam and myself and finally, with persuasive clarity, charged the painting with being too sentimental.

'I don't think that is quite fair,' I argued. 'The painting's purpose is to show the fragility of life in a hostile world. Not only are there forces of nature to be withstood, but also the marauder, man, has to be watched out for. I'd say there is no sentiment about the painting at all.'

'But look at the attitudes of the ducks. What plucks at the heart strings?' North replied. 'I don't go so far as to equate the picture as a highbrow cipher for flying ceramic ducks stuck on the living-room wall, but almost ... If you want threat and power, look at some of the nineteenth-century European artists, Blake or the dark Fuseli.'

North's views were not tentative. What he knew, he propounded with assurance. He argued without dogmatism and had a charming way of acceding to argument without giving the impression that he might have been defeated. You suspected that his retreats were tactical or, at least, that there was some covert purpose in his withdrawal from debate. I caught his eye and he fixed my glance. It was somehow disturbing, as though he were assessing means of control by delving deep into your soul. He turned to Jenny and smiled at her. She responded immediately and raised her glass to him.

'When were you here last, North? Do you feel that your roots are really here or on the west coast?'

'I was here as a very small boy, with my mother. But I feel I belong everywhere. I am at home here or in LA or San Fran. Naturally, for the moment, I prefer UK-side. That is where I feel at ease and at one with my companions.' He spoke with a soft, firm, liltingly musical Anglo-American accent, infinitely attractive. It was extraordinary that one so young could speak in such a way, with such quiet authority, that his listeners would want him to go on speaking and they to go on listening.

His last remark surprised me. I have already observed his aloofness. It seemed to me that he kept himself apart from his classmates. I had never seen him socializing with others. I imagined he maintained a studied distance from those he was forced to meet on a daily basis. Yet, I suppose he must have had friends. If so, I was not aware of them. Who were his companions? His private life was a mystery. I was not at that time his confidant.

'I love it here.' Jenny spoke with delighted enthusiasm. She was irrepressible. I always liked her for that quality of vivacity. She used her femininity to advantage. Her numerous love campaigns had earned her an accomplished flightiness. She teased us all, and those who were in her thrall in the affairs of love must have been in extreme difficulty knowing exactly how they stood with her. She avoided 'tear floods, and sigh tempests'. These were not part of her artful usage. She teased and entertained. I loved her for it.

'What will you do, North? You have so much ahead of you. I think you are already so distinguished. I don't mean in accomplishments, but in your nature and manners. I see you as some magnate in business, or even as some important politician.'

'I just don't know. We must wait. The time is not right for me to predict my fate. I am ambitious though. I do have my vision and premonitions. There is something special that awaits me.'

We all wondered. There was a silence, not awkward or embarrassed. We were all thinking and looking into the future. I recognized North's words as prophetic but, although a slight cold *frisson* ran down my spine, I had no idea what was in store for him, or for those of us who grew close to him.

We were nicely waited on by a plump black lady in black dress and white apron who was friendly and jolly without being over-familiar. She knew the form of the place, loved her job and respected the conventions of the club. I had chatted with her before, at breakfasts when she cooked over a spirit flame, on the spot, your eggs, scrambled, fried or as an omelette. Bacon, mushrooms, fried diced potatoes in plenty, stood by in heated tureens. You helped yourself. My dinner companions had puddings of ice cream and fruit, a lemon torte, while I preferred a Scotch woodcock as a savoury with which to finish the wine. We all took coffee, 'which makes the politician wise,/ And see thro' all things with his half-shut eyes', according to Pope's perceptive poetic dictum.

At about ten o'clock, we decided to part. The following day we were due in New York. We were to travel by train, up through Philadelphia to NYC: it was an early start. I wanted to retire to my room; the others were going to make their way back to their hotel in Connecticut Avenue. I pushed back my chair and stood. Jenny made to get up. North immediately rose, drew back her chair and, without hesitation, held her arm and kissed her, first on the right cheek, then on her left. You could see her delighted surprise. She laid her hand gently and quickly on his left lapel, not as a mother would, without thinking, touch her son, but as a close, an intimate friend. It was a momentary gesture which at once registered with me. It was not quite right, inappropriate in a sense, superbly so in another. North seemed to transcend his youth. He held within himself some unusual power which set him far apart from his contemporaries.

My mind was still dealing with this occurrence as I escorted them to the tall swing doors which led out on to the semi-circular drive in front of the building. On the steps outside, North turned and embraced me, gave me one of those very companionable hugs of which Americans and Continentals are so fond, thanked me for the evening, and retreated to join Jenny on the pavement. It was the first time that I had had physical contact with North, and there was something strange about it. There was no awkwardness, no artifice, no assumption of alien manners: it was entirely as it should have been. What I noticed in that hug was a warmth, a potent affection, and yet, at the same time, a thrill raced through my brain which I knew, deep inside me, meant danger. Outwardly I remained calm; inside, my mind was in turmoil. I did not understand this boy, this phenomenon.

Jenny was enjoying herself. She had tucked her arm into North's and they were waiting for Sam, who was reminding me of our departure time the next day. They spoke together in low whispers and I could not catch what they were saying. In that beautifully fresh, crisp evening, I sensed that everyone was content, pleased with themselves, happy; and yet I knew there was something wrong. It had to do with North but I could neither define nor express it. What I did realize was that the more you got to know him, and when you had felt his touch, the more you wanted to be with him, the more you wanted to explore his mystery.

The following day we arrived in New York City at Penn Station. The twin towers of the World Trade Center then still dominated the skyline. The city was its usual noisy, boisterous, crowded, dirty self. Apart from the quiet, staid formality and reserved propriety of the Upper East Side, where dog-walkers are led by half a dozen different breeds along the sidewalks and Woody Allen lives in guarded seclusion, the bustle of New York life in general speedily tires the newcomer. It was no matter, we had rested on the train and we looked forward to three days, which would give us time to visit the Frick, the Metropolitan and the Guggenheim. Such treats. I knew that the Met would give me a sort of art indigestion. There is too much there to be able to take in on one visit: you are overcome by a surfeit of artistic excellences. It is necessary to choose a few delicacies on a particular occasion. Otherwise it is like

20

indulging to excess in a box of chocolates: there are so many sweetmeats to be tasted that 'the appetite sickens and so dies'.

We had discussed our plans on the train, and in a brief conversation with North he had told me how much he was looking forward to seeing the Guggenheim which, as it happened, was the least favourite of the three for me. The tasteful Frick, with its portraits of Thomas More and Cardinal Wolsey, was the one I wanted to revisit. It has a fabulous collection of art and artefacts established in Frick's old town house. If there are not too many people there, you can imagine that the house is yours. It is just right: compact, organized, delightful.

The Guggenheim is altogether different. Its architecture is modern, belonging, to my mind, more to Mediterranean Europe than fashionable NYC, and it stands as a contemporary curiosity opposite Central Park. On a good tourist day it is like the tower of Babel, its circular staircase spiralling to the top, and the resonances of a hundred different languages echo down to its atrium. North was in awe of the architecture at first sight. Outside, he viewed the building at close quarters and from a distance. Inside, it was as though he were listening to music. With the reverberant hum of conversations which filled the grand central space of the gallery building in his ears, his eyes developed a misty, glazed expression and he wandered to and fro across the wide floor. I watched him and wondered what passed through his mind. At one point he sat elegantly cross-legged in the middle of the floor and, after a few moments, stretched out on his back, one knee raised. He stared up to the topmost height of the structure. He gave an impression that he was practising some mannered form of yoga. A short while later he got to his feet. He rested a hand on the shoulder of one of his contemporaries and asked him to brush off the back of his clothes. I noticed that the favour was performed with almost awe and reverence. I could not understand his relationship with his school friends. He did not seem to dislike any of them: he was prepared to take all of them into his orbit.

This American trip was the first time that I had come into a daily contact with North and been with him for any length of time. By the time we had finished the visit, I was engaged with him in a curious way and could not work out exactly why. He was like a magician: he attracted you, enchanted you, and, as I have said before, made you want to get to know him and listen to him. He also disturbed me. Deep in my soul I was alert to danger, and I could not understand why. The peculiar stature of his personality is rare in mature adults. I had never chanced across it in a student. Others never seemed to be conscious of incongruent elements in his nature, never aware of the indefinable sense of danger that he inspired in me. For my part, the thrill of knowing him, which others also clearly felt, was balanced by a faint but persistent fear; though, at this time, I could not articulate it or explain it.

That Washington and New York trip was definitive in that it established a relationship between North and me. I could see, too, that some bond had been made between him and Jenny. Yet no matter how much she enjoyed herself and loved the flirting, she was wise enough to stay on guard. She was like war-wounded. Her marriage and one or two other relationships had left her with scars which gave her a wariness about the people she liked. She was on her guard: she did not intend to be hurt again. Others did not have her mature defences and this proved to be to their peril.

On the last evening in NYC the Hilton hosted a fashionable cat-walk show. Sam, through one of his art and design friends, whose apartment he and I had visited just off Union

Square, had acquired half a dozen tickets for the show. He, Jenny, and this time Sue, myself, North and another boy, who was destined for the Charing Cross Art School, all went along. It was a spectacular of ritzy glitz and gloss, expensive, chic, precious in the sense that no one could walk down the street in half the ensembles that were presented there. Stage-managed projection, a crafted glamour, a carefully contrived conceit, indeed, an intentional deceit, characterized the performance. It might have been the devised artificiality of the presentation which appealed so much to North – a thought which occurred to me later.

Some of the great designers were there, and several of the world's leading fashion houses brought out their best models. The peculiar breed of designers, a race unto themselves, variously drifted or flounced their way around the vast reception room, converted for the evening into an ornate auditorium. Strange creatures, some seemingly neither man nor woman, pronounced in lilting tones about lengths, folds, shadows and attitudes struck by their model stars. One male designer, whose face was made up – a trace of lipstick, eye shadow, blusher – with the wide-eyed stare of an idiot or *illuminé* might have been transported from Berlin of the 1930s. Chanel's Karl Lagerfeld, his leathery mahogany skin and pony tail, lavender cravat and high-collared black coat, all of which made him look like a voodoo priest, marshalled his model charges into line. Some of the greatest and most glorious faces, some of the most cultivated and elegant female physiques in the world were there: that scion of the English aristocracy Stella Tennant, Kate Moss, Laura Bailey. North knew that the latter's father went under a different name and was a distinguished professor of law. I wondered how he knew.

'How do you know about her father?' I asked.

'She was at school in Oxford. The girls there now, obvi-

23

ously talk about her because many of them would like to be like her and lead the sort of life she does. They think that it is desirable.' North quoted Milton, 'Fame is the spur'.

'What do you think of this world, North? Does the glamour attract you? Could you live and work with people like Lagerfeld?'

'Easily. Their reality lies underneath. Their existence as we see it on the cat-walk is all veneer, façade. It is an act, a beautiful act which deceives many but is basically false. They create an illusion. They work the magician's art. But yes, I do find the glamour attractive.'

Milton was on his mind – I knew he was studying *Paradise Lost* – because he went on about Milton's view of evil, about vice 'with all her baits and seeming pleasures', and about the great puritan wayfaring Christian who learns to see behind an 'excremental whiteness'.

He had clearly thought about it. I wondered what his exterior appearance shielded. That exchange remained in my memory. I could never quite understand what went on in North's mind.

It was on this journey to the States, as I have mentioned, that our relationship began. It was intimate and reserved at the same time. Our American conversations, as I liked to call them, began the foundation of an understanding between the two of us. Our knowledge of the way each other thought accounted for the slight nod of recognition he made to me when, later, he was to keep his assignation with Bernie at Quod. He had no embarrassment, no self-consciousness. He knew he could trust me, rely on me: he knew I would be discreet.

Bernie went on enjoying herself. She had many admirers.

In the teachers' common room, several masters, one or two young and quite handsome, one or two not quite so young, or past the first attractive flush of adulthood, courted her favours. She was simply nice to talk to, pleasant to be with. She looked good and she made you feel good – your self-confidence grew discernibly. She was one of those women who exerted a benign influence on you by her presence and attention: your morale increased and you felt immediately able to deal with the problems of the world. So, she was never short of company.

One person who sought her out, and it became increasingly obvious that he was keen to monopolize her, was our young Head of Physics, a clean-cut, athletic, ex-Cambridge sportsman, Monty Ross. He was a runner and rower. He had been an oarsman at his college, had captained the boat, and rowed for the university's second eight never quite making it to the glory of the Boat Race at Putney. He was also a born-again Christian. He possessed in all respects the attributes suitable for a rapid, glittering career in almost any walk of life, but in school teaching everything he had done was to be especially admired. He was patronized at an early stage and promoted quickly. He was liked by his pupils, their parents, most of his colleagues, and by his headmasters. What more could you want for a startlingly successful career? As such, wearing his Hawks' Club tie, he was entirely acceptable to Bernie, even though he was a married man. A born-again Christian, he thought his motives and behaviour beyond question. He was a paragon of uprightness and virtue.

When Bernie first arrived, Monty was on hand. He showed an obvious sympathy for her as a young girl in unfamiliar surroundings. He confessed to me later, on one of the few occasions when he sought me as a convenient confidant, that he understood her isolation in a new place. He described what happened in this way: he offered to show her where things were, what the customs of the school were, how the system worked, and she hastily accepted. She was grateful. She had arrived from her former school in a state of shock. She had applied for the post at the suggestion and vigorous prompting of her then boss. She had not expected to be appointed. Internal politics had helped her: there were two strong internal candidates and it would have been invidious to give either the job to the exclusion of the other. The rest of the short-listed candidates had turned out to be worthy but lacking fire, sparkle, originality. Bernie appealed because she was unusual, feisty, even provocative: she would be the first woman head of department in the school's five and a half centuries of existence. All this made no difference to her sense of loneliness when she finally arrived to take up the post.

She had found lodgings with a girl research student who had advertised to find someone to share accommodation and expenses. There was no meeting of minds, no, what the Americans like to call, empathy. It was merely a convenient, practical financial arrangement. The researcher was a developmental economics postgraduate whose interests were far distant from Bernie's. Bernie looked to the social life of the school, and there was not much. Sometimes in the evenings, after various activities, chess, drama, sport, had taken place, several members of the common room would retire to a local pub, the Port Mahon or the Half Moon. On a Friday evening, one or two sixth formers and some members of the teaching staff would meet and play five-a-side football in the sports hall. The two best players were a French assistant, Raymond, and one of the senior boys who had been playing soccer since he was five. He was fabled because he had recently had trials for a number of professional football clubs – he had just spent an exhausting, demanding two days with Birmingham City – and, hence, he enjoyed the esteem of the smaller boys. At the same time, he annoyed the sports masters who ran the official school sports, rugby and hockey: they had only just found out about his soccer prowess, which he had been keeping from them. Raymond and the semi-professional sixth former ran each of the Friday evening sides. Bernie joined in, the only girl, and almost always played for the sixth former.

It was at these games that she first began to develop a reliance on the sympathetic ear of Monty. Naturally, as a good sportsman, he played in these games after he had finished coaching one of the rugby teams. He cut a good figure in his rugby shirt and shorts. He was a twenty-something Adonis. Bernie fell for it. You might describe that hour from five o'clock till six as the casting of live bait. Bernie was hooked and she was played in to the Half Moon.

It was there one evening that the trouble started. Alcohol relaxes the spirits, gets rid of social inhibitions, induces mild euphoria, some might say hysteria, and definitely eases the conscience. Monty told me that Bernie found she could talk freely to him. She sat next to him on a bench seat and lamented her fate in having to live for the moment with the dreary research student. How much nicer it was to be in the Half Moon with Monty and the others than back in her neatly dismal flat.

'When do you have to get back home, Monty?' Bernie asked.

'I have some time. Jess will be back about six, but she likes to relax and literally put her feet up for a bit. You know she's pregnant?'

Bernie knew this. Jenny had briefed her on various members of the common room. Monty's marital status and what was going on in his domestic life was no secret. Jenny's intelligence was first-class and reliable.

'Are you looking forward to the baby? Jess must be excited.'

Monty agreed and said, although with little conviction,

that he relished the prospect of a precious, vulnerable, little human life in his charge. It was noticeable though that he was more interested at that moment in looking at the evenness of Bernie's teeth and the profusion of her hair. Any close observer could watch the testosterone take over. Bernie had retreated into the showers after the soccer match and had emerged clean and spruce, smelling delightfully of Yves Saint Laurent's *Rive Gauche*, newly burnished with Lancôme flash bronzer, and with just the faintest touch of blush on her cheeks. There was no doubt that she knew how to present herself, how to capitalize on her already good looks.

'What will you do when you get home?' Bernie was full of questions.

'I don't know. Probably watch telly or a video. Jess won't want to do much. She gets tired in the evenings. It's a bit boring really. It's just a stage she's at. It's supposed to get better.'

'Oh dear, poor old you.' Bernie took a sip from her vodka Martini which was her special Friday night drink, too powerful for ordinary weekday nights. 'You'll have to ask me for entertainment.'

Monty looked at her, appreciated her coquettishness, touched her arm and half-jokingly but more than half-seriously, said he would take her up on that.

He told me what she said. It was as though he remembered every word she spoke to him that evening. 'I have a nice line in entertainment,' Bernie said, looking askance at Monty. 'There are many admirers who have enjoyed the delights I offer. And, don't forget, audiences at my entertainments are expected to participate.'

Monty knew that Bernie was leading him on, but how seriously? It was difficult to tell. More than likely she did not realize the danger she was courting. She felt the power of her attractions, but did not know their full potential. It was, of course, as those of us who have experience of the world know, a potential which could have catastrophic consequences.

Monty drank from his beer-mug and with some internal confusion of thought looked at the floor. He breathed deeply and stretched his legs. He felt in good condition, supple, relaxed and at peace with himself. He sat surrounded by his friends, next to a charmingly beautiful woman. He turned and looked at her. She caught his glance and admired the translucent blueness of his eyes. His face was handsome. She thought to herself that she would like to touch it. Thus are the fires kindled. Why should she not touch him? He was a friend and confidant. He had touched her arm in a gentle, considerate, compassionate way. She would respond. Very briefly, as though it were the most natural thing in the world, she brushed his shoulder with her hand and for a moment let it rest there.

'When you go, can you give me a lift? I don't think I shall stay too long here tonight. I am going to visit my parents tomorrow. They are going to have a lunch party. I shall have to set out early.'

He went on to tell me that all his senses had registered the brush and pause of her hand. He knew instinctively that there was more than just casual gesture in the movement. His mind was blank about what the next move was. Monty knew that he had embarked on a long chess game of the emotions. At least, he assumed it was going to be long. He was no grand master, able to bring off a rapid coup, but checkmates often appear out of the blue for the inexperienced player. The fact was, he did not know what to expect.

'Of course. Let's give it another half-hour, then I had better make tracks back to Jess.'

They chatted on. Jenny came in, mentioned that she was going to Southampton to see her daughter the next day, and then would be in London on Sunday, visiting a sick girl friend

29

who, in order to counteract deepening depression about her illness, had bought herself a white Mercedes sports car. One of the sports masters joined them for some minutes. He complained about the Principal.

'That bastard Aitken has cut our budget for next year. What do you think of that? How am I supposed to produce first-rate teams with no resources? He has to be mad; but we all know that.'

Monty sympathized and made the appropriate noises. His mind, though, was on trying to work out what was to happen next with Bernie. He knew what he should do: make the short detour to her place, let her out of the car while he remained in his seat, say a cheery goodbye, hope to see her on Monday, and be on his way home to the pregnant Jess. His sense of propriety, his evangelical Christianity and conscience directed him back home. Yet what he did was different.

His mind worked ceaselessly and he convinced himself that there was no harm in being totally at ease with Bernie. She was a friend, after all. Why should she not be a really good friend? If she were that, then when he parted from her he could, and indeed should, kiss her. He thought of the sign of peace in the reformed formularies of the Church's services. The kiss is the natural way of showing friendship, care, respect, of saying farewell and of greeting, and displaying affection. His thoughts avoided the word love, a dangerous word. It was particularly perilous in this context. He hoped that Bernie would rest her hand again on him. He found it difficult not to put his arm around her, merely in a familiar way, but he knew he could not do that in the presence of others. He was amazed at his capacity to run his mind on an independent course of thought as he was leading an entirely different one in conversation with others. Was this part of the duplicity, the deviousness of human nature? You never know what people are really thinking. He did convince himself that it would be perfectly legitimate to kiss Bernie, in the continental manner, when he left her shortly: that much was certain. It fired him in the last few minutes in the pub. Never had he seemed so animated, elated: internally he had made a decision which no one else knew about. Jenny noticed his ebullience but put it down to the fact that he was celebrating his wife's pregnancy. The irony of the situation was hidden.

Surely enough, when his sky blue Fiat Punto reached Bernie's lodgings, he got out, opened the passenger door for her, held out his hand, took hers and escorted her to the door of her flat.

'Thanks for the lift. Have a good weekend and love to Jess.' Not that she knew Jess: she had met her once at a reception for new members of the common room. 'I'll think of you tomorrow when you're refereeing. The weather forecast is appalling – rain and sleet.'

'I'll think of you with your parents. Anyway, take care.' He half embraced her, drew her to him and kissed her on both cheeks. He experienced a throb of emotion followed by the strong feeling that he would like time to stand still. He felt her tense and then, very quickly, relax and respond. There was more to that embrace than mere friendship. The wicked word, love, arose in his mind. Images of Jess confused themselves with Bernie. He knew what his body wanted, and it was not the same as his conscience.

Monty's mind raced. What could be done about this? She seemed to him to be on unfamiliar territory. She clearly responded to his touch and kiss. Should he allow his physical inclination to proceed unchecked? Or should he draw back and leave her to go her own way? If he did the latter, would she permit it or do it? What matter if he took her into care, as it were, gave her comfort and pleasure, which she obviously wanted and, to his notion, deserved. Nobody else need know.

There would be no harm. Jess would not know. She could not be hurt. He explained to me that it is easy to convince yourself of your own sincerity, your own integrity. The stark, real, underlying motives are readily concealed. They are only ever revealed after there is a violent, disrupting explosion, which, of course, is bound to happen, but which the victim of that ambiguous word, love, is blind to. It is in this way that those suffering from the self-delusional disease of love, which has been written about by the ancients, by Chaucer and Shakespeare, and by our own wry contemporary observers of the human condition, argue themselves into a state of physical enjoyment for the moment at the expense of secure, permanent relationships.

He then described how Bernie, flushed and elated, not quite understanding her own emotions, waved, opened the door of her flat, and disappeared inside.

Those of us confined within that small community of the school could see the liaison between Bernie and Monty grow. They pretended it was nothing out of the ordinary: they were just good friends. Anyone could see from the body language, from the way they stood when they spoke to each other, from their facial expressions and eye movements, that there was more to it than that. They thought themselves discreet, and to a certain extent they were, but they could not hide a particular intimacy which others did not share. Too often, if you were concerned in a conversation with them in a group, you realized that you were somehow on the outside. They became French and Italianate in their public bodily contact. They touched each other's arms and hands. When they met first thing in the morning they would brushingly kiss each other. Why did she not greet me in the same way? Naturally, as someone many years older than herself, I lacked, for her, physical attraction; and that was the whole point. Monty with his athletic Hawks' Club polish was extremely attractive.

Then came North. He, as part of the senior community of students, was not slow to understand what was going on between Bernie and Monty. They all knew and made their private jokes about the loving couple. At some time North decided to make his move. We often spoke. As we passed in corridors, we stopped and talked. We met by chance in the library, passed remarks, made observations, debated the news, and discussed the stock market. He had seen me studying the *Financial Times* and checking the state of play on the Internet. He was curious, wanted to master the money markets and asked me about them. I was delighted to inform him. I had learned investment know-how by myself and had often thought that I could have done with a mentor in my early days. North quickly saw that the whole business was similar to horse racing: it is necessary to know form, to have command of as much information as possible, to benefit from sources close to the centres of the markets. Analysts, brokers and, above all, financial journalists are necessary supports in the building of a successful portfolio and turning it into a considerable fortune. North, in conversation, revealed to me a vague outline of his family circumstances, the sort of money he received from his estranged father. North was prudent and shrewd. I admired the way he was coolly determined to make himself self-reliant as quickly as possible.

North watched Bernie. He watched Monty. He said nothing to me, or to anyone else. He made his move, and it was the move of a practised master of the game: it was as though he had decided to attack on a military front after studying the maps and defining his strategy. He acted unilaterally. He did not discuss with other generals and he took no political advice. He certainly did not confide in me. He knew my response – tread carefully, too young for action, leave them, she is out of her depth now and you will be if you pursue this course, concentrate on your work, there are more important things; that way madness lies. He knew all this. It was not that he was afraid to hear it; it was simply that he did not need to. His calculation had been made: he knew the odds and knew he could win. When I saw him move, I did not comprehend that Monty was in the complicated equation that he had constructed. That came as a complete surprise to me; and North's desired outcome never occurred to me.

His advance slowly accelerated in the Quod restaurant and thereafter gathered momentum. After I had returned, disturbed, to my study, he and Bernie had talked for a long time. She had spoken warmly of Monty, and, as she sipped her wine, her heart glowed to make her want to talk more. He told me all this a few days later, when we were walking home. I had met him emerging from a brilliantly lit, glass and steel sports centre which had recently been opened. He kept himself fit. He exercised on the machines in the Nautilus room, a huge warehouse of a space with a glass roof in which there was a vast assortment of industrial fitness gadgets. He ran for miles on the spot of a machine and toned up the muscles of his upper body on weight machines.

He told me that he had just taken advantage of a full body massage. A young twenty-seven-year-old Physical Education assistant employed by the centre, which was independently run from the school, was a qualified masseuse. She charged him a special cheap rate. He had just spent three quarters of an hour with her. She, I knew, was good-looking. How could he control himself? The sort of full body massage that I knew about was highly dubious. What were we talking about? Of course, he knew what I was thinking.

34

'You don't have to worry,' he said. 'I know what I'm doing. She is professional. I have a purpose for being there. I am single-minded.'

What he meant was that he was disciplined. He certainly had a purpose, although that was yet to be revealed. Still, my mind raced at the thought of this facility on offer, on site, and being used by North. He was elegant, dark, seductive: the masseuse, both literally and metaphorically, could surely not keep her hands off him.

I decided on a switch of movie on the screen of my mind.

'Did the lunch with Bernie go well?' I asked.

'Perfectly. She's so nice. She encourages me, never talks me down, is interested in me as a person.'

I have never heard anyone talk him down. It struck me that this was something he was saying because he thought it was appropriate, the sort of thing that a contemporary of his would say.

'Did she talk about herself? Do you think she is happy here with us, or does she regret her move?'

'She's getting used to it, although she is still distanced and separate from most of the other teachers. She loves the teaching, or rather the people she teaches. I like her a lot. I find her moving, touching. A bit of a pun, but don't you think she's eminently tactile?'

This last question came as a shock even though I had watched them embrace.

'What do you mean? Do you want to touch her all the time? Does she entice you in that way? I don't understand. How do you react to that?'

'Exactly. I mean that I want to touch her. So do others, most of the others, and especially, as you know, Monty Ross. And she wants to be touched. There is no doubt about that. She becomes aroused when I hold her or kiss her.'

This was amazingly frank. It was a confidence I had not expected. I had hitherto avoided or diverted such confidences when there was a risk of them being offered; but this was different. There was a maturity in his commentary, a depth of analysis which was curiously, objectively adult. He knew what he was talking about. He mesmerized me with his urbanity. I wanted him to go on.

'You are, then, an experienced monitor of the tell-tale signs of sexual arousal. Amazing in one so young.'

I detected a suppressed bridling on North's part, a glimmer of contempt, but the moment passed. For him, my remark was of no real importance, certainly not worth debating. Such trivial discussion of what is universally obvious and completely natural did not merit discussion.

'So where do you think all this leads you? You can hardly, as one of her students, have an affair with her.'

'It's possible. It has been done before. Not with her, perhaps, but with other teachers. Anyway, there is a spirit of competition in the air. I should like to stymie Monty Ross. He is such a self-regarding preacher-man. I want to expose his hypocrisy.'

'Well, you are a devious schemer. How can you waste your time on these plots? Concentrate on your main ambition.'

I felt myself shifting into role of advisor, which I did not like. It immediately changed the nature of our conversation and relationship. I decided to put things right. 'That's what everyone else would say, but I am not going to give you advice.'

'Don't worry. This Bernie stuff is relaxation, leisure time activity. It's no effort and gives me entertainment. I shall be careful, discreet. I shall, however, provoke Ross.'

'Extraordinary. I admire your self-possession. Watch out, though. People get hurt in this sort of adventure.'

'I think I know what I am doing. I can look after myself.'

I had no fears about that. I have never met someone so

inspired by his own abilities, someone so much in control of his mind and emotions. North, in this respect, was unnerving.

He rested his hand on my right forearm as I was about to press the switch on my ignition key holder to release the car door locks. It was an intimate gesture of friendship and trust.

'Don't worry. It will be fun. I'll keep you informed. Watch and listen.'

He turned and walked away. Where to? I wondered. Was he going now to his home and his American mother? What was his private life really like? Did he do ordinary things, sit in front of the TV set, kick a ball around? I doubted it; but then, if he did not perform the mundane habits of life, what did he do? The workings of my mind invented for him an exotic private world which I knew in reality could not exist.

As I drove away I thought about North's attitude towards Ross, and about his admonition to watch and listen. It was curious that he should take me so much into his confidence. Did he know my mind? After all, why should I not go straight to Monty Ross and warn him of North's threat? As I considered this possibility, of course it showed itself as an impossibility. Ross would not be inclined to admit his growing infatuation with Bernie and he would refuse to believe that North could have any influence on grown-up affairs. It was obvious then that North knew the lie of the land: he knew that I would not reveal what he had said to me. It was clear that he had absolute trust in me. I was flattered and impressed.

So, North would provoke Monty. He would have to show Monty that he had entered the field. It was not long before North acted.

Bernie had organized a theatre trip to London, to the Savoy

Theatre to see *Iolanthe* performed by the D'Oyly Carte company. We had a special deal whereby we took dinner at Simpson's in the Strand beforehand. About twenty of us went, mostly sixth formers, Monty, who was officially helping Bernie, and me. At table, North was to be found sitting opposite Bernie, and to Bernie's right sat Monty. I sat next to North, opposite Ross. The conversation started with art because of an exhibition of Vermeer, currently on at the National Gallery, which most of us had seen. I complained about an illiterate introduction the director had written for a screen description of the show: it was full of floating clauses, non-sentences and illogical conclusions. I was derided as a pedant by Monty but supported by Bernie. North offered no view and no comment. We talked of other Gilbert and Sullivan operas we had seen. A year previously I had enjoyed a production of *The Mikado* at this same theatre, energetic, vibrant, with an original set: it had been a magical evening after which I had taken my guest, a feminist literary critic from Yale, to my club for champagne. She liked the champagne but not the club – because it did not elect women members.

North's frequent eye contacts with Bernie did not go unnoticed by me and I should reckon that they were not missed by Monty. The effect on Bernie was to make her extremely talkative. She became vivacious. She teased me about my *goût* for champagne. I explained that it is a good, clean drink and, although it might be a little more expensive than other drinks, it can be relished, made to last longer, and in the end cheaper because you do not drink so much of it. That was not my main reason though; it is my drink. I like it more than any other, and I buy it because I happen to have developed the habit and can easily afford it. The last point is hardly worth mentioning.

As I sipped my wine, Bernie chattered on. Suddenly, Monty reacted to North's reticence in conversation.

'What's the matter with you North? Your mind seems to

be on other things. And you hardly look at anyone other than Bernie. She is not Venus or Aphrodite.'

North turned his electrifying gaze on Ross. Monty had a youthful face. There was a faint fair stubble on his cheeks and chin, the drink had brought a glow to his looks and he leant easily back in his chair, his legs apart, relaxed and rested.

'You are right she is not. They belong to the gods. Bernie does not. In the absence of goddesses, Bernie is worth looking at.'

He raised his glass to her. I had ordered for them a modest Piper Heidsieck. Bernie blushed. It was a nice compliment. North had made Monty's remark seem callow and out of place. Nonetheless, Ross continued to lounge in his chair with an assumed superior confidence which I knew was misjudged. North was embarking on his strategy.

'We should all try looking deep into her eyes,' North continued. 'Surrounded by so much grief and ugliness we should be grateful for what Bernie has to offer in the way of diverting beauty. Mr Ross you should not criticize me but follow my lead.'

North always called me by my Christian name. It was very American. His contemporaries called me merely Doctor, or Mister Doctor, in the fashion of Queen Elizabeth I when she addressed some of her bishops. A few used my first name in their final year. North's 'Mr' stood out as if he were making a point. He had pricked Ross.

'For goodness sake, North! Don't call me Mr, especially on an occasion like this. It is a social do. Call me Monty. And don't look at me like that. It's as though you are looking inside me.'

I noted that Monty was irritated and almost nervous. I knew that disturbing quality that North could bring to his penetrating gaze: he looked behind the mirror of your eyes into the depths of your soul.

We had to rush the chocolate pudding and coffee, but we all managed to settle in our seats with a couple of minutes to spare. North had positioned himself between Ross and Bernie. I sat next to Bernie on her other side.

The production was not a success. The leading lady and leading man were both too wooden, and he had difficulty hitting his bottom notes. I was used to the rich, deep bass voice of my friend, Robert Lloyd, an international opera star who lived in London but travelled the world stunning his audiences in the role of Boris Godunov. The quality of this man's voice was very much inferior. The young hero had just returned from hitch-hiking through India, Nepal and Thailand during a gap year away from opera. Perhaps he should never have returned. Two Gilbert and Sullivan buffs sitting next to me laughed, cheered and shouted at every conceivable moment: nothing was to deter them. Words and music were enough for them: stage presence and acting meant nothing.

I would not have been surprised, in one sense, if North, at the end of the operetta, had embraced both Bernie and Ross. He did not: he behaved with modest decorum. In the interval he chatted with both, with me, and with his contemporaries, moving comfortably between one group and another, between one person and another.

In spite of the poor performance, we all enjoyed the evening. When we arrived back in Oxford it was late, about one o'clock in the morning. Our party dispersed in the High. North hovered in the shadows of University College's walls before he vanished back home. Bernie made towards her lodgings, inevitably escorted by Monty. North had watched them start off before he, almost literally, simply disappeared. He had said goodbye, but suddenly he was not there. I had expected him to walk part of the way with me – we lived in the same direction; but he had gone. I walked easily back, relaxing after the theatre, the journey and the mental exercise of considering what was in people's minds.

I knew that North would be deciding his next move. I wondered what it would be. Bernie would simply be enjoying herself, not thinking beyond the next minute. Monty would be nursing his hopes, his desire to become more intimate with Bernie. He would not admit to himself that he was entering into a long act of betrayal towards Jess. He could mask his conscience: his liaison with Bernie was trivial, of no account; Jess would not know.

I now put all these thoughts out of my mind. The air was fresh that early morning, balmy. I breathed deeply and felt an absurd elation, a peak of physical fitness. I celebrated within myself my independence. I did not have to worry about anyone else. During my married years, my concerns had always been shared. They were not just for myself and my own interests but for my wife's also. Marriage had taught me altruism. You had to think of someone else's interests all the time. It had not been a bad thing: it was entirely commendable. Now, after Giselle's accident, it was all different. There was no point in occupying your mind constantly with considerations of her: there was nothing to be done. She no longer knew who I was, nor who anyone was for that matter. Her world either did not exist at all, or it only existed for her. There was no communication – nothing. Her consultant told me early on that I should not expect any improvement. This was how it would remain. Her brain was so damaged that there was no chance of recovery. I had come to terms with this after a long time of total dedication to the shared interests of the two of us. They had been good years, but they were now in the past. She had commanded all my faith and loyalty. No one had led me away from her. Now it was just me, and there was often an exhilarating thrill of freedom to be experienced. At other times, of course, there were black moods of despondency and acute loneliness. One or two good friends saved me from those periods of despair, which occurred infrequently, and most recently North had come to my rescue on one particularly dark occasion.

It was as if he had known that an overwhelmingly desperate mood of isolation had come over me. He had telephoned me. It was one or two days after our Savoy visit. I was so depressed that I had almost not answered the phone. When I picked up the receiver, North's voice with its soft, friendly Anglo-American timbre greeted me.

'Hi, it's North. How are you?'

As quickly as those rare moments of gloom descended on me, this one melted away as I re-engaged with the real world of people I knew. The dreary interior monologue I had been engaged in stopped abruptly and a huge relief came over me. North's voice was reassuring. There had been no reason I knew of for him to ring me at that particular time, but his voice called me back from the pit of despair.

'Pretty bloody, actually. But all the better for hearing you.'

'Can we meet? I wouldn't mind your views. What do you think?'

I had no idea what he wanted to ask. I suggested coffee in a central low-ceilinged, comfortable coffee house, tucked away in a recently renovated, antique Elizabethan courtyard. The bar, too, would be open all day, which would be useful if I found myself in need of a bracer. It was a place I frequented when I was in town and felt the need of a quick fix of caffeine or alcohol. The manager was an Italian I had met through a neighbour. When he first arrived in the country, she, a Neapolitan, had put him up for a few weeks until he found his feet. He always remembered me and made sure I received excellent service.

My black mood dispersed. North was entering the courtyard as I approached. We hailed each other, clasped hands, he held my arm and we went in. Like Churchill, I decided on a cognac with my coffee. North preferred a Coke. I sipped my espresso, alternating the taste with a sip of water and the strong kick of the cognac.

On the surface it seemed that North's worries were to do with *Hamlet* and some essay he had to write on the imagery of disease and desire in the play. It was odd. He could have asked me about it at any time during the coming week: there was no urgency for him. As often before, he could have buttonholed me at a time during the working day. Yet he had rescued me from the torture of my soul by bleak despair. His telephone call had sounded at just the right time. It was as though he had sensed that I was in trouble and needed company. Hamlet was just an excuse. The black prince would absorb my melancholy. On reflection, the incident was unnerving; or rather, North was unnerving.

As I suspected *Hamlet* was an excuse. The conversation soon worked round to Monty and Bernie.

'You watched our two fond lovers the other night. What do you really think of Monty?' he asked.

'Well ... to be frank, I think he's a bit of a fool. He is deluding himself if he thinks nobody notices what's going on. People are going to get hurt, particularly his wife, and then, of course, Bernie.'

'I think I may be able to stop him before the damage is done.'

How on earth could North stop this affair developing? I could not see it. Surely he lacked the experience? He would be out of his depth. Or at least, he ought to be out of his depth. That was the frightening thing about North: what you might have thought to be beyond his reach, out of the range of his perception and understanding, often proved, in the end, not to be.

'How would you propose to do that?' I asked rather scornfully.

'I have my suspicions that he is a man susceptible to certain approaches, someone who is not quite sure what he wants but is prepared to find out should a person he thinks sympathetic to his interests lead him on.'

'This is all far too deep for me. I don't see what you are driving at.'

'It is simply that I think I can divert him. In fact, I know it. I can deflect him from Bernie. And it would be fun – an entertainment for me, and also for you.'

'Very considerate to think of me, but I don't see how you will be able to do it.'

'You will have to wait and watch. I am not going to tell you. But do you think it would be a good thing?'

He seemed to want my approval. He certainly wanted me involved, complicit, bound up in whatever it was he was going to do. I was intrigued. So this was why he had rung me up. He had wanted to sound me out, test me, rather, on his ideas about strategy. He needed to know how I would react. Frankly, I could see no possibility of him succeeding in his aim of disrupting an affair which, I knew by experience, would have to run its course. Cupid is chaotic and mischievous, not by design but by chance, and once his arrow wounds, the cure and convalescence is long. North, I reckoned, could do nothing. If he did do something, it would make no difference or it would cause more distress and confusion than ever. I did not know then what he had in mind.

He looked at me, put his hand on my arm.

'Don't be so sceptical. Don't doubt me. Monty is vulnerable.'

I wondered what he meant by that remark. North had this odd maturity about him.

'What do you mean, "He is vulnerable"? You sound like his therapist.'

'I can't tell you. You'll find out if I am right. Just tell me this, do you think he appeals to other men? And do you think other men are attracted to him?'

'What a crazy question. How should I know? I am sure there must be some guy somewhere who would find Monty attractive in what I suppose is the way you mean. He is a good-looking chap. I have no idea about his inclinations in that respect. I haven't detected any tendencies towards the boys he teaches, and certainly not towards any of his male colleagues. But then, these matters tend to be personal and private.'

'I agree, but it is worth thinking about. As you say, he looks good. You never know.'

'What do you mean by that?'

North was not saying, but he had planted a little seed in my mind. Its gestation took some time, and its full flowering longer. I remember wishing that I knew precisely what was going on in North's mind.

Anyway ... he diverted me, took me out of myself: he gave me something to think about beyond my own personal worries. His company was pleasant, flattering. Objectively, why should this young man want to spend time with me, an often humourless adult? It is true he had no father to turn to, that he lacked the company of grown men in his family life. At least, I supposed he did. I knew nothing about his domestic arrangements. His delightful mother I had met on a few official occasions and, at the most, twice casually. From what he confided in me, I assumed he and his mother lived together. I had no idea if she had a partner or a lover. I thought not. It occurred to me that North might be positioning me as his mother's lover. He obviously liked me and, I thought, respected me. In his eyes, it might have worked. He did not understand my mental hang-ups. When I asked him about what happened at home, he always answered willingly, but his answers were never detailed, only general. Yes, his mother had friends who would come round of an evening. She went to an Italian class one evening during the week, she belonged to a novel-reading and appreciation circle. That was the limit of my knowledge. I wanted to know about the interior of their flat. Had she any intimate friends? Was she well off? Were there expensive paintings on their walls? My curiosity failed to penetrate the interior of their living space. It was like being on a train journey at night, looking out at houses with brightly lit but veiled windows. How the imagination works on what goes on inside those obscure rooms.

Later that night, I knew that the black, funereal, mood of depression would not descend on me; and I knew it had something to do with North. My meeting with him had expelled the demon; but still I did not quite understand why he had called to meet me. It crossed my mind, and it pleased me to think so, that he knew by some paranormal power that I was in desperate need of help and he had contrived the means of my soul's salvation. This was fanciful, and yet, when I thought about what he had discussed with me, I was convinced that there was a reason for our meeting which I did not see. He had made it clear that he saw the break-up of the Monty and Bernie relationship as necessary and inevitable: he would be the instrument of the dissolution. He also wanted me to know that he questioned the nature of Monty's sexuality. Did he think I would be shocked? Did he think that I would try to stop him taking action? He knew I would not. He read my psychology correctly. I had ceased interfering in other people's lives years ago. I looked on objectively. What path he chose, provided that he knew the options, the choices, the implications, was up to him. As for Bernie and Monty, well, they were certainly old enough to look out for themselves. The more I pondered our meeting, the more I became convinced that North knew precisely what he was doing, and I knew that he was either testing me or trapping me – perhaps both. Whatever his reasons were, he knew I valued his company and would never turn down an opportunity to be with him. That, of course, was his trap.

Things moved swiftly.

One morning there was consternation in the common room. Tensions were running high. Some people were on edge and extremely jumpy, quick to stand on their dignity and to take offence. Others were uncharacteristically stand-offish and disappeared to their rooms and offices without greeting. I had arrived after most of my colleagues that morning, and it transpired that there had been a row between Monty and Bernie. He had seen her the previous evening, coming out of a cinema in town with North. It was not just that: they had been arm in arm, talking intimately and, once, while they waited to cross a road, she had rested her head on North's shoulder. He had witnessed that little act of intimacy because he was so shocked at seeing them emerge from the film that he had followed them a short distance, making sure that he was not seen. He could not have mistaken the lover's tones and gestures on North's part, reciprocated compliantly, even enthusiastically, by Bernie. The rival was jealous. Stunned by what he saw, he was unable to make a fuss, but he was incapable of containing himself when he saw Bernie the next morning. How could she behave like that with a boy? Did she not know how old he was? She was bound to be seen. Indeed, he had seen her. Her actions and the relationship were ridiculous and juvenile. What did she think she was doing? Why did she not grow up?

Needless to say, Bernie bridled and rounded on him furiously.

'Mind your own business, Monty! It's nothing serious. Don't tell me what to do.'

47

'I'll tell you if you are doing something stupid. And you are. I can't believe it. North is like a kid brother to you. And what about his mother? Does she know? What would she think? You're being really stupid, Bernie.'

'Look, I am not going to discuss this with you. What his mother thinks, or does not think, is no concern of yours. The only person it concerns is North. He is quite old enough make his own decisions and look after himself.'

The fact was that North would be eighteen in a couple of weeks time. Bernie was aware of his coming birthday and realized that she was on difficult ground. It made her reaction to Monty even more extreme. I thought of the old Roger Miller song which advises, 'You're treading on quicksand. Walk slow.' Bernie was in no mood to go carefully.

'Come on Bernie, be your age. And be careful. You might end up in a lot of trouble.'

'Don't preach at me, Monty. I can't stand it.'

Apparently she stormed out of the common room and went to her office.

So, I thought, the secret is out. To mix with the scent of hyacinths on that lovely spring morning was a corrupt whiff of scandal. Later, when I saw North coming towards me, and he stopped and we chatted, he showed no sign of anxiety, discomfiture, embarrassment. I do not know if he was even aware of what was going on between Bernie and Monty. If he did, it did not disturb him. I restrained myself from asking what was happening on the Bernie front: he would tell me in his own good time.

During the day the atmosphere among my colleagues mellowed and became more stable. The mundane affairs of working life took over and dulled the edge of scandal. By the late afternoon, Bernie and Monty were talking normally again, audibly about school matters and in whispers about more personal ones. The eruption of that little volcano seemed to have subsided.

At the weekend Sam organized a trip to an art gallery in the newly developed canal basin centre of Birmingham. It was a trendy gallery, brand new, on three floors, and its director was famed for breaking new ground. His progressive, avant-garde, tastes often repelled and offended more establishment critics and patrons. The left-wing city council lavishly supported the gallery. It was not vast in space but it was well laid out. The architect had put the stairs to one side of the building and they curled upwards around a lift. The ground floor was used mainly for administration, but there was one fairly large exhibition space which was usually used for lectures, meetings, poetry readings and any miscellaneous cultural event which appealed to the director

When we arrived it was lunch-time and our party sat on the side of one of the busiest of the canals leading into the junction basin and ate sandwiches. Most of the usual art lovers were there: the sixth-form students who were studying art history, together with those who considered themselves culture addicts. Those who were genuinely interested in art, music, literature, those who always went to Stratford Shakespeare productions and the latest plays in London, were all present. It was a good mixture of people. Sam did well in organizing such trips, and other colleagues looked after the theatre and music visits. The students were fortunate in having their cultural experiences expertly provided for them. Naturally, North was one of the students with us. Among the adults were Sue and Bernie, but on this occasion there was no sign of Monty: he had been required to look after some Saturday afternoon sports fixture, and Jess was fattening to her task of parturition.

I sat and talked to North about the modernization of Birmingham city centre and pointed out the building that I knew the Oxford proprietor of Quod was converting into its replica. He was cashing in on the expanding, booming business of the bar and restaurant service industry. This was a financial sector which I studied carefully and had done well out of over the past few months. North had brought along his own prepared lunch, sandwiches cut in inch-and-a-half lengths and a couple of apples. He had no drink with him. Nor did I. Sam told everyone to make their way into the Axis Gallery after they had finished lunch and had a walk around the locks, over one or two of the humpback footbridges: we were to re-assemble at four-thirty when the coach would arrive and take us back home.

Sam, North, another student who was destined for Downing College in Cambridge to study history, and I, went into a Café Rouge. Sam drank a Carlsberg, North and his contemporary drank Cokes with lemon, and I took one of my habitual glasses of champagne. Sam told us that we might expect to be shocked by what was being shown in the gallery. The newspapers of the day before had made news out of a local city councillor complaining of the impropriety, vulgarity, obscenity of one exhibit in particular. The artist was a Spaniard, Santiago Sierra, who had been creating his art in Mexico. His compositions were mostly made up of photographs or video films. I had read about the complaint in *The Times* and knew what to expect. I was not sure how people were going to take it; but then, I had not seen the particular, allegedly offensive, presentation. I was reserving judgment.

When we went in, a West Indian poet was declaiming his rancorous, strident odes of complaint from a wheelchair in the lecture room. Sierra's works, which were described as ' "performances" that explore the value of labour', were on show in the first floor gallery; and on the second floor there were large-scale abstract paintings by a German artist called Katherine

Grosse which she had 'performed' directly on to the gallery walls. She had filled the spaces with intense colour using different methods of application. We were not told what they were but in the case of one wall the paint had dripped liberally down the surface and puddled on to the floor.

Sierra presented as one exhibit a series of photos, the first of which showed a huge articulated truck jack-knife across a busy street. The subsequent photos showed the patterns of other vehicles that arrived and had to turn about. Another set of photos showed a line of bread loaves laid across a road and how they fared as traffic ran over them. So, this was the cutting edge of contemporary art. There were also a number of video monitors in the gallery which showed a number of continuous video loops. One concerned a large number of Mexicans, who were all having their hair bleached. But the work which Sam had warned we might find shocking showed ten young Mexican men, seated in turn on a cheap plastic and metal chair and masturbating. I found myself standing watching this piece of 'art work to do with the value of labour' next to a middle-aged woman. She could not take her eyes off the screen, and for some minutes nor could I. Only one of the film stars reached the stage of climax, and in the end, because of the repetitive nature of the loop, it all became intensely boring. I could not quite determine what the artistic purpose of the presentation was. I was not embarrassed by this public display of a private act, but I was vicariously embarrassed for the woman who was standing next to me. I rationalized this and decided that she herself was not discomfited and, consequently, I ceased to think of her.

Naturally enough there were plenty of ribald jokes among our party but, when the discussion became serious, the burden of it was to do with what the artist makes out of the ordinary acts of life. Nobody could understand quite what it had to do with the value of labour, even less to do with the dignity of labour, unless the loop was showing a form of release and relaxation from work. We all agreed that we should like to hear Sierra expound on his motives for making the loop.

While I was contemplating a movie image of a tramp repeating a series of phrases about crisis management which was thrown up on to one of the walls, I noticed that Bernie and North were viewing the masturbating Mexicans together. North leaned towards Bernie at one point and whispered a lengthy, considered phrase or two into her ear. The anxious look on her face lifted and she smiled gently. After a minute or two they moved off in soft conversation. I wondered what they were saying and longed to discuss the images with them. But before I could catch up with them they went out of the Sierra exhibition, and so I lingered a little before going upstairs to see the Katherine Grosse wall pictures. After I had seen those decorated walls, there was no sign of Bernie or North: they had left the gallery altogether.



Since there was another three quarters of an hour before we were all to meet to make the journey home, I decided to go for a walk. I sauntered through a paved precinct, nicely laid out with trees and a few flower beds. A monumental piece of modern sculpture, rather Soviet in conception, that looked like an industrial worker carrying a railway sleeper under one arm and balancing a sledgehammer over his other shoulder, dominated one end of the open space. As I approached this massive tribute to twentieth-century endeavour, this latter day tribute to socialist realism, I saw, seated under a tree behind it, Bernie and North. They were sitting cross-legged on the grass facing each other and holding hands. From a distance, they looked as though they were in a concentrated yoga exercise. I shifted to one side so that the statue obscured me from their vision, and saw that they were talking in subdued tones to each other. North was looking straight into her eyes. He had captured and captivated her. He certainly looked charismatic in his dark, elegant, way. Bernie was entranced. She looked relaxed and happy. As I shifted behind the massive worker, North rocked forward and kissed her gently, first on her left cheek then on her lips. It was not a quick kiss, but prolonged for several seconds. Bernie did not shift away. She submitted completely. There was no doubt that she was spellbound by him.

I turned and walked back towards the Axis, making sure to keep the sculpture in between me and them. Although I knew that this was coming – it could not be a surprise for me – nevertheless it was difficult to reconcile what I had just seen with reality. There was no doubt about the intimacy of their attitudes and gestures, no doubt about her submission to him, to his will. That was obvious to any onlooker. Yet I still could not satisfy myself intellectually that this liaison between an eighteen-year-old boy and his mid-twenties teacher could happen. On the face of it, the relationship was absurd, inappropriate, unbalanced, ill-considered. My internal criticisms took no account of North's strange and different presence. To meet him was to begin to understand him, and then you knew that anything was possible.

In the middle distance, across the paving, I saw Sue. I went up to her, stopped, and chatted. In a few moments we were joined by others of the party. Sam approached us, swaying from side to side in the slow, ambling gait which always reminded me of a drover marshalling his cattle.

I had positioned myself to keep an eye on the direction from which Bernie and North would appear, and sure enough they came into view. As soon as North was aware that they might be noticed he unlinked his arm form Bernie's. They arrived, Bernie elated, North composed. They joined naturally into discussions about the gallery, about the architecture and layout of regenerated Birmingham, and no one detected that there was anything to their relationship other than the friendship to be expected in such a situation between a pupil and his mistress. In my mind the irony of that phrase was not lost. I kept what I had seen, and what I thought, to myself. There was only one person with whom I could legitimately and unconcernedly discuss what I had seen and what I now felt – and that was North.

I now knew that North was on the move. I experienced a tremor of excitement, which, at once, I thought ridiculous. Why should I bind myself up in this business so much? It was no concern of mine. I could choose to remain outside events which concerned North, Bernie, Monty Ross. There was no reason for me to involve myself, worry on anyone's behalf, to occupy my mind with the fates of others. My reason for continuing to be a close observer was North's personality, and the fact that he wanted and intended me to grow more and more involved. I realized that he would not allow me to withdraw. It was as if he had me fixed by a basilisk stare. Like Bernie, but in a different way, I was captured by his mesmeric personality. In any case, to take myself off into splendid isolation would have been boring.

I resolved that the next time I met North by himself, I would tell him that I had seen him kissing Bernie. I think it was a relentless prurience in my own imagination which made me want to know what he would then confide in me.

A few days later, Jenny asked me in the late afternoon for a drink in the Café Coco. We sat relaxing after what had been for me one of those fraught days when little went according to plan. With every intended course of action, there had been a problem: not a large one, but one significant enough to put me out of step. A general mood of dissatisfaction had settled upon me.

Jenny was tired but cheerful. 'When are you going to invite me to dinner in your college?'

I had a college connection which gave me occasional dining rights. Once, I had asked her and another teaching colleague to dinner. It had proved a bibulous evening of great fun, a lot of leg-pulling, interesting other company – the head of MI6 had been a guest of the Master – generally entertaining. Some of us had been warned in advance that the security chief would be there and that we were not to reveal who he was. At drinks in the senior common room before dinner, we had been standing around sipping dry sherries when he came in with the Master. He had immediately stepped into the middle of the group Jenny and I were in and introduced himself as head of MI6. So much for discretion. He had gone on to tell of his recent visit to New Zealand, where he had been in discussions with the Chief Justice on tightening security arrangements in the wake of a ship being blown up in Auckland harbour.

Jenny had been fascinated by him, and since he was recently widowed I had fancied that she might make a play for him. Physically he was her sort – chubby, hirsute, gravel-voiced. In the event, she had held off, or so far as I know she had. She had really enjoyed herself, but afterwards never stopped gently and relentlessly pressuring me to take her again, varying that demand with one for me to take her to my London club.

'I shall have to look for a suitable date. Don't worry. It will happen. You mustn't be too eager. It will probably be a disappointment next time.'

I ordered a couple of *tapas* dishes, a dry white wine for Jenny and a scotch and soda for me. I resisted the temptation to have a triple of a light-coloured whisky, like J & B, which looks as though you are drinking something weak and innocuous.

It was a pleasant half-hour and put me in a rested, satisfied mood after my difficult day. We talked mainly about her children and her sick, London friend.

As we left, I was conscious of an elegant, black presence moving towards us and, sure enough, there was North. It might have been that he had materialized out of thin air or arisen from the depths underneath the pavement. My good mood made him all the more welcome to me. Jenny waved to him, blew him a kiss, and said she must rush off. I waited for him, he embraced me, and I suggested that we might walk a little of the way through the main street together. This was my first chance to speak to him alone.

'So. How are things with you? How are you?'

'Good. Good. And you?'

'Yes, I'm OK. Jenny acts like valerian on my behaviour. I always feel calmer when I am with her. She relaxes me. I feel light-hearted, less serious. The world is an agreeable place.'

'You should marry her,' North quipped, glancing at me to see how I would take this piece of advice.

'You must be joking. I am not able to be lived with, certainly not at the moment. My former loyalties are still in place. G is still with me. She won't go away and I don't think she ever will. Besides, I value my independence.'

This was the answer that he had expected. I had talked to him before about the financial independence which made it possible for me to do virtually what I liked. I continued to teach because of the company, because I enjoyed the cut and thrust of debate with my students, because I liked to be able to talk about the literature I enjoy, and because there were one or two colleagues whose presence reassured me. I could not believe that he did not understand that I could never undertake a full-time relationship with someone like Jenny. Companionship was a different thing. I valued her occasional company and knew that it was good for me. I enjoyed her teasing, her flirting: she knew how to raise my spirits when I was low.

'But what about you, North? How do matters rest with Bernie? Or should I rather say, how is your strategy working with her?'

'All goes to plan,' he asserted. 'I can tell you she is eager, attentive, responsive to my needs. I don't think she has had much experience.'

I thought this bizarre coming from North, who could not have had a great deal of experience himself. He had immense confidence. It was as though he qualified in the world on the basis of one successful mission, whereas other people would need many tries, false starts, failures, experiments. North assumed complete competence, mastery, after only a brief excursion into the field, whatever the field might be.

'She looks after me, knows what I like. She would like to be with me all the time. She likes to convince herself that I really do exist, if you like. She can't stop touching me.'

It occurred to me that the sex must have been good if he had got that far. I was soon to learn that it had.

'She is very sensual,' he continued. 'In our moments of *intime* passion, it all works very well indeed.' He touched my arm, 'Her flat is a convenient refuge. Her flatmate is never there.'

My mind raced. I took this to be his avowal of the consummation of their tryst. In my imagination I saw them in bed together on, let us say, the previous afternoon, when other students might have been playing games or have been engaged in some public-spirited activity. Bernie would have been able to organize her time to make herself available. I found I had no difficulty imagining her naked and engaged in the toils of love; but I did have trouble projecting such images of North. I could not visualize him in the carnal, sweaty business of love-making. It was too inelegant, too gross for me to handle. Bodily fluids and awkwardness, physical and emotional, did not sit comfortably with my image of him. I could not even imagine him naked and involved; he seemed too remote from such base activity. I could her. There was no problem there. Bernie's body lived vividly in my mind.

North came across to me as a supreme manager. He orchestrated matters as he wanted them to turn out. He did it easily.

'What about Monty Ross? Where does he fit in the picture?' I asked.

'He bubbles gently,' North said. 'He suspects something is going on, but doesn't know what. His jealousy is coming along nicely. It grows, it grows. Bernie knows he is upset, but there is nothing she can do about it. I tell her to take no notice but just to be nice to him – she mustn't repulse him too severely. For me, it is important that he should be kept simmering. He will see eventually what a fool he is being.'

In a major sense I was appalled by his calculation. He spoke as if he were an agent of Nemesis. He was of the gods. His was the awful power of retribution. I became somewhat uneasy for myself. What did he think of me? If he was able to manipulate people in the way he seemed to be doing, why should he not somehow have taken me into his calculations? Was I part of his conceived plot? But I thought I could look after myself: at least I understood what North was doing. I was not in the dark. He held no secrets back from me. He appeared to need me to talk with. I was privileged: a neutral party, with no close loyalties. If I owed loyalty to anyone, it was to North: he trusted me with his confidence.

'The blessed Monty is in trouble,' he continued. 'He can't see very far ahead of him.'

There was something prophetic about that statement and

it chimed with what I had been thinking for some time. There were all sorts of rocks in Monty's passage, some visible, some half-submerged, and some, I reckoned, completely hidden. There was Bernie and his obsession for her. There was the problem of Jess and the fact that her suspicions were bound to grow. The complications were multitudinous. Then there was another phenomenon which I had been observing, brought to my notice by Jenny.

One Saturday morning, I had met Jenny by chance in Magdalen Street. She had been shopping at Boots the chemist: buying eye shadow and liner for her daughter. Then she had been to Marks & Spencer for some lunch items: she was having her sister and brother-in-law to lunch the following day. She had bought delicious-looking pâtés, a pheasant and apricot and a coarse one with chopped gherkin in it, rocket and watercress salad, and ciabatta with olives. She told me that she was reckoning to offer this, together with some smoked salmon she already had in, and a chilled bottle of Chablis which she knew was a good year; she had bought a dozen bottles and had tasted it the previous weekend.

I took her bag, which was not heavy, and suggested we spent a little time looking at some of the masterpieces in the Ashmolean Museum and then have some lunch in the basement restaurant.

'What a good idea,' she had agreed. 'I do like meeting you. You are never in a hurry and you think of such nice things to do.'

I reflected on some of the black moods that I endure. I follow, or at least try to follow, the advice of Dr Johnson that you should always try to be cheerful. Indeed, we have a moral duty to be cheerful. Our cheerfulness affects other people for the better. We went into the ancient classical building, the monument to Dr Elias Ashmole's connoisseurship and generous patronage. It is an exotic treasure house of great works of art and curios. On the ground floor, in its cool corridors and enormous rooms, vases, urns and bowls, artefacts from antiquity, are stationed amid splendid statuary. Ancient figures attest ideal proportions to the human form. Male and female beauty is celebrated, often erotically, for the satisfaction and delight of those who look on. Most viewers, malproportioned, bent, lame, short-sighted, obese Americans bred on burgers, dwarf Japanese – the women in short tartan skirts and long, dark blue socks, the men in Harrods jackets projecting bony shoulder blades at their backs – mooched and shuffled around the displays in the calm silence of that temple to art and sculpture. Jenny and I made our way leisurely upstairs to the pre-Raphaelite room. We whispered about Holman Hunt, Millais and DG Rossetti. We looked at glass work and jewellery in another room, at the Alfred jewel, the Finzi Bowl, considered the tiny painting of St Nicholas of Bari rebuking the tempest by Bicci di Lorenzo, and then in quiet contemplation went downstairs to the restaurant. We discussed the wonderful detail of Uccello's *Hunt in the Forest* and Cosimo's *Forest Fire*. I ordered for Jenny a glass of dry white wine. We chose some light sandwiches, and I took a strong double espresso coffee and a large tumbler of water in the Levantine tradition. Our conversation turned to Bernie and North.

'Don't you think those two are rather too close for decency's sake? Too close for comfort?' she asked. This was before I knew, before I was convinced, that they had become lovers.

'I don't know about comfort. I should think they are very comfortable. North doesn't seem to have any problems in his relationship with Bernie. Why should we worry? I don't really think Bernie knows what she is doing, but then she will find out.

60

'What about her position with Monty? I think she will run into trouble there. If he is going to pursue her, no doubt at the cost of Jess, there must be complications. I don't quite see what they are, but there will certainly be some.'

Jenny looked into the mid-distance, thinking, and remarked, 'Did I tell you about Monty and Aitken? Now this is interesting, and I have a theory. We were in the Half Moon the other evening after finishing at the school. There was quite a crowd: the deputy was there, Monty, the French woman, our maths and geography colleagues. We were discussing the proposed building plans and the expansion of lab space for chemistry and physics, when who should come in but Aitken himself.'

I knew that it was unusual for the Head to join those evening drinking sessions, which he knew were a way for his staff to wind down. He steered clear of such occasions as a rule. It was surprising that he had called in.

The deputy offered him a drink. He took a half of bitter, perhaps to show that he was part of the common crowd; but it did not convince. Jenny reported that he joined the group discussing the labs.

'He explained the acute need for an increase in lab space to cater for increased numbers of students and the new demands of the national curriculum: there was no alternative. More room was the priority. I thought,' Jenny added, 'that he'd come to launch a PR initiative on behalf of the scheme and to convert waverers to his cause. But I'm not so sure. What do you think about this?'

She paused, looked again far away, brought her attention back to me, sipped her wine, and said, 'I think he's gay and was on the prowl. He was tracking Monty. I think he fancies Monty.'

'How do you work that out? I don't believe you. As usual, you're teasing me.'

'No, I'm not. Listen. We were standing in a small group,

six of us. Monty was opposite Aitken. Aitken only had eyes for Monty. What Aitken said was as if it were just directed at Monty. After a short time, Aitken moved round next to Monty. It was totally weird. Monty, of course, being the sort of person he is, was all ears and eyes for Aitken. Monty is on the make. He listens to his master's voice. I shouldn't be surprised if Monty doesn't fancy Aitken back.'

That was meant as a joke, but we could both see that if the premise was right about Aitken being gay, then who knew where all this would end: Monty might well reciprocate. Neither of us trusted Monty: he might respond to Aitken's advances simply because he was on the make. Monty had the ability of adapting his morality to his interests. He was entirely unscrupulous. Now we had the picture of a homosexual liaison between the Head and his dashing young physicist. There was no doubt that Monty was his blue-eyed boy. Monty had been patronized and brought on at a rapid rate. Aitken evidently liked him, admired him, and was prepared to promote him over other people with more justifiable claims to position and power.

Aitken himself was a ruthless, late-thirty-something go-getter. Clever, calculating, focused, he saw his career in clear terms laid out before him and was determined that no one and no thing should stand in his way. He was the product of a big inner city comprehensive school and had gained his position in the independent sector through ability and efficiency. He was one of those institutional administrators who cannot bear to have power delegated to those below him. Aitken was clever enough to give the impression that others were making decisions but, on closer scrutiny, you could see it was all an illusion: Aitken was the decision maker. This did not endear him to his senior colleagues.

He had married early a Spanish girl from a well-to-do

Madrid family. They had three small daughters. His wife's admirable Spanish energies were all taken up in nurturing the three daughters: she had little time for her husband's school or for society in general. Hence she kept very much to herself. My relations with her were cordial. We always stopped and spoke should we meet. I felt she was isolated, but concluded that she preferred her way of life to one of involvement in the school. I knew that she and Aitken had fierce rows from time to time: one of the secretaries had told me of a number of times when she had been witness to some loud, unseemly squabbles. Jenny's intelligence did cause to cross my mind the possibility of a *marriage blanc* which hid from public view his real proclivities. The more I contemplated Jenny's theory that he was gay, the more I liked it.

Monty was a suitable target for a predator. Jenny said that Aitken could barely keep his eyes off Monty. She particularly registered what was going on because Aitken usually responded to her innocent flirting and enjoyed bantering with her. This time he had been impatient with her, had brushed her off almost, off-handedly shifting from standing beside her to move next to Monty. She said that Monty's eyes had glowed. Aitken gazed at him. It was as if the others were not there.

'How could he not take notice of me?' Jenny complained playfully. 'I'll tell you this: something is going on between those two. A woman always knows these things.'

'Fascinating. I wonder if anyone else has noticed.'

'Oh, well, I mentioned it to Sue. She half agrees. She doesn't know Monty as well as I do. But she has noticed Aitken's attention directed at him. She reckons that there is an exclusiveness to Aitken's chats with Monty. You know, that you are not wanted to join in.'

I took a sip of my strong, bitter coffee and drained my glass of water. My mind wandered into a region of multitudinous possibilities for Monty. His life, in my eyes, was becoming a maze. Central to his operations were himself and Jess; then there was his relationship with Bernie; then followed the possibility of an illicit relationship with Aitken; and then there lurked in the dim background himself and North. The last I mention because North was later to make a remark about Monty that made me uneasy, though I could never be sure that this was what North had intended. At that moment, a friend of Jenny came across to our table. I stood and invited her to join us, which she did for a short while. She was one of Jenny's arty friends, the wife of a television film director who painted and exhibited in one or two galleries in the Cotswolds and, very occasionally, at a gallery behind the Tate in Pimlico. Her pictures were not bad, and I had once considered buying one of her still-life interiors. When I had made up my mind to buy, I found that I had been pre-empted; a London collector had seen it, liked it, and taken it away immediately.

It was impossible for Jenny and I to continue our conversation, but for the rest of the day my mind tracked various lines of thought and their implications for the rest of us at the school.

If it were true that Aitken was gay, in the present climate of opinion in education he was extremely vulnerable. Monty was certainly at risk. The whole prospect was amazingly outrageous and preposterous, but there was a relish to hoping that it was all true: life would be more interesting than hitherto.

North's remark about the 'blessed Monty' worried me – not too intensely – but it was constantly there in the back of my mind. Was he cursing Monty? Or was he indicating that Monty was blessed by the attentions of Aitken and was therefore one of the chosen? Whichever way it was, North seemed highly critical and was not happy about Monty's favoured position in relation either to Bernie or to Aitken. I began to imagine North as a junior Iago. Then I also began to see that I could not reconcile North to a role of resolute, unmitigated evil. He was far too likeable to be a complete villain. As I have said, he inspired you to want to be with him. But then, what about the Prince of Darkness, the fallen angel, was not that true of him also? I longed to talk to North and discuss these matters with him. What did he think of Aitken?

The opportunity occurred when North sought me out on the Sunday. I was seated at my writing desk in my study when the phone rang. I had to nudge my black cat, with his red collar and identity disc, away from the receiver, against which he had been lying. He refused to be disturbed by the ring. He had taught himself to continue dozing through the noise. I sometimes wished that I could cultivate my cat's indifference to the world's demands. These days I was conscious that it could be North at the other end of the line. I always had an eagerness to speak with him.

'Are you busy? Could you do with a visitor for a short time? I want to walk out for a bit. I was going to call on Luke but he has gone out somewhere with his parents.' Luke was a fellow student who, of all his contemporaries, was, I suppose, the person he talked to most. I hesitate to call Luke his closest companion because North, it seemed to me, did not have close companions: his contemporaries were acquaintances.

'Sure, that would be nice. I'd love to see you. Drop by. I'll put some coffee on.'

'Great. I'll be with you in five minutes; and thanks. I always feel good talking to you. I feel that anything is possible. You inspire a quiet confidence.'

Now, I was not sure about the sincerity of those last sentiments even though, of course, I was pleased to hear them. We had just been reading an account of some educationalist, a prominent national writer, who had concluded from his researches that young aspiring students often felt that the whole world, indeed the whole of the universe, was open to them when in the presence of their mentor. There were no bounds to possibilities. North could have been giving the writer's views as a spurious reason for wanting to see me. He could have believed it all. Possibly he was being ironical. Knowing what I did of North, I suspected the latter. Nevertheless, I was infinitely pleased that he was coming round.

I finished the paragraph I was writing and turned the top sheet of my writing over so that the blank back of the page was uppermost. I put a kettle on to boil, then sat, ruminated, and waited.

North arrived. He was wearing a deep midnight-blue, open-neck shirt under a loose-shouldered, black linen jacket which looked expensive. It possessed a contrived, expert casualness which belongs to only the most expensive of tailoring houses, Ermenegildo Zegna perhaps. Again, I wondered how he could afford to dress in this manner, or how his mother could fund his image. Image, though, is the wrong word. No one felt that North cultivated an image the way others did. North was North; it was as simple as that. Everything about him was effortlessly North. There was no image, just North. I noticed that he was wearing around his neck some sort of black leather bootlace, attached to which there might have been a medallion or tag, but nothing was visible. His trousers were a pair of very dark bottle-green, almost black, needlecords; and he wore his customary black boots – he must have possessed quite a few pairs.

Perhaps my proximity inspired him. His presence certainly exhilarated me.

He obviously did not have anything specific to talk about.

I saw my chance to ask him what he thought of Aitken. He was curious to know why I wanted to know. Admittedly, I was not very subtle in my lead in.

'What do you make of Aitken? Does he strike you as an agreeable sort of man?'

'Why on earth should you ask? You know more about the guy than I do.'

'Yes. But from your perspective, is he likeable? Does he talk to you and the seniors very much?'

'Well ... not much. He talks to us a lot when he wants things to go his way without any fuss. Otherwise, we feel his mind is on his career. He spends most of his time doing what seems to him is the right thing. But he's an odd guy in a way. His relationship with his wife is a bit odd: he doesn't actually seem to care for her. And you rarely see him with his daughters. I reckon he's disappointed he hasn't got any sons.'

It was quite clear that everyone saw that Aitken was intensely ambitious. Even his senior students realized that he was clever, articulate, dedicated and ruthless. In spite of his gift for literary appreciation, his love of Milton and the Romantics, he was amoral: there was no religious burden to his thought. What North had to say reflected all this.

'Sure, he is amoral. Nothing stands in the way of what he has calculated he wants. Do you think he is without morals, though, in his dealings with those who are close to him?'

I gave this view and asked the question with North standing just in front of my desk, coffee cup in hand, looking out of the window. I could see that below him in the next door garden was my neighbour, a woman in her late thirties, lesbian, who had been quickly divorced after an experimental, disastrous marriage. Free from the encumbrance of her husband, she allowed a svelte young lover to move in. The lover, half the age of my neighbour, was an attractive, model-like blonde who wore a single pendant earring in her left ear. She customarily wore jeans and a bomber jacket, yet she was the sort of girl you might have dreams about. My neighbour was lucky to get her hands on this one, and lucky to have this one's hands laid on her.

North remarked of my gardening neighbour, 'She looks pretty amiable. What's she like? Do you communicate?'

I thought of the cries and shouts of pleasure, heard through the wall, that sometimes kept me awake in the early hours of the morning, or even woke me up. When she was being pleasured she knew no restraint, and certainly no modesty. I had no basic objection to what she did, but I did worry about any guests I might have staying in my house. I should not want them disturbed by her enthusiasm. My theological training had instructed and warned me against enthusiasm and in this instance, I saw it as a very bad thing. I was in the process of composing a note to her, diplomatically making it clear that I was aware of her liaison and enjoyment and asking her to think of those of us next door who might not want to hear her shouts and moans of gratification. It was a difficult project and it was taking me some time to write. Also I was concerned to choose the right moment to deliver it.

'Yes, she is nice. Is her lover there? I mean, of course, her female one. She's blonde and looks good.'

'No, she's on her own.'

'Look, North, in a sense I shouldn't be saying this, but do you think Aitken fancies any of the boys sexually ... as it were, homosexually?'

'Difficult to say.' North was not disconcerted by my question. He responded as though it were a natural follow-on from what we were saying. 'Some of the lads think he's got to be gay. He has just a very slightly camp manner which on the whole he keeps in check. They feel he'd love to let himself go. He never will: he's much too smart. He is never going to get caught with the boys. He's too focused on his career. He would never let himself down in that way. But they think he's in love with Monty.'

I could not believe my ears. It was as though North knew what I was thinking and what I was going to ask him. Anyway, the road was clear: he had brought up Monty; not I. I played cautiously, all the while convinced that North knew the cards I held in my hand.

'Good Lord!' I exclaimed in a sort of mock seriousness, 'Why do they think that?'

'Well, Aitken can't leave him alone. He's always in and out of his classes, asking him about something or other. They go into close huddles, turning their backs on the class. There is a lot of looking deeply into each other's eyes. These things do not go unnoticed. Another thing is that the only sports sessions and matches which Aitken ever turns up to watch are Monty Ross's. So, the consensus is that he fancies Monty.'

'What do you feel about that? What about Monty and Bernie then?'

'Don't worry. Bernie and I are all right. We know what we are doing. At the moment Monty doesn't bother me. I don't think he's interested in Aitken and any advances which might come from him; but he must be careful. I appreciate that. Monty wants to look after his own prospects. I might just encourage him to satisfy Aitken's desires in the interests of his career.'

He spoke his last thoughts jokingly, but I knew they had a ring of truthful intention as well. I was not sure that Bernie knew what she was doing. North, I was sure, had calculated all the odds so far as he was concerned; Bernie, I felt, was naïve and almost certainly confused. She, paradoxically, was relying on North, her young student, to guide her.

I commented to North that I had reservations about Aitken's alleged gayness. 'I think we should watch this space, so to speak. I intend to observe those two pretty closely from now on. I needn't bother to add, North, that some of my other colleagues, well, Jenny in particular, think something is going on.'

'We should listen to her,' North said. 'She's good. She knows what's going on.'

We then dropped the subject, but both of us knew that there was much more to be said and that the business would come back on some future agenda.

North talked about his mother, who had just gone away to Venice for a fortnight. She had been invited by an old, wealthy American friend to stay in a splendid palazzo near St Mark's. She was looking forward to the Danielli, where she and North's father had one evening on their honeymoon been entertained by her father-in-law. Venice possessed a romantic, artistic, literary atmosphere for her. She loved the place and would have dearly liked to live there. Oxford was second best.

'What will you do? Stay with friends?' I asked, knowing with a deep certainty that he would not.

'No. I'm looking after myself.' He turned and looked straight at me. He gently flicked back his long black hair – it had a slightly burnished, brown hue to it which relieved the blackness – he beamed that superb, brilliant, engaging smile he reserved for what he considered his most intimate moments, and said, 'I shall be able to see more of you. I delight in our conversation.

'Bernie and I will find everything less restricted. I shall not have to be so careful, although my Ma would leave me alone anyway. She thinks I know what I'm doing. Bernie will find it easier: she is basically conventional. Monty ... well, I don't know.'

I was not sure what he meant by his last remark. I was pleased that he had flattered me. He had the great gift of putting people at their ease and making them feel satisfied that they are wanted around the place. He never failed to make me feel elated.

We talked about sport. North was a natural, talented, sportsman. He played games, particularly cricket, with consummate style. He did not have to try: he had a natural eye and timing. Others had to practise, put hours in to achieve anything like the level of expertise that he had. Yet he was not fundamentally interested in playing the game to a high competitive level. We discussed this lack of enthusiasm on his part a number of times and were always returning to the subject. He thought there were better things to spend time on than sports: it was a mistake to become too professional and consequently spend a great deal of time on these games. He considered people, their souls and spirits, more important. It was better to read and learn, even if it were only novels, expand one's knowledge of human nature. You had to know how the mind works, understand the tricks and devices of a person's thinking. If you did, then you could compete in the far more important game of life. Sport was merely an adjunct, part of a means to an end: you should not waste too much time on it.

'For me, Monty Ross is suspect in this way,' he said. 'He is too keen on games. They have dominated his life in the past and he now gives them too great a prominence in education. I think his over-emphasis on them in his university days has damaged him. I know religion has taken over, or has seemingly done so. But I think the world is more important for him than his religion. It will take a back seat when the chips are down and he wants to pursue his own personal ends. We've already seen it happening. And just you wait: you will see how his religion becomes a matter of convenience. I bet you I could lead him astray. I already have when you think of his jealousy towards me and Bernie; but I bet I could seduce him too. I reckon there is something in the Aitken story, the more I think about it; and I reckon Monty is not all that disinclined to find a variety of sexual pleasure.'

North spoke with conviction and some passion. He seemed to mine a depth of knowledge about the way people behave which was beyond his years. I sat back and looked at him in admiration, this handsome boy, fresh and entirely open, and yet emitting a dangerous aura of analytical shrewdness. Again, he looked steadily straight into my eyes. It was as though he was settling quietly any anxieties, insecurities, I might have been experiencing over what he said. Later I would think that I should have done as the southern Italians of Apulia do to fend off the effects of the evil eye: they make the sign of the devil's horns with the first and fourth fingers of the hand and point them downwards to the ground. No one was immune from possessing the evil eye: even one of the Popes is said to have done so.

It was dangerous talk. Here was an eighteen-year-old proposing to me the homosexual seduction of one of his teachers. What was I doing? I should have been scandalized; but I was not. The discussion and the suggestion that a seduction might be possible at all seemed to spring quite naturally from the position we found ourselves in. There was no surprise. Anyway, at this point, the idea was academic. In any case, eighteen-year-olds were now grown up. Their position in society was significantly different from the one my contemporaries held at that age. We had been conscripted into the army and told to fight for our country and democratic values. We did not vote. For North and his contemporaries there was suffrage, there was freedom to have consenting sex, with either sex, from the age of sixteen. Why should I be surprised or shocked that he, or any of his student friends, could contemplate the sort of thing he had just mentioned?

North had removed his jacket and stretched out on the floor. He lay full length, flat on his back, his hands behind his head. He was totally relaxed. He had made himself completely at home, and was clearly gaining strength from his recumbent rest. It was like a yoga session for him. He was not self-conscious in any way. He assumed he belonged in my surroundings. He had assimilated them, and they had assimilated him. He was at one. He closed his eyes, but I sensed he was not asleep. I turned to my desk and looked at what I had been writing so that in the lull of conversation, while he took his rest, I might consider what I should write next. I tried a sentence or two, but although the ideas were there I could not find the right expression. North's presence was inhibiting. It was like not being able to urinate in front of others and not being able to analyse why you cannot: it was a mixture of reasons to do with embarrassment, anxiety, insecurity, lack of nerve, of confidence, and, maybe above all, an unspecified feeling of threat.

I turned the sheet back over and put on at very low volume a CD of Bach cello suites played by Tortelier: No. 2 in D minor, No. 3 in C and No. 6 in D. The music soothed my soul and, I thought, would have the same effect on North. Still awake, his breathing assumed the rhythms of one asleep. We listened to the music in complete silence.

When the recording had finished, I asked if he would like to listen to some more. He made no comment, merely nodded an affirmative. His eyes wide open to the ceiling, he continued his careful relaxation; and he was obviously thinking. I found a German recording by Harmonia Mundi for the French market of Beethoven's *Sonate pour piano et violoncelle, Opus 69*, the cello played by Christophe Coin. We listened to the haunting airs of variations on the theme of Handel's 'See the conqu'ring hero comes', and until the close of the variations on 'Bei Männern welche Liebe fühlen' when North gently rose and said that he should make tracks back home. He admired the music we had just heard. He was an eighth-grade pianist and a guitarist. He had told me that his mother had made sure that he was taught classical music, classical guitar, but that it gave him an edge in his more popular music playing. His tastes were eclectic. He was not a stranger to the club scene. He had told me on other occasions that he had been to both Birmingham and London to some of the clubs there, Palumbo's Ministry of Sound, and God's Kitchen in the second city. He was no punter: he viewed the scene and knew what was going on.

As I saw him to the door, he checked his mobile phone for messages. There was evidently a text message which he scanned briefly and smiled at. I wondered who had sent it. I imagined his mother might have been in touch, telling him of the architectural grandeurs of Venice, about the friends she had met, the art historian from Chicago and Lady Duveen, a left-over of the Irish aristocracy. It might have been Bernie, keeping in touch, unable to be out of contact for more than a morning at a time. Who knows? He gave no clue: just the faintest of smiles. Had he been an agent of a foreign power, it might have been from his controller, the message immediately erased. Perhaps he was the devil's emissary, communication maintained by terrestrial means. It did not matter: it was no concern of mine. He turned at the door, thanked me, apologized for, in his own words, not making an effort, and said that he would spend the evening with Bernie, which troubled me slightly.

'It should be good, and might even extend into the night. I don't have Ma to think of. Bernie would like it.'

'She certainly would. You would make a young girl's heart happy. Mind you if Monty were to know, there would be problems. Anyway, I envy you your lot.'

I did not in fact. There were too many complications in

this sort of situation. I could see most of them clearly, but some were vague and ill-defined.

'Don't worry,' he said, 'I'll make Monty happy too. He might feel disconsolate now, but he will have his reward.'

I did not know exactly what North meant, but there was something a little salacious intended in his remark. Was Monty to be diverted and satisfied by North's sexual attentions, a tactic in North's wider strategy? It seemed possible.

He held my shoulders and gave me his usual hug, and walked away homewards.

Later that evening I saw Bernie and North. I had tired of my desk and had arranged to have a drink with an old friend, the ninety-year-old widow of a famous, Nobel prize-winning, medical scientist, who still lived by herself in a large house in Headington. I decided to walk the mile or so, and as I walked down the High, past the Queen's College, I saw Bernie and North emerging arm-in-arm from a café. Bernie looked splendid. She was looking very 1950s-ish, wearing the chic drabness of what looked like an Eley Kishimoto spotted dress. Of course, it was not Kishimoto but it created a similar impression, and it made her look extremely sexy. All this for North. She was entranced by him, there was no doubt in my mind. I had noticed over the last few days, the way she presented herself for him. She tried consciously to complement him. His elegant darkness needed to be set off against her emphasized femininity and she instinctively knew how to do it.

They were murmuring in conversation, North holding her hand. Since I was there to see them, I thought, why were not others who belonged to their world? Why were they not seen, for instance, by Aitken? Admittedly, he was hardly ever around in public except on formal occasions. But the deputy might see them, surely. Were they just lucky that scandal avoided them? Did North lead, then, a charmed life? I began to think he did.

I watched them go, a pair of lovers disappearing into the night. They gave off a romantic aura. It was how life should be. Theirs was the perfection of youth: to those who did not know the reality of their mundane lives, they must have appeared an ideal couple. As I continued to watch, they slowed down, paused, she turned to face him, and he gave her the gentlest of kisses on her lips. She responded by inclining her head and resting it on his left shoulder. She brought her right hand down to his waist, then to his thigh, and she stroked him tenderly. She looked up into his eyes, kissed him firmly on his lips, a long, insistent kiss, raised her hand, caressed his cheek, turned, put her hand through his arm, and they resumed their walk. I felt that somewhere in the background there must be a film director who was setting up this scene specifically for me. Yet they did not know I was there; they did not know I was watching.

Monty Ross must have been in turmoil. I did not know him very well, just as a colleague. I noted when he was appointed that he was a personable young man. The fact that he was a sportsman was an advantage for him in my eyes. I was still a keen player, mostly of squash and tennis, though I had to be careful about playing squash, nothing too competitive. My opponents needed to be potentially good players who were still improving. That way I could pace my game and make sure my blood pressure did not hit the top of the scale. It meant that coaching the game was perfect for me, although I was only any good with natural players, otherwise I lost patience. Monty had played before, but not very much. He joined one or two of us who played a few times each week. At first I could hold my own in contest with him; but it was clear that before long, if he were to play regularly, he would outlast me and reach shots which I could no longer quite make. That was how I knew him: on court, for a short time afterwards, in the common room, and elsewhere in passing.

I watched him about the place. He was keen and energetic. He reminded me of advertisements for schoolmasters which appeared in the national press, 'young, vibrant, energetic teacher required to teach (whatever), able to help with games, drama, societies, and the Corps Cadet Force'. That was the head teacher's idea of the perfect schoolmaster: someone who would fill vacancies and solve a whole bunch of problems. I reckoned that such people did not really exist; but then I realized that Ross was the sort of person those potential employers had in mind. It was no wonder that Aitken was so pleased with him, and no wonder that Monty got on so fast. I watched his rapid rise to positions of power in the small, restricted world of the school. He became head of his department. He was put in charge of the Christian Union Society. Aitken soon made him a housemaster, one of the youngest ever appointed. Monty Ross was the shining star.

At the same time as witnessing his promotion and enjoyment of Aitken's patronage, I told myself, and one or two others, that he was the sort of person you would avoid sitting next to at dinner in an Oxford or Cambridge college. His brand of bright evangelism would stick in your craw as he tried to entice you to attend the next Christian meeting: 'Come on. Come and listen. Don't be afraid. Listen to the witness of those who believe, those who are saved, those who have Jesus as their friend. It is an open house: you can share your doubts with all of us and we shall help you.' I always considered this sort of approach to be audacious. It required a naïve nerve. I belonged to a religious way of belief that put great store by quiet reserve. You did not press yourself on people uninvited. You did not initiate conversations on the topic of religion, which should be considered a personal, private matter.

Anyway, because of my reservations about him, I did not get to know him very well at all. I gleaned what I did know by what others said about him and from my own observations. His ability to talk himself into a position in which he could espouse his religion, continue to lead his intimate domestic life with pregnant Jess and want every moment of the day to be in the presence of Bernie failed to impress me. I thought he should come clean to someone – Jess, Bernie, Aitken, but mostly to himself.

Jenny was a prime source of information. She kept company with some of the younger female teachers, who were all extremely envious of the budding Monty and Bernie relationship. To a woman, Jenny exclaimed, they would all like to bed Monty. The very sight of him in his coaching kit, slightly sweaty but with still a hint of Givenchy aftershave, clean-cut, handsome, fit, made each one of them lust after him. The fact that Bernie, relatively new to the scene, should have got to the bait before them, annoyed them intensely. Some of them expressed their anguish and jealousy in the crudest of terms. Jenny and I who had been confidants for years never held back: she told me exactly what they said, and I was surprised, if not shocked.

Jenny also knew Jess and occasionally went to see her, now that she was pregnant. The one subject which she avoided in discussion was Bernie, but she knew that Jess had her suspicions. Jess's problem was that she was preoccupied with her condition and the developing life within her; she could not devote her attention to making sure that Monty was in line.

She felt, anyway, that he ought to be, without her having to whip him in. Jenny was sorry for Jess, but could not see the way out of that particular moral mess and so did nothing.

She knew Monty far better than I did. She would seek him out and chat with him, tease him in her own inimical way. She had the gift, sometimes dangerous, of making people, particularly men who were younger than her, say things which they later wished they had not. Monty, with his self-serving, naïve enthusiasm, she could lead on quite easily.

'He hates what Bernie is up to,' she told me one afternoon as we were unwinding from the stress of teaching that day. 'He is even prepared to mention North by name. He said the other day that he hated that 'precocious Anglo-American boy'. He could not understand what either North or Bernie was doing. I told him not to worry, that it was nothing; that it would soon fizzle out. I didn't believe myself, but that is what I told him.'

Apparently the conversation continued like this. Monty responded crossly, 'I hate the little bastard. What does he think he's doing? And what is wrong with Bernie? I thought she liked me.'

Jenny cut in, 'Of course she does. But come on, Monty, she knows you're married. The North thing is not serious; it won't last. And, in any case, you are good friends with her.'

Jenny acknowledged to herself that what she had said was risible. Good friends: it was obvious to everyone that Monty was in serious trouble with Bernie so far as the affairs of love went. On the other hand, how did you play it all down? Monty somehow had to be stopped from making a fool of himself. If he really began to hate North, there would be big trouble. She tried to diminish the level of Monty's jealous anger. Jenny thought that the obvious person to sort out this mess was North. Someone should speak to him and point out that there could be chaos. At one stage, she even appealed to me to talk to him. My immediate response was that she clearly did not have any idea about the nature of North, no understanding of what makes him tick.

'Being friends with Bernie is all very well,' Monty said, 'but if you know that she is canoodling with some trendy late-adolescent then it makes it difficult.'

'You don't know if there's really anything to it, Monty. It's probably all perfectly innocent. Stop worrying. Pursue your own course. North doesn't stand a chance.'

'Oh, yes he does. Look at him. He's attractive. He's good-looking, polite, charming. She goes for him. He knows it. If she's hooked, he'll do something about it.'

Of course, Monty was right. He was a lover who could sense danger; and Jenny did not believe the content of her own soothing words.

'It's a complete bastard. I'd ring his bloody American neck if I could.'

When Jenny told me this, I knew for a certainty that there would be trouble, and I knew that was what North was deliberately contriving.

There were times when Monty could not keep still. He became frenetic. I observed him. I found it difficult to conceive that he could have any peace of mind in the same building, the same institution, in which North, who was, in a sense, his rival, lived and worked for most of the day. He must suffer that disease of love that the ancients describe as the 'loveris maladye of Hereos'. Even if any other grown man were unable to take the idea of North philandering with Bernie seriously, Monty certainly did. He was sick. He found the experience torture; and he did see North as a rival. There was no doubt about that: he took it very seriously indeed. Perhaps he should have laughed it off: I thought that I would have done. As a young man, I might have been as deeply obsessed, preoccupied and captivated by Bernie as he was. Slightly older, I would have left Bernie and North to it or, conversely, done something positive about it: I should have played North at his own game and worked out a strategy to set him up in a destructive position which would have left him exposed to public view and humiliation. After all, North was a mere youth.

My thoughts were all very well, but Monty was not me. I think I have a harder heart, and I ponder with the hindsight of experience. Then there was the nature of North to consider. I certainly had never before come across anyone like him: in all my years of teaching, lecturing, meeting people professionally and socially, I had never met anyone so coolly confident as him. North had a disconcerting, dangerous quality about him. So there was that to reckon with. Monty did not know what to do and it showed.

He did not teach North. They did not come into direct contact. Monty just felt his constant presence. His agitation was extreme. The only times that he calmed and recovered his confident personable manner was when Aitken was in view. Then, Monty was noticeably in control of himself. It was as if an autopilot detected the head's presence and took over Monty's steerage. Everything else, including North, became subservient to Aitken's view of Monty's world. Monty was not going to let anything disturb Aitken's benign view of him. No questions were to be asked by Aitken.

On Aitken's part, Monty was to be talked to and encouraged at every turn. The tone and timbre of Aitken's voice changed subtly when he spoke to Monty, or when he spoke of him to others. I remembered what Jenny had said and North's opinion. The circumstantial evidence was adding up to Aitken's queerness. As I listened to them speak to each other, I could feel that they were absorbed in each other. Had I, or the others who happened to be around, not been there, I sensed they would not have been able to keep their hands off each other. The atmosphere was as loaded as that. My imagination raced.

Aitken sought Monty out on every occasion possible: at lunch, during the lesson breaks, he turned up to watch training sessions and matches, as any good head should do, but always managed to single out Monty to talk to. He often called Monty to see him for meetings in his study. In public, Monty could be seen to look him straight in the face, tilt his head to one side and engage Aitken fully with his deep blue eyes. Body language, eye contact, all physical gestures signalled admiration and affection: in two people of opposite sexes it would all have added up to a heartfelt, conventional love. Perhaps that's what it was. North said so: he saw clearly what was going on and was never afraid to use the term. He knew the two of them were inhibited because of their backgrounds, upbringing and career ambitions, but he read the signs; and he convinced me that the true nature of that mutual attraction was homosexual love.

What I did not understand, and never succeeded in working out, was how such a young person, with little experience of the world, could have a knowledge of human behaviour such as North appeared to possess. Indeed, it was not a case of appearances, he did have such a shrewd understanding that you wondered how he had passed his teenage years. Where had he been? What fire had his intelligence been forged in? To my knowledge, he had spent the time with his mother. She had brought him up in difficult and disturbed circumstances after the arguments with his father and the eventual separation and wretched divorce. When I approached the subject with North, and expressed my wonder at the level of his worldly knowledge, he dismissed it all: he suggested that I was a little out of touch with the contemporary lifestyle of young people. He knew that this was a deflection, because he knew that I was not out of touch: my young friends were numerous. I, of all people, knew what was going on in the fashionable, media-dominated, music-motivated society that the young lived in, not just during the day, but also at night. I still believed that someone of North's age could not ordinarily acquire the maturity of vision and judgment he had; but, of course, that was it – North was out of the ordinary. Rules that apply to everyone else did not apply to North.

The fact was that North did possess an understanding that was mature. Human nature held no mysteries for him.

'If you are intelligent, if you read as I do, if you study how people react in different situations, then you can see what is going to happen. All the rest is easy: some people are kind and cheerful, others morbid and cruel. Some are excitable, passionate, sexy, others static, insipid, neutral so far as sex goes. You can see around you, some people are rampantly voracious heteros, and some are crafty, predatory gays. A few,' he added, 'like me, act according to our own agenda.'

'So,' I concluded from this discussion on that particular occasion, 'you have learnt from what you see and from what you read. You are remarkable. When I was your age, by comparison, I was a greenhorn, a tenderfoot. I knew nothing of the world.'

'Then you had not read Milton. The complete tragedy of human existence is embraced in the *Paradise Lost*. It is my bible. Adam and Eve are fooled around with by an unforgiving, vengeful God: they are sorry victims. Then look at the stark intelligence of Satan, whose complaints against the Almighty are extremely reasonable. He refuses to give up in the face of an overwhelming, unremitting force, which in the end is bound to crush him. Or so the legend would have it. Poor mankind: what an awful mess we are in.'

He was right: I had not read Milton at his age. I could barely grapple with the great Puritan moralist until I was in my early twenties. That was a difference between North and me.

Apart from times when he was in the presence of Aitken, Monty was, I reckoned, losing control. He was losing patience and his frustration was making him careless: he took less and less account of what other people thought about his actions, speech and general attitudes. He grew more and more outspoken against North. If North's name cropped up in conversation, Monty was bound to make some tart remark about him. If he happened to see North in the distance, he would bring him to notice by talking him down, speaking adversely of him. It became an obsession. I pointed it all out to Monty one morning and warned him about making it too obvious that he disliked the youth. It would do him no good: everybody would notice his obsessive criticism and, parents particularly, would take exception to what would be seen as an inappropriate personal vendetta.

'Monty, you must not go on so much about North. For goodness sake, take no notice. You are making your objections too strong. People won't like it, and if they complain to Aitken, it won't do you any good.'

'But he's such a brat, such a nuisance. You don't understand. He's intolerable. Why doesn't he keep out of the way? What is he doing messing about with Bernie?'

Monty's ambitions so far as Bernie was concerned were all too clear. He could not see what a spectacle he was making of himself.

'Look Monty, ease up. You are not behaving rationally. If you like, North is a puppy. His Bernie affair won't last, probably not the week; and even if it does, it isn't serious. She'll send him packing. Don't let it eat away at your soul.

'Anyway, why should you care? Look, keep Bernie as a

friend. Don't get mixed up in anything more spiritual or sensual. You have Jess and someone else to think of now.'

In my heart I knew it was too late for advice such as this, and this was probably the reason why I gave it. I have made a point of not giving advice: it usually works to your detriment. You set yourself apart, the advice is more often than not ignored, and you begin to be perceived as a critic. The friend you have advised grows distant and ceases to be a confidant. I stopped dispensing advice early on, becoming instead someone who would explore possibilities, discuss options, debate ways and means. In this way, by clarifying the issues but not preferring one before another, I could remain close. I took no hard and fast moral position. I kept my friends.

With Monty it was different. I must have recognized him as a lost cause. So, I gave him advice, which I knew there was no chance of him taking.

'Bernie is a friend,' he almost shouted, 'and Jess doesn't mind. She likes Bernie. They get on well. She knows there is nothing in it. She can rely on me.'

How many times have I heard that sort of protestation in my life, just before disaster, when a marriage has collapsed in chaotic ruin? There was no doubt: Monty was blind to reality. He did not know that he was mortally infected by a disease which could prove to be terminal, a disease of love whose symptoms were obvious to onlookers but undetected by the sufferer.

'Well, don't waste your time on North. He will go away. It isn't serious.'

I mouthed the words but did not believe their import. North's intelligence was superior to Monty's. North was not obsessed: his interest in Bernie had nothing to do with love and everything to do with calculated pleasure, not just sexual but intellectual as well, as in a game of chess. Monty was totally involved physically and spiritually; North was engaged in a strategic game, which he thoroughly enjoyed, but from which, if he felt like it, he could maintain a distance and, if necessary, stop playing immediately. My only remark which seemed to make any impact was the one concerning Aitken.

'I don't like him,' Monty continued to attack North. 'You don't really think that my dislike is so noticeable that people really would mention it to Aitken, do you? It isn't that obvious, is it? I'd like to know what Aitken thinks about North. I'm going to ask him. Perhaps he can cut the little pervert down to size.'

'Oh come on Monty. Don't be so extreme. North is not a pervert. If you ask me, he's a pretty normal sort of a guy. Get a sense of proportion. Aitken – well, be careful what you say about North to him. Remember his mother has powerful friends. That ferocious chairman of governors is a friend of hers. She moves in influential circles in this community. Turn the pressure down, Monty, you're overdoing it. And yes, I do think people would mention your personal animosity towards North if they notice. I'm not sure that they have done so yet, but if you go on as you are, they will. Don't let it get to Aitken.'

I continued, 'He thinks too much of you, Monty. He holds you in high regard,' and before I knew what I was saying, I added, 'He likes you. Build on it. Cultivate him, Monty.'

Subsequently, I realized that by expressing my thoughts like this to Monty I was performing part of North's task. I was becoming a tool in the implementation of North's strategy.


A few days later I drove into London. I went to meet an old friend. We were to dine at our club in St James's. It was a classical, elegant, building of the late eighteenth century, with high-ceilinged rooms of lavish proportions, comfortable chairs, and good service. The incumbent secretary kept telling us that he wanted us to feel that it was our London home, a place to escape to from the noise, the hurly-burly, the litter of the crowded city. He was right: it is an oasis of calm. The great casement windows seem to shut out the clamour of the metropolis. The eye of the Great Wheel and the sentinel Big Ben look in from a short distance at the drawing room with its relaxing, recumbent men and women. I had driven up to town from Oxford in my BMW 325i, a comfortable, lively car, rather old but, nevertheless, reliable. I meant to renew my car but could not decide what to buy. As the BMW functioned superbly, there was never the pressure or urgency to change it. I stayed loyal to it.

The journey into London had been straightforward. In the late afternoon, early evening, the traffic is rarely bad: the bulk of it goes the other way, out of London. So, you pass queues of traffic, congested and stationary, facing out of town, while you glide with a minimum of delay into the centre. I had listened on Radio Three to a contemporary I had known at university who now hosted a two-hour concert programme. He had treated me, among other delights, to Beethoven's Piano Trio in B flat major, Opus 97 'Archduke', and Schubert's Piano Trio No. 1 in B flat major. I always find that while driving or cycling some of my most constructive thoughts arrive, and on that occasion I suddenly had an idea about what to do in Monty's sad, agitated case. The music soothed my mind and my soul, and I saw clearly what should happen.

Certainly Monty should be careful about what Aitken thought and learned about him; but why should not Monty and North somehow be friends? Monty had to see that the business between North and Bernie would not last, that it was ephemeral, unimportant. His own preoccupation with her, too, was fleeting. What mattered to Monty was his continuing relationship with his wife. That was important. Aitken should not think badly of Monty in any circumstances. What I had to do, and others as well, was to make it all clear to Monty and make him calm down. Perhaps if I spoke to Bernie it would help. Could Jenny be brought into the scheme? Hers was a gentle, agreeable approach. Monty might listen to her. All these thoughts crossed my mind. I grew convinced that Monty and North should be brought together. Monty had to see that North was a friend, not an enemy. After all, in a year's time North would not be around. He would have gone off to a university miles away, perhaps even back to the States to some Ivy League college like Princeton or Yale. He was no threat. His presence was short-term. Bernie had to know that too.

The meeting with my old friend was hugely enjoyable. We reminisced about our days on national service in the army. He had served in a distinguished northern infantry regiment and spent most of his time as a subaltern in West Germany expecting invasion from behind the iron curtain, while I had been drafted into intelligence and worked for eighteen months in Cyprus, the greater part of the time spent in Nicosia dealing with field intelligence and interrogation of EOKA terrorists. I had never kept up my army connections, but he had: he was concerned with the regimental association and had chaired a committee responsible for raising funds to refurbish the regimental museum. He represented the regiment at various meetings abroad, where he would appear in smart, pin-striped suit, bowler hat, furled umbrella and regimental tie. He was good company. We dined to the accompaniment of a decanter of the club's best house claret and parted company at ten-thirty. As I drove back to Oxford, I determined to talk to Monty, to North and to Jenny. Bernie I was not so confident about: I did not know her so well.

The following day I ran into Monty just after lunch. He looked worried and preoccupied.

'Hi, Monty. How are things? Are you OK?'

'Not great. Nothing seems to be going right. Everything was such fun here. Now, I don't know. It's all going wrong.'

'Oh, come on. Don't be so despondent. What's specifically is worrying you?'

'Jess is suspicious and crotchety. Bernie is hard work: she is difficult. She still wants me, but North gets in the way. Once we do get together, after a short time, everything is OK. She says I am very special; but then she says that about North, only in a different way. She likes his youth and is flattered by his attention. She says she wants to understand him, that he is so young and beautiful that she wants to make the most of him now. She knows it can't last.'

'Well, there you are,' I commented. 'He will go away. It's as I told you. And, since she knows it, you have nothing to worry about. Take it easy. If I were you, I'd talk to North. You would find him pleasant company. I know you would. You had, though, better be careful about Jess, if you value your marriage. She must have got wind of what's happening. It is impossible to keep this sort of thing under wraps. Thank goodness I am past being involved in all these *affaires de coeur*. I wish you joy.'

He carried on about how difficult it would be to talk to North. He still had a gut feeling of enmity towards him. I told him he was mad, that he should try dialogue. It was like an exercise in diplomacy. There were warring parties: the only way to peace was through discussion. Once embarked upon talks, trust and friendship would grow. I told him I was convinced of it. He must try. We went on for some time. It was one of the longest talks I had ever had with Monty: as I have said, he was not one of my close associates.

I think he listened and probably saw that there was nowhere else to go: his present entrenched position with regard to North was self-destructive. He repeated that Aitken should not become aware of any trouble, any scandal. He had, as it were, to treat with North. His was the advantage: North would soon disappear. I reminded him that in most people's view, it was Jess who would command sympathy if the whole complicated muddle broke cover and came out into the open. He thought, as all such lovers do, that he could handle Jess. His attraction to Bernie was not as fundamental as that to Jess: Jess would understand if ever it became known; but it never would become known. Of course, he was deluded: these entrapped married lovers always are. Fiction becomes truth in their minds. They are in constant denial, as the therapist I once consulted in Los Angeles would assert.

Later, as I remembered the conversation, I was pleased that Monty was setting out on the right road. I was sure he was. Even if it was only a beginning, it was a good thing. Soon after meeting Monty, I met Jenny, and, as we were chatting, North came along and joined us.

It is extraordinary, the way I could sense his approach. I would feel my back tingle, but I could never decide whether the cause was fear or excitement. In other circumstances, with other people, I would have decided fear. The sensation made me recall a time in Cyprus when I was accompanying a patrol and we came face to face with a group of Cypriot youths led by two older men. I had turned to speak with the second lieutenant in command of the patrol when I experienced that spinal *frisson* for the first time, and, sure enough, when I faced round one of the two men had hurled a hand grenade towards us. Fortunately, it hit the ground, bounced twice, and rolled down an alley between two shops, one of them, appropriately, a coffin maker's, and exploded. Shattered wood and glass was the result of the grenade, and one Cypriot shot in the thigh, lying immobile, but screaming, in front of us. The lead soldier had quickly levelled his Sten gun and shot the culprit; the rest had fled. The patrol fanned out and went off in hot pursuit. That *frisson* was fear: the cause was unseen when I experienced it, but I recognized what fear was from that moment.

With North there was no fear; there was exhilaration, excitement. The nervous tingle, which spread upwards and made my back tingle, anticipated delight, also before the source was understood. I cannot explain why I should react this way, but I did: my spirits soared. At the same time, there lurked in my mind a question: where was the fear? I should have expected fear, and yet I was experiencing the opposite. I was aware of the strange effect that North had on me. Paradoxically, I detected danger, but only slightly. It was impossible to explain, to define, but it was there, faintly present, obviously, definitely, associated in some way with North but insubstantial no matter how deeply I thought about it.

Anyway, no matter: because North's presence gladdened me. This time there was no formal greeting. Jenny asked him how he was and I acknowledged him with a nod and hailed him.

'Hello. Good to see you. How are things?'

North smiled at us and said, 'Fine. Good. I'm keeping myself busy with work and play.'

Jenny ribbed him. 'I hope you maintain the balance. Too much play can make you tired. Don't let your work suffer.' She said it with a knowing look, and I wondered what was passing through her mind. Jenny would not have been averse to enjoying the delights of North's sexual attentions, but she was a realist who knew what she could expect at her age. She confined her enjoyment of North to her imagination.

'I can manage, and manage very well,' North said. 'My sense of balance is well developed. You needn't worry about me.'

'Well, I certainly don't,' I offered. 'You seem to me to be in control.'

Jenny asked him about his art work and mentioned an exhibition which was due to open at the Museum of Modern Art. The American artist was known to North's mother, so North had met him and was about to do so again at the pre-view party. It was at this sort of event that North had learnt sophistication at so young an age, by conversing with artists, writers, political commentators. He was lucky to have been surrounded by articulate adults whose views and manners must have given him a polish which most of his contemporaries lacked. Jenny made her excuses and went on her way. I said that I would meet with her later: we should have tea or a drink when the school had closed down for the day.

I strolled with North towards the sports centre where I was heading to fix a squash game with one of the sports coaches.

'I've told Monty Ross that he should talk to you as a friend. He thinks of you now as an interfering nuisance. You know this, of course. I reckon he should get to know you: that's what I've told him. It might make things easier.'

'Good idea. That's what I want. It would make me happy.' He spoke with deliberation, and went on, 'And I know that I can make him happy.'

I felt a panic sweep across me momentarily. I remembered North lying on the floor of my study, stretched out and relaxed, and his remark then about being able to make Monty happy. He had made some remark about Monty reaping his reward. What was going on? What did he mean? I was strongly aware of North's sexual power. I felt sure that he was announcing his intention of seducing Monty. He had captured Bernie. That conquest made, he could advance in the chess game of love. I thought mischievously that if Bernie were the queen, then perhaps Monty was a bishop, a low-church, evangelical one. Who, then, was the King in this game? Aitken, I thought, without a doubt.

'What do you mean? How can you do that? Really, I don't see what power you have to make Monty happy.' That was a lie: I could see very well. I was going through the conversational requirements of someone of my age and position. I was being conventional and orthodox, and it did not deceive North.

'You know very well. You're no fool. You know me. I have no secrets, at least not with you. I'll bet Monty will want me, and I could make it to the exclusion of everyone else. Yet I don't want that. I want him to keep an interest in Bernie, and I don't want him to leave his wife. If I can give him pleasure, though, at the same time as enjoying myself: why not? I reckon it's on the cards.'

I was sceptical of North's altruism but did not say so.

Of course, I have heard and read about children who have sexually seduced adults – that is to say, who have been the initiating partner – but I had never encountered one. Not that North was such a child: he was not a child – he was eighteen and he knew perfectly well what he was doing. He acted with a grown-up's rationale and deliberation. Yet it was almost as if he were controlled by an alien spirit, subtle, sophisticated and supremely competent, so much did the workings of his mind belie his external appearance. I dismissed this thought as fanciful and considered the reality of the situation. North was about to embark on the seduction of one of his male teachers. Though Monty did not actually teach him, he did work in the school North was at. In one sense it was absurd; in another it was catastrophically awful. I had visions of headlines in *The Sun* or the *Mirror* 'Boy Leads Master Astray' 'Boy Seduces Beak'.

Yet such sensationalist claims did not describe the situation. What North was engaged in was the politics of love. There was a campaign going on: moves had to be made, tactics conceived and performed. Its politics were giving way to warfare and the strategems of a general were being brought into play. North was no minor thoughtlessly following some basic instinct; his was a superior intellect making conscious decisions in matters of personal relationships and, what to most of us seems to be that arbitrary element, love.

When we reached the sports hall and parted, I knew that he was primed to respond to any advances or overtures that Monty might make towards him. He would have responded anyway. One remark of his during that conversation lodged in my mind, the one about not having any secrets which he kept from me. Did I believe him? I was not sure. We all have secrets we guard carefully from even those who are dearest to us. Yet again, he knew how to flatter me: I felt immensely privileged. Who, then, did he keep secrets from? And why? Why had he adopted me as his confidant? North was such a complicated fellow. He contented and calmed me with his presence and simultaneously created so many questions that I wanted to know the answers to.

I met with Jenny again later on. She immediately asked how everything was in the personal stakes between Bernie, Monty and North. I told her that I knew little about Bernie's feelings, but reported most of what I had picked up from the other two. She said that Bernie had spoken to her and had seemed perfectly happy. Bernie enjoyed both her men in different ways. She loved North's freshness and his mind, but she was attracted to Monty's physical strength. There was a physical chemistry she could not understand which made her want Monty's body more than anything else. I thought it amazing that Bernie should have spoken to Jenny, someone she did not know all that well, and reveal such details of her preferences. Jenny said that other female colleagues, inspired by jealousy, were planning Bernie's downfall: some of them were determined to make trouble for her with Aitken. They were envious of her success and happiness. In this equation it was not North who featured very much, but Monty. He was the one they wanted, not the person they saw as an inexperienced youth and of whose interests they were ignorant. If only they had known. I felt that North actually contrived to reinforce their view of him. He remained aloof. When he had to have dealings with those female teachers, he was polite to the point of formality. There was never any sign of sexual interest. He made himself unavailable by his manner. Rather like a chameleon, he appeared differently in their presence than when he was with Bernie. Monty was their man: his handsome good looks and athletic physique made him desirable, his Christian credentials rendered him wholesome and drew those young women to a challenge. They told themselves that they knew his game and they could defeat his principles: the defensive walls surrounding his moral keep would easily fall to their wily attack. Therefore, how irksome it was to find him so utterly abject before the demands of a newcomer. Bernie drew their hatred. North kept intentionally to the shadows.

Jenny told me how her pet project was developing. One of her students, a boy whose mother was Jewish and father Croatian, had won a number of local poetry competitions and had been invited to attend the youth section of a literary convention to be held in Ravello. He was to read some of his poems alongside a selection of other young, aspiring international poets. Since a number of famous writers and poets were supposed to be showing up there – one American novelist was running a number of creative writing seminars, and an Australian poet was helping judge a competition – Jenny was trying to organize a five-day trip to the Italian resort. It would be out of season, so the place would not be stuffed with tourists. Apparently there was also going to be a conference of heart specialists in town, and they would be using the main public building, the Villa Rufolo. But two other hotels, smaller but just as distinguished – each had seen former glory as a residential villa belonging to noble families, both Italian and English – were to be given over to the literary convention. Jenny had booked ten places and arranged cheap air travel with a low-budget, no frills airline. The core of her party was much the same as that of Sam's art expedition to the States.

Our Croatian poet had pride of place. Sam did not go: he had a prior visit organized to Rome. Sue said she could not afford it. I would have liked somehow to pay for her, but I knew that she was not at all keen on poetry and probably would not take the patronage anyway. Jenny asked Bernie and Monty, expecting Monty not to accept. He did, saying that Jess, who was near the time of her delivery or, should I say, deliverance, said she did not mind. Her mother had moved in for the duration and, as there was a little tension between Monty and his mother-in-law, Jess thought it better that Monty was out of the way for a time. I accepted the invitation with alacrity. Ravello is one of my favourite places. If, like Gore Vidal, I could afford a villa there, I should move tomorrow. Jenny had consulted me on who else she should ask, and I at once suggested North. She replied that she had obviously thought of him, but for the sake of a quiet life considered that he should be left out. I countered with the view that it might bring matters to a resolution; besides which, it would be extremely good for North and, in any case, he was good company. Our Croatian poet needed someone of his own age and intellectual calibre: North would fulfil the role perfectly. Jenny acceded, and the party was completed with a few other senior students. It was a congenial party, and one for me which was full of interest and full of potential.

North loved the idea of the trip. It was not too long and, therefore, would not distract him from his work. He had never been to Ravello, but he knew about people who had. He asked me if it were my idea. I made it clear to him that it was Jenny's, but that I had strongly supported his inclusion in the visit. He was immensely pleased.

'Thanks, my good friend. You look after my interests more than you could know. You seem, if you don't mind me saying so, to be facilitating my plan. Bernie will be on the trip – a distinct bonus for me – and Monty. Perhaps I shall find the opportunity to be alone with him. I think he and I are destined to be close companions,' he said, looking at me directly. There was no ambiguity in his look. His deep, dark blue eyes shone and sparkled with electric energy. His mind was working on lines familiar to both of us.

'I know what you mean. I suppose all goes according to plan, but be careful. I'm not sure this trip is the time to make a move on Monty. It may be too soon. Take the temperature.'

I paused. I was doing something that I had renounced: I was giving advice.

'Take no notice, North. Do as you see fit. I trust your judgement. You will know when the time is right.'

'Of course. And thanks. I value what you say. I don't underestimate the importance of what you say. In every way, you are essential to me.'

It was the first time he had said anything like this to me. I was pleased that he said he needed me but could not quite work out what he meant. Did he value me as a true and proper friend? Or did he see me simply as a tool to help him in his enterprise? He did not elaborate. He remained an enigma. It was true that I had proposed his invitation for the visit to Ravello, knowing that it would put him in proximity with Monty Ross. Miles from home, distant from familiar places, the provision of bedrooms and secluded gardens, I knew perfectly well all those factors provided the opportunity and the space for two people to feel that they could safely meet in private. No doubt, in the complex game started months before, I had become a support player who, for the most part, sat on the sidelines and watched, but sometimes was called on to participate. Perhaps I had just done that: taken part, helped to set up a move that would lead to some sort of eventual victory. Whose victory, though? I was not sure. Nothing, at that stage, was clear.

We all looked forward to the visit. Aitken gave it wide publicity. There was a piece in the local press: Jenny was interviewed with our fledgling Croatian poet; their photograph was in a central, culture section of the paper. The school took more credit for the encouragement of the poet than, in fact, had been the case. Aitken had a keen sense for the exploitation of anything with favourable publicity potential. He was education's Max Clifford, determined, unscrupulous, effective at catching, and staying in, the public eye.

A regional poetry magazine, not very famous and printed on low-quality paper, decided to publish a couple of our poet's poems. Jenny loved it all and was also interviewed on the local television channel about the school, its poetry output and her planned visit to the literary convention.

They set off a few days into the mid-term holiday in a minibus for Stansted airport. That was the part of the venture that I baulked at: I told Jenny and the others that I would meet them there. I made an excuse about having to go into London for some reason or other. I would drive myself out of London to Stansted, leave my car in a mid-stay car-park, and meet them at the airline desk. North, when he heard, immediately understood that I wanted to avoid minibus travel and wanted to come with me: he said it would give us time for a good long chat, but I thought that his presence with me would not do. It would be seen by most of the others to be inappropriate. I told him it was not possible and explained the reason frankly, which he accepted without demur. I told him that in the close confines of a minibus he would be able to bond with the others: there was no alternative, apart from committing murder, in that close proximity. He took the point and said he rather looked forward to the experience: he would contrive to sit next to Monty. I doubted that he would be able to do that. I thought that Jenny or, maybe, Bernie would seek that pleasure.

'We'll meet at the airport, then,' he said. 'Don't be late. If you fail to turn up, I'm not going.'

I do not know if he meant that last remark or not. Of course, I like to think he did; but I am not sure. He knew how to gain desired effects by saying certain things to certain people. He knew the effect it would have on me.

'Don't worry. I'll be there.'

According to North, when he recounted the journey to me later, they had set out in good time and drove the M40 to the M25. They passed the Hillingdon railway station, with the famous piece of graffiti on one of its walls: 'Ken Dodd's dad's dog's dead'. The driver negotiated in and out of the traffic lanes on a stretch of the M25 to minimize the delay caused by a jam to do with an overturned van. Several Eddie Stobart lorries had been spotted. They reached the M11 and were dropped at Stansted with more than two hours to take-off.

The most important news North gave me was this, he had successfully managed to sit himself in the bus between Bernie and Monty. Jenny had apparently sat in the front with the poet and the driver. North told me, with a smile, that he had deliberately positioned his right thigh against Monty's leg, and Monty, far from moving his leg away, had responded to North's move. North was adamant that Monty had definitely been interested in the physical contact: it was obvious, he said; Monty had enjoyed the sensation. North had carried out one or two test moves to make sure that Monty was keen to maintain the bodily pressure. He had inched away at particular points in the journey, but Monty had resettled himself so that their legs were touching again. The situation turned out to be as I expected; and North did not lose his chance to start his assault on Monty Ross in that war of relationships, or, should I say, of love. Monty was doubly ensnared, although he did not know it. He refused to recognize that Bernie held him in thrall; and North now had him engaged. Naturally, they had talked about many subjects during that journey, made observations, discussed ideas. North had been careful to ask Monty's opinion on various topics, general and specific, and by the time they had reached Stansted they were getting on well. Monty's view had changed: North was worth knowing.

I told North that I hoped he had not neglected Bernie, and he had not. He told me that, while talking to Monty and establishing physical contact with him, he had surreptitiously held Bernie's hand on the seat between them. I marvelled at his competence in these matters; indeed, I was slightly shocked by his deviousness, and I said so. He was surprised, and argued that I should not think badly of him: it had not been deviousness. He accused me of choosing the wrong word. In that sort of affair, all was permissible. He justified his behaviour and pointed out that both Bernie and Monty were well satisfied.

It was true. Jenny commented to me at the airport, as we were checking in, that the pair of lovers, Bernie and Monty, were unusually happy.

She added, 'And Monty seems to be getting on so well now with North. It was fortunate that those two were able to sit next to each other on the bus. I think Monty has lost most of his animosity.'

I agreed that the seating arrangement had been a fortuitous coincidence and suppressed my instinct to tell Jenny that it had been by North's design. I noted that during the flight to Naples, North cleverly managed to sit with the poet and another of his contemporaries. North was subtle: he did not make his moves obvious. I wondered what was going to happen about sleeping arrangements at the hotel. I knew that some of the party were to share double rooms. This was another part of the excursion that I opted out of: I had made my own reservation in one of the two five-star hotels in Ravello. The Palumbo is a distinguished old villa, now converted into one of the world's best hotels. Since I could easily afford it, I had some time ago decided to stay as comfortably as possible when travelling or visiting places. Gore Vidal, whose villa was close by, was a friend of the proprietor. The manager told me that, when he was in residence, Vidal would often stroll up to the hotel and take an evening drink in the bar. Sadly, while we were there, he was in the States. So when we walked the short distances between our hotels and the Villa Cimbrone, along the narrow alley hung with drooping wisteria, the scents of that flower, early jasmine, and vibernum filling the air, we had to make do with the ghosts and shades of Richard Wagner, Ezra Pound, DH Lawrence, and Greta Garbo with her lover Leopold Stokowski. It was singularly appropriate, I thought, that Bernie, Monty and, particularly, North should have come to this spectacular, almost inaccessible hill-top town, following in the footsteps of the great Garbo, who, according to a plaque on the villa's wall, came there to escape the 'clamore di Hollywood' and to pursue 'segreta felicita'. Secret happiness, secret love: these Ravello promised for my precious group of lovers.

In the hotel where the others were staying, I learned from Jenny that she, Bernie and Monty had rooms to themselves. The others shared rooms. Jenny asked North to go in with the poet. When I later spoke to North on a walk with him, he was perfectly satisfied. He thought it a good thing to be with our celebrity, and he was close enough to Bernie and Monty to be pleased with the prospects. Bernie was in a room across the passage-way. Monty was a matter of yards away around a corner, at one remove from Jenny, whose room was separated from his by a service cupboard.

North teased me. He said it was a perfect set-up for his liaisons. Should he want to, he could slip in and out of the various rooms at will. The poet, he said, was discreet and broadminded, and in any case, he revealed, he held some privileged information about the Croatian which meant that the poet owed him countless favours. That intrigued me, but North was not forthcoming. It was typical of him that he held some currency, valuable in the commerce of love. I had been in no doubt that North would want free movement between the rooms. Everything seemed to be set to North's advantage.

The convention proceeded smoothly enough. There were one or two good sessions, though I did not attend them all. There was one excellent young American female poet, who read some of her own works and talked lucidly about the way in which she exploited and refined her inspiration. She was good-looking, with a head of hair full of tiny plaits interwoven with coloured ribbons and minute strings of beads. She was intelligent, focused, modest. She had a voice that you wanted to hear. North and the Croatian, and a number of American college students talked endlessly to her after she had finished her lecture. I felt she would be a huge success in American literary life in the future. I also enjoyed another session in which a moderately successful Dutch novelist who wrote in English gave a seminar on his approach to the novel. Again, he attracted a large crowd: it was clear that his reputation as a teacher was well known: the audience had been primed to listen to him.

Since I am an old conference hand, I opted out of many of the other events and contented myself with wandering the paths and streets of the small town, exploring the less well-known back streets and byways. I spent hours in the two great gardens in Ravello and decided the Cimbrone was by far the best. The villa had been bought in 1904 by an English intellectual and aesthete, Ernest Beckett, Lord Grimthorpe, who regarded the dwelling as a jewel and decided to turn it into 'the most gorgeous place in the world'.

On the second day, in the middle of the afternoon, I walked in the town, passed by the cathedral, entered the Cimbrone's grounds and, very leisurely, made my way along the beautiful, picturesque avenue towards the Temple of Ceres at its end. This elevated belvedere gives out onto the fabulous Terrazza dell'Infinito. The terrace is adorned with a series of marble busts atop its balustrades and looks out over the sea to a vast distance. The blue Mediterranean dazzles. It is rare to behold such beauty. When I had just about reached the Temple, I noticed Monty and North at the far end of the terrace. They were looking away from me, out to sea. They stood close and intimate. They were deep in conversation, neither looking at the other. North shifted his stance slightly and raised one foot onto the edge of a low, stone seat. He leant against Monty in doing so, but then did not move away again, as would usually happen. He stayed leaning against Monty's arm and shoulder. Monty looked down at him, and then put his left arm around him.

I froze: I felt as though I were intruding in a solemn and private ritual. I determined not to be seen. No one else was around: I had passed one or two other walkers as I had wandered along, but they were returning to the house in the opposite direction. I kept, for the moment, to the Temple and obscured myself behind the central statue. They were completely unaware of my presence. They went on talking until, eventually, North stood straight, disengaged himself from Monty's hold, turned to face him, embraced him with both arms and kissed him on both cheeks. Monty looked elated. My own feelings were ambivalent. In a way I was cross that North's plan was succeeding so easily; but then I realized that I was just a little jealous that Monty was enjoying an embrace from North which I should certainly have appreciated. I dismissed my vexation. Then I wondered if North was really as entranced by Monty as he seemed. Perhaps he had discovered that he really did like Monty. Perhaps his behaviour was not just a calculated part of his strategy. But what of Monty? How did he feel? Was he confused? Was his conscience troubling him? He looked to me to be very happy. I wondered if he was sexually aroused.

They both turned and started to walk away from the terrace, back down the avenue towards the villa. They had not seen me. I was thoroughly disturbed by what I had seen; and yet, objectively, I could not understand why I should have been. What had I expected? The answer was: something similar to what I had just witnessed. It should have been no surprise. I calmed myself and waited for some minutes before returning to the Palumbo. My peace of mind had been totally destroyed. I wondered if I dared tell North that I had seen him. I did not know. I decided to wait until I met him, and then decide.

As the late afternoon wore into the evening, it became clear to me that I would talk to North about the terrace incident. It would not surprise him, nor would it embarrass him. Since we shared interest in his scheme, and since he totally confided in me, there was no reason not to discuss what I had seen. The opportunity would come soon enough.

I had told Jenny that I would join her and one or two

others for dinner. I suggested that they should come to the Palumbo at seven for a drink beforehand. Jenny arrived with the poet and Monty. I ordered a bottle of champagne, a Roederer which was reasonably priced, perfumed, and sharply nutty in flavour. It went down extremely well. We lingered, going over the day's events. Jenny and the Croatian were having a terrific time. Monty made no mention of his walk in the Cimbrone garden.

Towards eight we walked round to a restaurant whose outdoor balcony tables commanded a fabulous view of the Gulf of Salerno. The evening was perfect: calm, warm and scented. We sat and discussed what was to happen the next day. In the morning there was to be an extended session of readings by attending poets: this was when our poet was to read three of his compositions. The two-and-a-half-hour recital was to be broken by a twenty-minute interval for coffee at eleven. In the afternoon, there was to be an organized visit to Positano, a centre for women's fashion about twenty five minutes away by road. Bernie and Jenny were eager and excited to make the visit. Bernie had told me that she was looking for a blue denim jacket, of original cut and embroidered at the breast and over the shoulders, which she had admired on a girl in Ravello. The girl had given her the name of the shop, which was situated on the narrow path that leads down to the short strand at Positano.

Our conversation flowed easily. Our minds had been relaxed by the good wine. The courses came and went, the dishes robust and subtle, with just a hint of *nouvelle cuisine* influence. About a quarter-to-ten we finished with coffee and walked back to the main square and dispersed.

I had asked Jenny, at some point, where North was.

'I asked him just before I came out if he wanted to come, but he said he would probably join a couple of the others at a pizzeria near the main road. I didn't press him. I thought it good that he should mix with those other two. The younger one, Michael, needs confidence. North could be good for him.'

I kissed Jenny goodnight and watched the three of them disappear towards their hotel. I was not tired. The evening was superb – there had been a brilliant sunset – and I decided to walk around the town. At the back of my mind was the possibility of running into North. I went past a souvenir shop which sold the usual kitsch objects to the unsuspecting tourists who are marshalled here and there by fast-talking guides and travel representatives, past a bar with one or two locals inside, and past houses and hotels. At the foot of some steep steps, roofed by trellis interlaced with grapevines and wisteria, I looked into the garden of a restaurant which had some of its low-lit tables still occupied. At one of them sat Bernie and North. For the second time that day, I found myself in the role of voyeur. Bernie sipped a glass of wine, North a cup of espresso. As is the Mediterranean way, it had been served with a tall glass of water, which he tasted from time to time. They chatted intently and quietly. Standing in the shadow of the gate pillar and its hanging wisteria, I could not hear what they were saying. I watched their body movement. I could see that Bernie's right leg was between North's legs and he held her tightly there. I noticed Bernie's look of placid contentment, and as I did so, North put down his water, reached across the table and took her left hand in his. He squeezed and caressed it gently. She responded by pushing away her wine glass and holding his hand.

There it was, I thought, the tryst of two lovers. It was a perfect scene from a stage set. If North had been a theatre director he could not have arranged things better. It was a perfect setting, and the two leads were performing most convincingly. Bernie did not need to act: it was real for her. It was North I was not sure about. How true were his feelings? I had wondered the same when I had watched him with Monty on the Terrazzo. I knew he relished the sexual aspects of these encounters, he had made that clear, but was he to be trusted when defining his emotional attachments? I was unsure whether I could fully believe all he told me. It was essential I kept an open mind about what he said. I even thought I might discuss my reservations with him. I knew I was going to mention his Terrazzo meeting with Monty. I now decided to let him know that I had watched him with Bernie. What would he think of me? In his place, I should have thought that I had been followed purposely. I had to convince him that my sightings of him had happened by chance.

As I watched, North finished his coffee. Bernie took her right hand away from the table-top and rested it beneath, on North's knee. She then, almost imperceptibly, moved to stroke the inside of his thigh. I saw him tense and sit back, upright. He sighed and looked at her full in the face. She inclined herself more towards him and whispered something across the table to him. For me to have edged nearer to them would have drawn attention to myself. A waiter approached their table. They asked for the bill. Within a couple of minutes, Bernie had paid with a credit card and I knew I had to move.

I walked, disturbed and disconsolate, back to my hotel. Again, I asked myself why I should feel this way. I imagined that Bernie and North were by now back at their hotel, and were either in Bernie's bed or had made an assignation for North to go there later.

I was to find out.

The following morning I was sitting at breakfast in one of the Palumbo's salons. The Gulf of Salerno view was presented through high French windows that gave out on to a small lawn stopped by a parapet, and then a sheer drop of several hundred feet fell away to a lower path on the cliff face.

I imagined what it would have been like to have been an owner of this house in the nineteenth century: what pleasure, what satisfaction, it would have given me. Design, decoration, landscaping, all embellishments would have been in my control. I would have wandered the great, high-ceilinged, tall-casemented rooms and contemplated the portraits of my ancestors on the walls. It gave me a vicarious sense of satisfaction just to have the privilege of staying there. I immersed myself in those surroundings and hid myself from what was taking place around me.

My breakfast reverie was broken when I became aware of a short *sotto voce* greeting from the grand vestibule, whence the manager was directing someone into the salon. I turned my head away from the vista of sea and garden to find the handsome figure of North standing over me. He was dressed in his usual dark clothes: black shoes and trousers, a very dark charcoal-grey shirt which hung loose. In his hair a neat little plait, of no more than four inches long, hung down by his right ear. He looked refreshed and relaxed. I stood up and he gave me his customary hug of greeting. When I invited him to sit and join me for breakfast, he said he would take some coffee.

'You're looking good,' I said; and before I could stop myself, 'You had a busy time yesterday.'

'Yes, I did. But what do you mean?'

I had not meant to blurt out any indication of my knowledge of his movements the day before, but it was at the forefront of my mind and I did so. Sometimes you are helpless in the face of your preoccupations: they dictate your actions without your conscious sanction.

The waitress brought a fresh pot of coffee for him and I asked for a bottle of mineral water. North poured himself a cup and added plenty of milk.

'I have adopted the Italian habit of taking lots of milk with my coffee in the early morning. The cup then becomes a source of nourishment and stimulation.'

'I agree – a good habit. Look, I have to admit, I saw you twice, as luck would have it, yesterday. I debated with myself whether to tell you or not. What the hell, why not? The first time was on the Cimbrone's terrace with Monty, the second was when you were finishing dinner with Bernie. I know you'll think I was following you about. I'm sorry, but I wasn't. It was utter chance. Quite extraordinary.'

North was not at all put out by this news.

'I wondered if we would be seen,' he commented. 'I thought it unlikely in Monty's case because everyone was supposed to be busy. More likely, of course, at dinner with Bernie in the evening. Earlier on I was hoping to see you, but I didn't know where you were. Still, as it happens, everything went well, although I don't know what Monty did yesterday night. He was probably with Jenny.'

I was pleased that he had wanted to see me the previous day and I was sorry that he had not found me. He had the gift of making me feel extremely important in his life. When I now consider some of the things he said to me, I wonder if his words were all part of his greater strategy: perhaps they had no meaning at all beyond the purpose they were supposed to be fulfilling in his plans. The personal implications were negligible compared with his grand design. At the time I chose to believe he cared for me and, indeed, others. Who knows? My doubts might do him serious injustice.

He sat back in his chair and said in a completely matter-of-fact way, 'I made it with Monty.'

I did not know whether or not that meant that the pair had reached the stage of physical – sexual – enjoyment which, I knew, was part of North's plan.

'What do you mean? How far did you go?' There was a slight tremor, a catch, in my voice. North recognized my anxiety.

'Not all the way … yet. Monty likes physical contact. He likes touching me. He likes the feel of me. He doesn't recoil when I touch him. I don't think he quite knows what he is after, but he soon will. Don't worry. You mustn't be anxious for me. I do understand what he wants and I know what I want. It's no big deal.'

What he said did not reassure me but I did not show it. I was unsettled. I could not see where his current line of action was leading. Or, at least, I could see where it led in the short term, but I could not see how it could end happily.

'You simply must not worry. You are most important to me. I shall let you know everything,' he declared. I believed him, but I could not quite work out his ultimate objective. It did not matter to me: I valued being taken completely into his confidence – it was unusual, flattering, and immensely valuable to my self-esteem. He made me feel good.

'I think Monty will be less absorbed by Bernie now. He has to divide his energies between her and me. He won't be so angry and jealous because I am involved with her. So long as he can enjoy me, now that he knows me, he is going to let much of what I do with Bernie slide.' He seemed sure that this was the way things would turn out.

'Yes. Well, what happened with Bernie last night?' I asked. I can't imagine that you slept in your own bed.'

What I said came out rather more crudely that I meant. I had not meant to be so direct.

'You're right.' He took no notice of my direct approach. He responded as though he almost expected it. There was no surprise, shock, affront on his part. His relaxed manner showed that he understood my psychology. 'We made our way slowly back to the hotel. Jenny and Monty were sitting in the bar. In a very proper way, I said goodnight and went to my room. I read my *Paradise Lost* for about an hour, by which time our poet had fallen asleep, and then I went to Bernie's room. She was expecting me. She's great; I love her. She's very attentive, and I know what she likes. We're pretty good together. About six-thirty this morning I went back to my room. The poet opened his eyes, raised an eyebrow and went back to sleep. He's a great romantic — no questions asked.'

I admired his control. He looked at me and his eyes danced. I was at a loss for what to say. He left me drained of intelligent response. I was left to utter the banal, 'What do you plan for today?'

'I've said I'll meet Monty just before lunch. I think I might advance matters. We'll have some lunch and then I might take him up to my room and see where we go from there. Do you think it time for a little overt sexual interlude with him?'

Why ask me? I thought. For me, it was new territory. The suggestion and the idea certainly made me uneasy.

'I can't tell you, North. You must judge; but be careful. I can't give you advice. You know this. You wouldn't take it any-way, if it wasn't what you thought. You have to make your own decisions. All I would say is: think about how Monty might react after the event.'

I was talking allusively. North knew what I meant. He had to keep Monty on the hook, or near enough to the bait to want to go back for more. He knew he would have no difficulty in making that possible and told me so. I believed him, of course. His charisma, charm, magnetic physical appeal would make sure of that. With these attributes he could master Bernie and Monty; and, I realized, in a different way he could use them to manipulate me. There was no physical side to our relationship; our connection was an intellectual one. We seemed to under-stand each other perfectly.

He told me that he intended to spend the evening with the Croatian in celebration of the literary achievement. After all, the reason for us all being in Ravello was his poetry. North said he was a nice chap, with an interesting international cultural background. He had learned much about the poet's family, his brothers, sisters and a half-sister by his mother's first marriage, who was now a television documentary producer at the age of twenty-four. He would leave Bernie and Monty together for the evening: he thought it good politics in the affairs of love to leave them alone for a time. He hoped he would find the opportunity to be with Bernie at some time during that night.

I did not doubt his ability to engineer that tryst. He and I knew that Monty, although he might join Bernie in her room late at night, almost certainly would not stay there overnight: he would be far too worried about being discovered. North was already a shrewd judge of Monty's character and he was learning more and more all the time. He was beginning to know him well: the way he thought, his likes and dislikes, his preferences, not just physical but also intellectual. Monty was fundamentally an ordinary, orthodox individual, who was temporarily deluded by the enticements of love. For the moment Monty was inextricably ensnared. Reality for him was behind a veil, lost within a mist: he could not see it. The here and now was, for him, his association in Ravello with Bernie and, strangely, North. He did not wonder at his love for Bernie: it had been established at the same time as trying to deny it back at home. The fact that it bloomed in Italy was quite natural. North was different. He had surprised himself. He had not known that he could ever be taken up in that way with another male. He shrugged the shoulders of his morality, accepted the experience and was determined to see what happened, and at the same time enjoy himself.

\* \* \*

We had a session on that last morning to do with imagist and modernist poets. Both North and I wanted to attend. I hoped to hear proper reverence paid to both Pound and Eliot. I told North that I would go to my room and tidy myself up; he could join me or stay in the salon. He said he would like to see my room, and, anyway, he was eager to see how I lived when on holiday. So he accompanied me to my room. It struck me how different was the purpose of his company with me from that with either Bernie or Monty. As I have said before, in my own way I was privileged, but somehow there was envy in my soul over the sort of intimacy North shared with them. As we went into my room, I felt a shiver of loneliness, even though North was there beside me. It was almost supernatural. Of course, I dismissed it as foolishness, freshened up, cleaned my teeth, put on some good shoes, and was soon ready. North had stood for a while transfixed by the astounding view from my balcony window, and then had looked around my room. He looked at the two books I had brought with me, a selection of Browning's poetry (I can re-read *The Grammarian's Funeral* as often as anyone likes) and the Estonian author Jaan Kross's *The Czar's Madman*. He looked at my clothes, some in a mess on the floor; at my cuff-links inherited from my grandfather and made out of old silver coins; he examined the labels of my shirts and jacket. He behaved as though he belonged in my room. He was completely at home in my surroundings, and I in no way resented his presence.

We made our way to the lecture room and heard a half-hour talk on Eliot's idea of the impersonality of the artist, a theory which I approved and supported thoroughly, and then, a little later, we listened to some Milanese academic make an excursion into Pound's Cantos and enthuse about his imagery, his learned yet familiar style, and, above all, his intellectual eclecticism.

In the late afternoon we were driven to Naples airport and took our flight back to Stansted. We arrived just after ten o'clock. As we stood waiting for our bags, North said he would like to go with me in my car back to Oxford. Again, I was reluctant to take him for fear of offending the others. He concurred but said I ought to know that he would have much preferred to travel with me in the BMW. I said I would follow their transport to Oxford so that I could say goodbye at the other end.

There was hardly any traffic on the road. Most of it comprised huge lorries, belonging to transport and logistics companies (I noted that road haulage had become rebranded as logistics) and the high-sided trucks run by private couriers and the Post Office. We reached Oxford just after midnight. I parked briefly behind the bus and we all made our farewells. It had been a good trip. Bernie had certainly enjoyed herself: even at that late hour, she looked flushed and her eyes sparkled. She looked in the best of form. Monty, too, looked lively and elated. He had grown: he now knew more about himself than he had done before. He had given himself some freedom and reached out to new experiences. I could judge that he was confident that no one, apart from North, knew what had happened. He was happy and eager to adjust to the new and, necessarily, more complicated situation. I had seen that on the journey home Bernie and Monty had sat next to each other in the front seat next to the driver. Jenny had sat with the poet, and North behind them.

Jenny was jubilant. She judged the trip a success. She thought that, when she reported, Aitken would be extremely pleased. I kissed her goodnight, kissed Bernie on both cheeks, shook Monty's hand, embraced North, and turned to go. I noticed that North, too, with immense confidence and persuasive command, kissed both women, embraced Monty and then the poet and his contemporaries. He left no one out.

I wondered how North would get home. I looked for his mother – he might have contacted her to come and collect him – but she was not there. As I was getting back into the car, he turned and asked if he could have a lift with me.

'Of course. Climb aboard.'

I started off and drove gently over Magdalen Bridge into the fairytale centre of Oxford as we made for the northern part of the city. The globe lights which illuminated the bridge and the floodlighting of Magdalen College gave the city an enchanted air.

'Where's your Ma?' I asked. 'I should have expected her to pick you up.'

'No. I told her not to bother. I told her to go to bed: that I'd be quite safe and make my own way home. Actually, I thought I might do something with Monty or Bernie. Anyway, there we are. I've ended up with you. I like the evening and the trip finishing in this way. It's better like this. I feel safe.'

Safe? Why should he have felt safe with me? It had never occurred to me that North would have any insecurities, that he might ever be anxious. Once again, I felt flattered by what he was saying. Then I thought that it might have been a conscious calculation on his part, that he knew the effect of what he was saying on me.

'That's important,' I said. 'Do what you feel is best.'

After a few minutes, we were outside his house. He travelled light. He hoisted out his soft travel-bag which he usually carried over one shoulder, put it on the pavement and came round to the driver's window which was open. He leant down and kissed my cheek, 'Goodnight. Thanks for everything. See you tomorrow.' He turned, picked up his bag and vanished in the shadows of the driveway to his house.

Rather stunned, I drove the short distance home. I mused on this strange young man. Somehow there had grown up between us a familiarity, close and certain, which we both accepted without reservation and which was becoming casual in its interplay. At the same time, it seemed to me, his life was growing more and more complex. Perhaps his remark about feeling safe had reflected an increasing unease with his developing relationships. I confessed to myself, in the many interior discussions I had with myself, that I could not grasp what his ultimate designs on Bernie and Monty were. I even considered changing my stance and warning both of them that they were proceeding into territories they knew nothing about. They stood a good chance of losing their ways. What they took at that time to be enjoyment and happiness might well turn to dust and ashes. The juice of the bursting grape, the lusty wine, might suddenly, at some witching hour, turn to the sourest vinegar.

With that worry in my mind, I did not find the good night's sleep that I had anticipated. My mind, as if haunted by some malignant spirit, refused to settle. The worst possibilities, the most detrimental of outcomes, constantly posed themselves as resolutions to the puzzles being created around me. It was not that I suffered nightmares but that I simply could not achieve a sound and satisfying sleep. I drifted in and out of light slumber, with visions of North, Monty, Bernie, and even Aitken and Jenny, catching the prolonged attention of my mind's eye, leaving me disturbed.

I kept to myself for the next few days. Everyone was busy: exams were coming up in a few weeks time. Students and teachers were preoccupied. I kept my head down. I even went to various lengths to avoid meeting North. I certainly did not want to talk to Monty, though Bernie was not such an awful prospect. Jenny I did not mind about one way or the other, but

I felt at that time that I could not, in that particular frame of mind, be sociable to the extent that I usually like to be.

As I went over in my mind the events of the last week, and then considered how the lives of those people I knew and worked with had been changed over a period of months, I saw vividly that the cause of complications in relationships was North. Monty would still, no doubt, have fallen for Bernie had North been nowhere in view, but the way things had turned out, as they stood now, was because of North's presence and intervention. I consoled myself with the thought that North would be gone in a couple of months. He would shift into a new orbit: Bernie and Monty would be left behind. Sorting out Monty's difficulties with his wife, which were bound to develop seriously in that prevailing climate, would be easier with North at a distance.

Of course, I did not personally relish the prospect of North moving on. I had grown to value his companionship, his trust, his open discussions, his compelling charm. He was so unusual that I did not want to lose his friendship. I knew, at the same time, that it could not last: he was bound to move on, pursue his own directions; indeed, to grow older. It was as simple as that: he would grow older; he would change. In one year's, two years', time, he would not be the same. Nevertheless, I wanted to make the most of him as he was at that time. It was like enjoying to the full the flowering of a rare orchid: while it is in bloom, it should be appreciated as much as possible. I felt exactly that with North.

I had not accounted for Aitken in the equation of personal relationships. I thought he would remain on the periphery: an external force, formal, demanding accountability, but not impinging dramatically on any one individual. I was wrong. He became a key player in that game of love. I do not know if he meant to keep himself apart, at a distance from what, I am sure, he felt to be unrelated to his main interests; but if he did, he found it impossible. He initiated a huge publicity drive in the local press and on local television about the Ravello expedition. It even featured on the regional television news. Aitken himself spoke to an interviewer and praised our home-grown poet. Jenny was shown introducing the Croatian, who recited two short verses of a symbolic poem about fritillaries in meadow grass – something to do with rare beauty appearing amidst the ordinary. The coverage was impressive. The parents and governors were pleased.

I met North's mother in the vast local bookshop and she told me how much she had been impressed by the trip, the school, the poet. She herself was a living advertisement, a propagandist, for the school. She told me how much North had enjoyed the experience of Ravello. I could not help marvelling at the irony. Here was this woman, so far as I knew, entirely ignorant of what her son was like, innocent of what he contrived, of his preferences and *amours*. I assumed that she lived in her own world. In order to survive, she had to follow her own interests, which were in the long term not the same as North's. So, if she saw that he was happy, she was satisfied and all was well: her concerns ended there. I wondered what she would have felt if she had known that her son was sleeping with one of his young female teachers and, quite possibly, at the same time with one of his young male teachers. She did not know. She thought he was a paragon of virtue.

I am not condemning North by saying that. He had to go his own way. How he did it was his own affair. I expressed no moral judgements to him. As I have said, if he asked me what I thought, I told him; but not otherwise. I recognized that great divide between the generations that exists always in matters of morals and social mores. I interpreted North's stance in the light of my experience. Others would not, and did not, agree with me. Jenny was one.

'You're talking nonsense,' she said on one occasion. 'You delude yourself if you think that basic moral values change. They don't. Or if they do, they change very slowly. North certainly runs counter to the norm. He's an odd-ball. If you don't see that, you're mad. How many other guys of his age behave like him?'

'Yes, in one way you're right. On the other hand, there are young people in each succeeding generation who create new rules, lay down new markers, break old moulds. North is one of those, and he combines his policy, and it is that because he has thought it out, with his natural charisma. These last few years I have told my students that everything is now over to them. My generation has had it: we are on the way out. We have given them nuclear energy and weapons. We used them to create peace in our time, or so some would say. Theirs now is the responsibility to take everything forward. They have to make the decisions, both on the wide, public stage and in the private parlour of personal morality. It seems to me that North is someone who is calmly and competently assuming his responsibilities; and without much reference to his Ma.'

As anyone would have expected, Aitken called Monty to see him. He wanted to know what Monty thought of the trip. Jenny reported this news to me: Monty had met her after the meeting and told her that Aitken was immensely pleased. Monty reckoned that his going on the visit had done him a great deal of good. Aitken had thanked him for joining in and said that it was just the sort of thing the school should organize for senior students.

'I don't suppose Monty mentioned his *affaire* with Bernie?' I asked facetiously. I thought to myself that Aitken would not have been unduly worried if he had known, unless he considered it bad for the school's reputation and, therefore, detrimental to his own career. Aitken was entirely self-interested.

119

I imagined that meeting, Aitken searching Monty's eyes for some signal of affection. As Monty described the events of those Ravello days, skilfully edited, Aitken would have wished he had been there. No doubt his imagination thrilled at the thought of the opportunities there might have been for him and Monty to have grown closer.

It was noticeable, at least to me, that Monty evaded North around the school campus, and North was happy for him to do so. That was not how it was with Bernie. She did not avoid North, and he was also quite happy about that. Nor did she avoid or repel Monty's advances. Bernie was busy, and pleased with herself. I think she realized that North's time was short and she had to make the most of him before he was away at university. So far as Monty was concerned, she enjoyed the notoriety she had for being so close to him, and, in any case, she convinced herself that no one knew what was really going on. Jess was seriously otherwise occupied. Bernie tried to give the impression that she was just giving Monty a sympathetic ear during the approach to Jess's giving birth. Few knew the degree of intimacy they had achieved. I certainly did: one or two suspected.

In the summer the University Parks play host to a succession of first-class cricket matches between the university and, mostly, county elevens. They become a glorious cricket ground. The wicket is expertly tended; the outfield is superb – always green and closely mown. The rest of the Parks is a kind of arboretum: handsome trees collected and planted over many years, sturdy English oaks and chestnuts together with rare species from all over the world. The flower beds are formally tidy and colourful according to the nurseryman's horticulture.

To the north and east there is a splendid backdrop of trees; to the south an early twentieth-century pavilion, brilliant white and green, watches over the square and field. Against the west stands the majestic chapel of Keble College: Sir William Butterfield's triumph of Victorian gothic romanticism abuts the Parks in its own peculiar, polychromatic splendour. You feel that after Butterfield's *tour de force* to memorialize John Keble that style of architecture had nowhere else to go.

It so happened that two alumni of the school at the university had been selected for the Blues side. Naturally, Aitken had made much of this. He had ensured that their photographs had appeared in the press alongside his own with the school's name sign looking down on the three of them. Since I knew the two cricketers, I thought I should see them play. One afternoon, on my way back home, I decided to walk through the Parks. It was a fabulous afternoon, the sun was shining and, a rare event, there was not a cloud in the sky. There was a small crowd watching, scattered at intervals throughout the ground. As I proceeded slowly round the boundary away from the pavilion end, my eye caught sight of Aitken and Monty. Aitken talked animatedly, while Monty listened intently. This, I thought, must be an official visit of Aitken's: he was no lover of sport.

My initial reaction was to ignore them, to walk behind them so that they would not see me; but then I decided it would be interesting to judge the nature of Aitken's response to my appearance. To that end I watched them both for some time from a distance. They were closely engaged, Aitken making most of the conversational headway. Both looked relaxed. Monty stood straight, shoulders back, arms folded, not tense but casual. He commented on the cricket from time to time. It was clear that he was of the *cognoscenti*, Aitken an initiate. The finer points of the game Monty could demonstrate: he showed Aitken how one of the bowlers altered the flight of the ball by differently fingered grips. A batsman was yorked: Monty explained. It was almost impossible to believe that Aitken could have been around for so long without learning some of the details of the game; but he was one of those men who viewed the games cult with contempt. He had done so while he himself was at school and continued to do so in his adult life.

As I watched them, they moved to a position of vantage behind the bowler's arm, next to a sight-screen. There, Monty was able to show how the ball swung in flight, how the bowler could make the ball move off the seam, explain the leg-before-wicket rule. I could see that, in spite of his prejudice against games, Aitken was eager to learn from Monty. He asked questions, which I could not quite hear, and made comments after balls had been bowled or runs scored. He was an intelligent man. He had no difficulty in understanding the object of the game. He put aside his disinclination to have anything to do with the alien world of sport in order to learn at Monty's feet.

Our two alumni were on the fielding side and one of them came to field deep, up against the boundary. He noticed us, nodded cheerfully and waved. I thought it necessary to reveal myself to Monty and Aitken.

'Hi. You're here to see these lads. I thought I would look in on my way back home. Who's winning?'

'Impossible to say at this point, although I'd predict that Gloucester will. I think they are teasing the game out. Another half to three quarters of an hour and I think they'll go for the kill,' Monty commented.

'You understand the strategy of the game, which is certainly more than I do,' Aitken said. 'Our two boys are doing well. They look the part anyway.'

I thought that a mindless comment and decided Aitken should not get away with it.

'What do you mean exactly? They're wearing whites, if that's what you mean.'

'No. I mean they fit in. They know what they are doing. They convince the spectator. They are not amateurs but professionals doing what they have to do.'

It was typical Aitken. He would intellectualize anything at any time. He had a shrewd, analytical mind. He looked at details and had an exceedingly good memory. You had to remember that aspect of him when you had dealings with him or you were lost. His grasp and command of minutiae made him able to control most matters of administration himself. He was reluctant to hand down real responsibility to others; their authority was only apparent. Control was always with Aitken: there was never operational delegation.

With me present, the atmosphere changed. I noticed it immediately. Aitken's body language altered. He stood marginally farther apart from Monty and became stiffer in attitude, more formal. I would not say that Monty grew awkward, but he was less at ease than he had been. I stood in my usual manner, affected when I was in the army and retained ever since, feet apart but parallel, straight back, hands in coat pockets. It was an easy stance, relaxed and comfortable, one which you could maintain for long stretches of time. It was now second nature to me.

I detected that Aitken was none too happy that I had turned up. He became fidgety and twice looked at his watch. Suddenly he said that he had better go back to his office and began to walk away in front of the sight-screen. Monty stepped towards him, held his arm and told him he could not go that way: etiquette demanded that you walk behind the screen so as not to interfere with the batsman's vision. Monty guided him to the back of the screen in what looked like an embrace. I heard Aitken thank Monty for saving him from what might have been a form of public humiliation and suggest that Monty looked in later, after he had finished in the labs. He then headed for the Parks' gates, walking briskly with his slightly odd gait, his right shoulder swinging perceptibly lower than his left.

Monty was cheerful. 'He really doesn't know much about the game – never played it. Now he seems to want to learn. Funny chap, but I like him all the same.'

I thought it time to tell. 'And he likes you too, Monty. That's obvious.'

Monty reddened a little, 'Yes, I suppose you're right. Well, I don't mind showing him the ropes.'

He went on to say that over the following two weeks he was going to bring our tyros, those young aspiring cricketers, to the Parks as often as he could to watch first-class cricket. No doubt Aitken would appear from time to time and Monty could give him instruction.

I could not determine what was in Monty's mind concerning Aitken, perhaps nothing. It might have been that Monty did not then realize that Aitken admired him and was becoming increasingly obsessed by him. When I look back, I become more and more convinced that Monty was innocent in that respect. He did not register what was going on in Aitken's head.

I gave Monty a pat on his shoulder and said I had better be off. I am not able to watch cricket for long before I am struck by the awful consciousness of time passing: 'And at my back I hear, Time's winged chariot hurrying near'. Almost always, Larkin's stern imagery, of wasted time being like a page 'torn off unused' comes to mind. It is the same with golf: after about an hour of the game, I start thinking of all the other things I might better be doing, my game deteriorates and I wish I had not begun.

I went off towards home. Monty continued to walk slowly round the boundary.

The next weekend I was in London. Early on the Saturday morning I met an old Australian friend for breakfast in the Oriental Club, just off Oxford Street. It is a club I greatly enjoy. I like its atmosphere of the East, its carved elephants and portraits of imperial adventurers. Robert Clive looks down as you sip your *chota peg* or taste your tiffin. Colonial governors and generals and imperial admirals contemplate today's members. My Australian, a Sydney surgeon, godfather to one of my sons, was a member. He had been in London trying to sort out a financial mess to do with being a Lloyd's name. He was catching an 11 o'clock flight back to Sydney that morning, and so we met for a lavish breakfast before he left. I had driven up to town early in the morning on virtually deserted roads and left my car parked just off Portman Square.

When it was time for us to part, he went off to his room to prepare himself for his flight home and I decided to stroll down to St James's and my club there. I doubled back and went into the food hall of Selfridges to buy some of my favourite olives and then took my way through Mayfair at a leisurely pace. It was a warm day, but I thought the exercise would be good. I went through Carlos Place and round past the Connaught, where I often have lunch with a writer friend who divides his time between Nice and Duke Street, St James's. I was about to cross Mount Street when I remembered Scott's Bar. I thought an espresso would be good to help me on towards Waterloo Place. I turned right along Mount Street and saw a familiar figure coming towards me. It was North's mother, Francine. She was hurrying.

'Hello there,' I called when she was some yards distant. 'What are you doing in these quarters? I didn't expect to see a local face here.'

'Hi. Great! I have just been to the embassy in Grosvenor Square and now I'm going to the Redfern Gallery to look at some paintings a friend has recommended.'

'You're obviously in a bit of a hurry, but have you time for a coffee? I'm just making for Scott's, along there.'

'I'd like that. I'm not really in a hurry at all. I always like to walk with a purpose, though. It puts off muggers and beggars. I'm in no hurry. I simply have to be there before one.'

So, we entered Scott's, North's mum and me. It was the first time that I had ever been alone with her privately. I could see much of her in North: eyebrows, chin, curious, deeply attractive slant of top lip; but his eyes were different, much darker in colour, enigmatic and, in certain lights and moods, dangerous. I imagined that those were his father's eyes, whoever he might be.

She was looking good: very smartly dressed, her hair fashionably styled. I complimented her on her looks. I was old enough to be able to do that without there being any suspicion of ulterior motive.

'I always admire the way you dress. It's so refreshing when, after all, we are surrounded by the usual rubbish at home. You don't compromise your standards. That's excellent.'

'Thanks. That's a real compliment. As a matter of fact, just before the embassy, I went into the place where, these days, I get many of my clothes. At least, it's where I buy the ones for when I really want to look good. Do you know it? Georgina von Etzdorf in Burlington Arcade. It's a bit expensive. An American friend introduced me to the shop.'

'Well, it does you well. I don't know it, but I'll take a look next time I pass.'

I wondered if her ex-husband picked up her bills there.

We chatted on. I drank my usual espresso and glass of water, iced with lemon in it. Francine drank a fruit juice with sparkling water added. I asked her how North was faring now that his exams approached. I wanted her perception of him. I was curious about how she viewed her own son, and I wanted to know if she realized the sort of life he led, the kind of power he had over other people. I knew what North felt about her. We had spoken about her and his home life many times. I had his perspective. Did hers coincide? Did she share my view of him? I was immensely eager to find out. All sorts of questions arose. If she found von Etzdorf expensive, how could she afford to kit out North, who was always expensively dressed? He had told me that the last pair of trousers he had bought came from Etro in Bond Street. They could not have been cheap.

She said North was unperturbed by the prospect of the exams. She could not understand him: he took it all in his stride. When she had been in his position she had always panicked and worried. He kept calm. She thanked me for talking to him now and again. She thought it important because he lacked his father's influence. She told me North valued my company and took good note of what I said. I was pleased to hear that. Again I felt flattered: it was as though North was intentionally courting me through his mother. It crossed my mind that North might have told her that if she ever talked to me, she should be sure to compliment me. Knowing his mind as I did, it was more than possible.

She certainly had a different view of him from me. She had no idea that he was involved in affairs of the heart. She simply knew that he had a number of good friends, some his own age, one girl younger than himself by two years, and some, like myself, older than him. She believed him to be a good boy. He was attentive to her needs. He rarely displeased her, he possessed a balanced temperament, never lost his temper. If he were out of sorts, he simply went quiet and ceased to communicate. That was scarcely ever and never for very long.

I said to her that, like her, he was always well turned out. She agreed. He had an uncannily exact eye for style and he bought all his own clothes. I commented that they looked to me to be expensive.

'The finance is his father's. There is no lack of dollar funding,' she smiled. 'He insists that North has the best, and North has this natural sense of knowing what to do. He knows where to go, he knows what to buy. He rarely asks my advice. When he starts going out with the girls, he's going to wow them, and he'll be generous in spending money on them.'

She had no idea that North had already begun to play the game of love. There was much I could have told her, but, of course, I was bound in confidence to North. The more we talked, the more it became obvious to me that, contrary to what I expected, I knew more about her son than she did. Quite clearly, he did not allow his sex life to filter into the zone of his relationship with his mother. What he had confided in me permitted me to see dimensions of his personality which were hidden from her. Once again, I felt immensely favoured. She did not know that he had slept with Bernie and with other contemporaries, that he was capable of seducing someone of his own sex, Monty for example, even if he had not slept with him yet. I could not be sure about that: perhaps he had chosen not to admit that to me.

She had her own life. She did not worry about North. She thought he was doing well and so she went contentedly about her own business. It was me who was worried and disturbed. I often had sleepless nights trying to work out how North's mind ticked. I am sure that he had never given his mother cause for such anxiety.

Then there was a different slant. I was, in a sense, complicit with North. I was keeping things from her which many would say she ought to know.

I asked her how she would manage when North went to university.

'I'll keep busy. He's a good boy, though, he'll keep in touch. He won't let his old mother vegetate. I shall probably go more often to America, certainly during his term time. I'll visit him, too. In a way, I hope he gets in at Oxford. He wouldn't live at home but he'd be around the place. I should feel his presence in the streets. Do you believe in spiritual contact, ESP and all that? I do.'

I told her that basically I did not believe in such phenomena. On the other hand, I knew deep within myself that remote thought contact seemed to be possible with North. There had been times when it had become clear we had both been thinking of the same subject. On one occasion, I had become suddenly aware that he was about to telephone me and, immediately, the phone rang: there had been North on the other end.

We talked on without a pause until Francine said she must go or miss her appointment at the Redfern. I kissed her farewell and she continued eastwards along Mount Street. I went down towards my club, convinced I knew much more about her son than she did. In fact, I knew him far better than she did.

As I walked down towards Piccadilly, I wondered about North's father. I knew nothing about him except that he was living in America with his second wife. When North went to the States he saw his father privately. He did not get on at all well with his father's second choice. They met independently of her, and North always stayed in a smart hotel or with family friends. His father must have been wealthy, otherwise North could not have dressed as well as he did; and he was never short of cash. His father kept him more than adequately funded. It would have been intriguing to meet North's father. I wondered why it was that Francine and he did not get on. What was it that had made them split? I wanted to understand them, all three of them. Later, I was to conclude that it would not have made any difference. What was to happen could not be so easily explained.

I walked down Sackville Street, past Henry Southeran & Co, the antiquarian bookshop, turned into Piccadilly and took the narrow street alongside Fortnum & Mason into Jermyn Street. It was then a few minutes walk to Waterloo Place where the magnificent equestrian statue of Edward VII, Rex Imperator, Emperor of India, stands sentinel and looks up towards the busy heart of commercial London.

I spent the afternoon in the club's library, had a late tea in the drawing room, and as I was leaving met an old college friend coming in. We diverted to the bar and I drank a glass of champagne with him. About six-thirty I walked at a leisurely pace back up to Portman Square, collected the car and drove back to Oxford. I had thought of spending the evening in London but the meeting with Francine was on my mind and, in any case, I had half-promised to call on Jenny that evening. I knew that because I had not telephoned her she would be expecting me. I do not have a mobile phone. I abhor the tyrannical objects. I refuse to be subject to them.

I arrived back in Oxford at about eight-fifteen and drove straight to Jenny's house. It was in a rather grand new development near a tributary of the river. Everything had been tastefully landscaped and it was a pleasant place to live. She had moved there when her marriage collapsed. Her daughter, then at college, had chosen to live with her, and her son, a twenty-eight-year-old over-educated vagrant, came and went. She had a cultivated interest in interior decor, so the house was agreeable to be in, comfortable and comforting. It fitted her personality. She was an easy, amusing person to be with. I could not understand her husband for either wanting, or agreeing to, a separation. We are destined never to understand other people's close relationships.

'I had begun to think you weren't coming,' she said as she opened the door. I caught the scent of lilies which I then glimpsed, arranged in a tall vase, on a hall table behind her. 'But I've learnt never to give up on you,' and she smiled.

'I hope I can be relied on. I would have rung you if I couldn't make it.'

'I know; but it's getting late. I tried ringing you but there was no reply.' She added coquettishly, 'I dared not think what you might be getting up to.'

I explained I had been in London and, after a moment's hesitation, decided to tell her how I had met North's mother. She was surprised, said that she had met her once but only briefly, and wanted to know what I made of her. I intimated that I reckoned she did not know most of what North did, how he spent his time when out of her sight, and certainly not that he was involved sexually with Bernie. Francine was a mystery. She was not sheltered, she was not naïve, but she seemed to lack imagination – especially about her son. She was bound up in her own life, that was sure, and she cared for North, but she was amazingly vague about his movements.

'Perhaps she's still in shock from the failure of her marriage and suppresses most of her real feelings in hyperactivity. That way she doesn't have time to concern herself closely with North's doings,' I suggested.

'It's a thought, but it's not very likely. I speak from experience, and as one who is still in shock. She'd be more likely to monitor him zealously, be over-caring. Her attitude probably has more to do with the way North behaves.'

'I don't quite see what you mean. Are you saying that North contrives to make his Ma unconcerned? That he engineers, encourages her apparent innocence about his leisure activities?'

'Exactly.'

By this time we were seated at table. Jenny served a balti curry of tiger prawns which she had concocted herself with the help of a proprietary sauce patented by some television chef. We had rice, flavoured with cardamom and cloves, and some French beans which, from their wrapping, I noticed had been imported from Kenya. She served a delicious Burgundy which we both sipped to begin with and then left until we had finished our curry and cleared our palates with a little green salad. As we savoured the wine, Jenny remembered some Jarlsberg cheese she had and we drank the rest of the bottle to accompany it.

Inevitably the conversation returned to Francine and North.

'I wonder where she was going after the Bond Street gallery? And what was she doing at the embassy on a Saturday morning? And where was North? What was he doing meanwhile?'

'Well, it's a mystery about her, but not about North. He could have been doing any number of things. Yes. The most likely is that he was in bed with Bernie. I wonder what Francine would think if she knew.'

'Precisely. I'm not sure how she would react. Of course, he might have spent the day improving his friendship with Monty. Either way, it's idle to speculate about Francine's attitude. We are never likely to know.'

'North might tell you,' Jenny immediately replied. She intuited that conversations between North and me went pretty deep.

We left the specific subject of North and his mother and went on to talk about the curiosity most of us have about the private lives of people we see every day. We see only their public faces. We do not see them in their leisure hours. We do not know what they do in the confines of their own homes. How do they spend their evenings? What sort of friends do they have? The experience, as I have said before, is similar to travelling in a train at night: the eye and the imagination drawn to the lit windows of the houses we pass, but we are able only to guess at what goes on inside. Mostly, we do not care; most people excite no particular curiosity. Yet some we want to know about because they catch our attention in some way and prompt our imagination. We invent friends for them, imagine how they live, and even, perhaps, conjure up heated images of what they might be doing in those upstairs rooms with the lights turned on.

Jenny and I decided on a little game. We chose people we knew and imagined what they might be doing at that particular time. It was about eleven o'clock. We thought of Monty. There were no holds barred in this game. I suggested that he would be sitting watching late-night soccer matches on television, Jess having gone to bed, worn out by her pregnancy and trying to store power for her coming labour. I added that he would be trying to suppress his desire to be with Bernie. Or even with North, I thought to myself. Jenny could see him finally making for the bathroom and giving himself his own solitary pleasure in the absence of a collaborator. We both decided that was nearer the mark.

Bernie? She might have been away at her parents' house. She would have driven there in the early afternoon and would be relaxing in the security of a familiar ambience. Or she might be at a club or bar, at the Cellar or at Thirst, trendy scenes where she would be immersed in the sounds of DJs playing funky, garage or house music. Thirst's resident female DJ would have attracted her — there were not many of them — and that was where we saw her. She would lose herself in the noise, rhythm and movement until two in the morning and then retire to bed to rise at lunch-time on Sunday.

So we passed the time, Jenny and I. North we skirted round: he was an enigma. Who could guess what he might be doing? It caused me no anxiety: I knew that if I asked him he would tell me. I said to Jenny that I might ask him. He would be direct and honest because, as he always told me, it made no difference; he could tell me the truth and what would I do about it if I did not like what he did? Nothing: he knew I would do nothing; it was none of my business. If you like, I was no more than a recording angel. He listened to my praise, censure or lack of comment, loved my approval and merely accepted, without complaint, the rest.

We tired of the game. 'Jenny, I must go. I'm tired.'

'Of course. We've not made much progress in sorting out Bernie's or Monty's problems. We must see what happens. Lovely to have you round for supper. Sorry you won't stay.'

She made the last remark jestingly, as she always did. She and I were good friends. In my own way I loved her, but there was no sexual motive. Neither was there for her, I thought, although I could not be sure. She was keen to marry again, or at least to have a man in her life. She missed the reassuring presence of a man whose company she valued, and she missed the intimate physical pleasure of a regular partner. That was the way she was, but we both knew that our closeness and understanding of each other would have been ruined by sex. We were destined to look elsewhere.

I kissed her on both cheeks and left. She waved to me cheerfully as I drove away. My mind moved rapidly to Francine: what a strange woman, slightly bizarre, very enthusiastic, and someone who gave an occasional false impression of attractive naivety. Then the image of North cropped up. What was his father like? That was the one subject I had never succeeded in discussing properly with him. He did not shy away, he just exercised masterful evasion. I wanted to speak to North but nothing was to be done: it was too late at night.

The following day, the first of the new week, I had no chance of meeting North for two reasons. One was that he was taken up with an art exam which was a marathon. Candidates were given five hours to work on a composition. They sat around for some time in the art rooms, preparing themselves mentally and practically, before they set about their tasks, taking only a short break for lunch.

The second reason was that Aitken asked me to go with him to meet an extremely wealthy alumnus, an American called Rathbone, who had been staying at the city's best hotel in north Oxford. In my early days I had taught Rathbone and since I was now a senior figure in the school, Aitken thought it would be appropriate for me to be there and bid him farewell. I had liked Rathbone as a boy; I hoped I would like him as a man. I was pretty sure that I would. I told Aitken that I should be delighted to meet him. Aitken said that the idea was to meet him for tea and perhaps have a drink with him, but a car was picking Rathbone up at around six to take him to Heathrow. Aitken suggested that we stayed on for dinner: there were a few matters he would like my views on. I thought that a good proposal. I had nothing arranged for that evening. I had anticipated going for a long walk and keeping to myself for the rest of the time. Dinner with Aitken would prove a diversion and, although he wanted to consult me, there were things I wanted to find out from him. I felt I could answer questions which had arisen in my mind, not necessarily by asking him overt, outright questions, but by leading him on in conversation and watching his reactions. I could, as it were, indulge in a little low-key interrogation. It was a technique which, many years ago, I had been trained to use, and something which I liked to think I was good at. I looked forward to the evening.

I met Aitken at his office and we walked to the hotel. Aitken could be an incessant talker especially when he was excited – when his adrenalin was flowing. As we walked through Oxford, past Magdalen College, through the incomparably beautiful Radcliffe Square, into the Broad and up past St John's, Aitken's conversation sped on at a mind-dazzling speed. There was no doubt he was clever. His brain was sharp, fertile and excelled at command of detail. He was articulate, clear and incisive. A short man, he was physically alert but not athletic. His conversation was non-stop. We covered government policy, not just in education but in the wider field of foreign affairs. Current initiatives were assessed, commended or dismissed. He could have been a politician.

We reached the hotel and found Rathbone seated at table, taking tea and reading the local paper. Aitken greeted him cheerily.

'Hugh. How very nice to see you. I hope we are not late.'

'Not at all. I just thought I'd get started: my schedule is pretty tight.' He turned to me, 'Great to see you. You haven't changed. Maybe just a touch of grey, but basically the same. Good for you. As you can see, I've put on a bit of weight.'

'Very good to see you, Hugh. We must do what we can to withstand the ravages of time. The trouble is we're not very good at it.'

'Right. Let's order,' Aitken suggested at once. 'Hugh hasn't much time. I don't mean that as a death sentence or a threat, it's just a fact in the present circumstance.'

That remark was typical of Aitken. His torrential conversational style was elaborate but precise.

'OK. I've got about three quarters of an hour,' Rathbone commented. 'Let's get down to business and see what can be done.' He had no illusions about the real reason for our meeting and clearly regarded me as a piece of comfortable padding. Aitken put forward a strong case for funds that would help finance students from families not well-off. Rathbone, like many of his contemporaries, took quickly to the idea of a subsidy fund to assist with the payment of fees, the cost of trips abroad and the purchase of games equipment. The result was that he pledged at least $75,000 over the following three years. He knew that was possible, but he would look at his charitable donations when he returned to the States and he would give more if his accountant approved. He was very well disposed to the school and said that, were it not for the education he had received there, he would not now be in a position to help. He felt he owed it to the institution to encourage and enable other intelligent students to attend it.

At six exactly, his car arrived. The hotel manager, whom I had got to know over the years, came to inform him that it was waiting outside. Rathbone's cases were fetched, our farewells made. Aitken thanked him warmly and Rathbone made his exit, glancing round nostalgically, lingering before briskly making for the door. We waved after him and wished him good luck.

I asked Aitken what he would like to drink.

'Whisky? A dry Martini? Champagne? The sun has just dipped below the yard-arm. We can get on with the proper stuff.'

'I'll have a Martini, please. I rarely do. Anyway, I should be buying. You're my guest.'

'Not for this round. These are on me.' I did not want to feel

137

totally indebted to him. It would have put me on a false footing with him in the ensuing conversation. He did not object. I ordered his drink and a glass of champagne for myself. The waiter brought us an assortment of black and green olives and a few pistachio nuts. Aitken mentioned to the waiter that we would be dining, but not for another fifty minutes or so. We settled down to our cocktails and I wondered where the conversation would lead us.

At first sight you would think Aitken rather dull. He was a small man, who always wore a suit. There is nothing intrinsically wrong in that, but the suits he owned were few and drab. In my youth there had been chain stores throughout the land that sold business suits off the peg or machine-made to your personal requirements after just one fitting from a shop assistant. You had to put enormous trust in the skill of the shop worker and, mostly, they had no training whatsoever in tailoring. So, anyone you saw wearing drab, dull suits, you knew had bought them cheaply from Hepworth or some other, similar store. These shops had their own cachet which was not enviable. This was not snobbery: it was fact. Their suits were never well made and rarely fitted properly. Aitken's suits were throwbacks to the Burton era.

He was clever. I was in no doubt about that. He had a first class mind; but I was not confident about his moral stance. His academic discipline, if you could call it that, was English literature. He was a Miltonist. He held the great commonwealth puritan in the highest regard. He quoted from his works. He admired *Paradise Lost* beyond any other work of literature after Shakespeare. The doomed struggle between Satan and God held enormous, ongoing fascination for him. From that work and the Bible he espoused Christian principles. He preached at chapel services, invariably bringing in the thoughts of Cromwell's Latin Secretary. Yet in his business life – the running of the school – he appeared to the close observer as amoral because everything was subordinated to his pragmatism and his ambition. When it came to personal issues to do with individual members of his staff, administrative convenience and what he viewed as the good of the institution held sway. It was as though his Christian morality was suspended. Yet he occasionally sought reassurance, and when he did he mostly came to me. Often I declined to give it: my philosophy was much opposed to his. It made no difference anyway. He would briefly consider what had been said and continue on his own way: no one should stand in his way. Although there were plenty of complaints from those who worked for him, the governing body was perfectly happy to let him get on with the day-to-day running of the school. In my senior capacity I rarely ran up against him. He did not administer the place as I would have done; but then I saw the wider view. He was not going to be in office for very long; he was extremely ambitious; he would soon move on.

The restaurant was adjacent to the bar where we had taken tea and where we were drinking. We finished our cocktails and ordered salmon fish cakes, a speciality of the chef there. We both had them, Aitken on my recommendation. Neither of us fancied a white wine. I ordered a good Burgundy which I knew the proprietor admired.

We talked about various aspects of the school. I asked him how he thought younger teachers were progressing. I led him on. I wanted to see how he responded to mention of Monty. I said that I reckoned he had been very perceptive about Monty Ross. I lavished Monty with praise: a vigorous, lively, sociable young man who was prepared to lend a hand in every enterprise – look at the way he had given support to Jenny and Sam when they had organized trips abroad. He was good at games and was invaluable to that aspect of activities. He was also academically excellent, able to run his department seemingly without effort, and he was good on the pastoral front. I extolled Monty and flattered Aitken for his judicious choice. What I noticed was the way Aitken accelerated when he discussed Monty. Already fast in talk and in riposte, he became excited and even more voluble. He loved talking about Monty. It was obvious to me that there was some sort of obsession there. It was the way that a lover cannot stop talking about his beloved. Jenny was absolutely right about them; at any rate, she was right that Aitken had fallen for Monty. The question that arose in my mind was whether Aitken could control his passion. Could he tread cautiously? Would he allow his career pragmatism to hold him in check or would he give way to his infatuation with the handsome young Cambridge blue? At that point, it was impossible to tell.

I asked Aitken if he knew anything about North and if he considered him up to scratch to apply for an Oxford college place.

'I don't know him all that well, but I should have thought so. I can only go on what others say and by his results so far. But he looks a good bet. It seems he should do well. I know his mother. I've met her socially. She's a friend of the chairman through an American connection.'

I was interested to hear that and wanted him to talk about her, but he kept veering back to Monty.

'She's a great admirer of Monty, you know; and quite rightly so. I encourage her to talk him up in the presence of the chairman. It'll do his career no end of good.'

'True,' I said, 'but you're the lynchpin. Without you to back him, he would be dead in the water. You've given him rapid promotion, and rightly so. With all-round support, he is going to reach for the stars. Five more years, then he can try for a headship. Is that how you see it?'

'Sooner, I think. I don't usually talk about careers in this way. Monty, though, is different: he is one-off. He's special. And I think you are quite right; I'll give him all my support. He should go a long way.'

There was no doubt about Aitken's enthusiasm for Monty. He simply could not stop talking about him. I wanted Jenny to hear all this. She would have to make do with my account of Aitken's fervour. While Aitken talked rapidly on, I leant back and wondered where Aitken's tacit admission to me, by his display of intense feeling for Monty, would lead. If ever Aitken planned to do anything about his passion, physically at least, he would have to be very careful. I was convinced Monty would respond. He was responding to North. In this relationship, Monty and Aitken both knew what they wanted; both would be careful of their careers. A crucial factor was that Monty would see acquiescence to Aitken's wishes as important to his getting on. Monty, gaining experience all the time, was not likely to baulk at giving or taking a little pleasure on the way. It was most difficult to come to a conclusion about Aitken. Would it be a throw of the dice for him: to risk all in the hope of gaining paradise? My hunch was that Aitken considered himself clever enough to calculate the odds and to be able to succeed with his gamble. These were high sexual stakes. By the end of the meal, I was convinced that Aitken would join the game.

Aitken had enjoyed himself. He thought he had done well with Rathbone: it was a success he could report back to the board of governors. He had talked, too, at length about Monty Ross, a subject he could not dwell on with most people. With me it did not matter. He knew I spoke to few of our colleagues and kept my own counsel. He considered me discreet. He did not reveal his true feelings for Monty, but I diagnosed an age-old sickness: it was a variation of the mania of love. There was little he could do about it: the frenzy would become more extreme before the fever had burnt itself out.

He settled the bill. I noticed he used a credit card sponsored by his old Cambridge college. He was the sort of person who might still wear a college scarf. We said goodnight and he walked towards town and his home at the school.

I decided on a walk in the Parks. It was a mild evening and an hour was left before the gates would be shut; there were few people around. Trees were in blossom, the air was scented, birdsong filled the air in those declining moments of the evening before there is silence. I breathed deeply and felt the exercise do me good.

Aitken was in a trap of his own emotions. I pondered his predicament. Monty was in a whirlpool. Where should he strike out to? Should he reach out for safety to the arms of Bernie, or North, or Aitken? Should he cease to struggle, simply lie back and settle gently into the stifling calm of Jess and domesticity?

As I walked across the Parks towards the tiny humpback foot-bridge which spans the Cherwell, I realized that I desperately wanted to talk to North. I knew he could tell me certain things I wanted to know. He held more of the pieces in this game than the others. Only he could answer certain questions, always supposing that he was inclined to.

I paused on the bridge and looked at the punts. In both directions: southwards towards the punt station at Magdalen Bridge and northwards towards Bardwell Road, punts floated slowly and quietly. Some punters were expert, some not so — their punts unable to make straight progress up or down river. Suddenly, I was aware in the middle distance of a punt making steady headway. It was propelled by a dark, handsome youth who was no novice to the gondolier's skill. I have to admit that an electric thrill went through me: it was, of course, North. He had been uppermost in my mind, dominating it, for the past five minutes and, now, here he was. With him were Bernie, Sue and one of the art students. As he flicked his hair back away from his eyes, North glanced up at the bridge and saw me, just as I was about to turn away to escape notice.

'Hi there! Come and join us.'

'Hello. How very nice. You carry on. I'm just walking.'

'Oh, come on. Don't be so dull. Join us,' he insisted. 'We're just going back to Bardwell Road. It'll be a short hop for you. I'll pull in over there and you can jump in.'

The others encouraged me with various remarks and I could not refuse. Not that I really wanted to. I went down on to the bank and carefully stepped on board. I sat next to Bernie and we glided smoothly up river to the Bardwell moorings. It was splendid. I thought to myself how lucky I was. I had dined well, drunk well, walked in those beautiful parks and ended up with the person I most wanted to talk to.

When we had landed, we sauntered up to the end of the boathouse drive where Sue had her car parked. She was giving a lift home to Bernie and the student. North and I lived close by. We said we would walk. It was ideal for me; an opportunity to talk with him, which is what I had wanted to do all day.

North kissed Sue and the student on both cheeks and said goodbye. He kissed Bernie, but it was a single kiss on her right cheek and close to her mouth. He lingered over it just long enough for me to notice. There was something different, of course, in that kiss for her: a suppressed, controlled passion, a promise of further, more dangerous intimacy. This much was obvious to me, and North knew it. His hands on her were serious, tender. He did not try to hide it from me. If there were an innocent party present, it was Bernie. She was a tenderfoot.

I think she scarcely knew what was happening underneath the surface. North whispered to her just as she was getting in the car. Perhaps it was an assignation for later that night. I do not know; and I forbore to ask.

'How do you get time to punt? I thought you were in the middle of your exams,' I said to North as we walked away towards our homes.

'We had just finished our art exam. I thought a short relaxation on the river a good idea. Actually, it was Sue's suggestion. She reckoned it a good way of winding down. Fortunately Bernie was around – she had been invigilating. So that was the way it went.'

'You have more nerve than I had at your age. I could never have done that. It would have made me too nervous. I admire your sang-froid in face of the enemy. You're like Drake playing bowls before the Armada.'

I asked him how his mother was. She was fine, mentally and physically preparing for a visit the following weekend of an old American friend, her best friend through university. She was very much looking forward to it: they had not met for six years. She was very excited.

The person I wanted to ask him about was his father. 'Do you hear from your father? When did you last see him?' I felt like the interrogator in WF Yeames's pre-Raphaelite painting *And when did you last see your father?* It hangs in Liverpool's Walker Art Gallery and always reminds me of the vulnerability of children. I want to know the answer to the picture's riddle: does the small boy betray, innocently and unwittingly, his Royalist father?

I immediately apologized to North, excusing myself with mention of the vivid image of the puritan tribunal's question. He knew the painting and said he was fond of it. Under its softness of background, its familiarity of surroundings was the

144

threat of death. He said the painting haunted him and he realized it had to do with his relationship with his father.

'I shall be seeing him most probably towards the end of the summer. I'm not going over there; he is visiting this country. I'll meet him in London, I expect.'

'What does he do?' I asked. That was the question that intrigued me. North always skirted round the issue.

'He's a money man. Finance. I don't know exactly what he does. But there we are, he is generous and exacting.'

'Exacting!' I exclaimed. 'What does he demand of you?'

'The usual filial things. I'm not complaining. He funds me. I think I fulfil his expectations.'

That was it. I could not entice any more information out of him. Not that I wanted any more: what he was prepared to give, I was prepared to take. If he did not want to go on talking about his father, then that was fine by me. I retained an impression that his father, like North, was a dark figure, one who belonged in the shadows and operated in an obscure market of securities, derivatives and futures. I have no idea if that was right. I never met his father and North never fully explained.

I tried to imagine what it must be like for North when he met his father. What did they talk about? What tone did they adopt towards each other? Monty came into my mind. I wondered how North was faring with Monty. As if reading my thoughts, North said, 'You're probably wondering how I'm getting on with Monty. Do you want to know?'

'Of course, if you want to tell me. He doesn't think you are an interfering little brat any more. I can see he loves to be with you.'

'He does. I like him, but I'm not sure he feels completely safe with me. He loves me in a sense. He loves the feel and touch of me; and he loves my personality, whatever that is. I say that because it's what he has said to me. We spent the early evening together the other day, in his office in the labs. No one else was there. The place was deserted: the caretaker and the cleaners had gone home. He was great. He has a fantastic athletic beauty.'

It struck me that if I had heard that piece of information about anyone else, it would have seemed grubby and trivial. This was different. This pairing was important in the intricate game I was watching. My interest in North made his involvement with Monty important. I was not jealous. Why should I have been? I had no ambitions for North's affection. I knew where I was with him. No one could share the sort of intimacy I had with him. I was not interested in a physical relationship beyond a hug or embrace. The physical contact of those gestures merely sealed our intimacy; no words needed to be spoken.

'How does he feel about you and Bernie? Do you sufficiently intoxicate him to feel indifferent? I can't really believe it. Presumably Bernie is unaware of what you two do. I don't see her liking it at all.'

'Sure, she doesn't know. He has reservations, but when he sees me all that changes. My presence alters his values. He can't bear now to give me up. It's an extraordinary power. Until Monty started fancying me, I had no idea I had it.'

'I'm not sure I believe that. You've always had tremendous charisma, but not shown in that particular way. Be careful though, I don't want to see you hurt.'

'I think I'm all right. There is always a temporary hurt if you feel strongly for someone and you end the affair. One party is going to be hurt, but it usually only lasts for a short time.'

North appeared to have the wisdom of Solomon. It was odd to hear such sentiments coming from him; but there we were − he had a supreme confidence in his own views, as though he were inspired from elsewhere. It was both a mystery for me to puzzle out and a mystery which he possessed. Sometimes, in the dark hours of the night, I half dreamed of him as supernatural. Fully awake, I always dismissed the idea as ridiculous.

'Don't get hurt. It would grieve me.'

We walked slowly along and approached where he would turn off to go home.

'I must work an hour or so before bed,' he said. 'I don't really want to leave you. I'm reassured when I'm with you. I can't quite explain it.'

'It's OK. You know where I am. Give me a ring if you like, later on.'

It was by now almost a quarter to ten, but I was planning on some reading. After that I would make my diary entry for the day.

'Great. I might just do that.' He embraced me as usual, kissed my cheeks and went on his way. He half turned and waved, and I went towards home.

There was so much to contemplate. I began to worry seriously how this muddle of relationships, which all revolved around North, would finish. The obvious end would be brought about by North going away to university. Supposing, though, he applied to Oxford and stayed in the city. What would happen then? In any case, one of the players in this game might break the rules: then there would be complications. It was possible even that they might all cheat. Who would be the most determined to win? Those of us who are students of love know how swiftly love turns to hate. Your old lover becomes your sworn enemy. Positions of battle are taken up. Rules of warfare emerge. I remembered Field Marshal Montgomery's instruction to the Eighth Army in North Africa, 'Seek out your enemy and kill him'.

That was it: I saw the possibility of a cauldron of boiling

emotions. On the other hand, all might pass off peacefully – North would go on his way and the catalyst would be removed.

The other concern that nagged away at my mind was what North had said about his meeting in Monty's office. He had mentioned that Monty was 'great': he admired his 'athletic beauty'. What had he done? I had to assume that they had been in physical contact. There was the 'touch and feel' evidence of North's reflections; to think otherwise would have been unrealistic. I wanted to know in detail what North had experienced. It was a natural, inquisitive prurience. I was sure that if I asked North he would have told me what they did, but I felt it would reduce my position in his eyes. I even had the feeling that North was tempting me to ask him. Perhaps he was intentionally leading me on, provoking my imagination, because he knew I would want to know. It would have been one more exercise of his relentless power. The more I pondered, the more it became clear that he could monopolize my thinking. He had no doubts over my concern for him, my care for him. G was no longer in the equation, my children were embarked on their own lives far away – I had no one else to think about.

This realization set off warning signals in my head, but I was not particularly inclined to listen to them. That was the trouble – I thoroughly enjoyed this torrid business of the sexes. It was fundamental to society, life, the whole of the human world. I wanted to know what had happened in Monty's study. Whatever the intimacy, the manipulations, the caresses, the endearments, maybe even the violence, the excitement, the delays, the crises and climaxes – whatever they were – I was curious. I resolved not to ask North. He would tell me and I would be rendered his subject. If he were to tell me of his own accord then that would not alter the balance of power.

\* \* \*

What I feared might happen began the next day. I met Jenny late in the afternoon, after a tiring and trying day. I had wrestled with a difficult seminar group in which we discussed Milton's view of God in *Paradise Lost*. We had two different groups in that examination year: North belonged to the other one. I wished he were in my group. I would have found his presence reassuring and he would have made me teach better. We had talked about Milton so many times, I knew what he thought about most topics to do with the examination text. He would have been a great help in that day's discussion group.

Most of the students sided with Satan, said it was entirely reasonable that he should have felt the way he did. The Almighty came across as an unjust God, who acted out of pique and made rules that meant that mortals suffered without choice: God was unreasonable. I posed the question, if that was so, why would Milton, a devout puritan, write the poem? He was hardly likely to denigrate God in the way they suggested. I tried to present the case for a wise, omniscient God, for a human creation supposed to exercise free will, for a fallen angel who, after all the storm and tempest, knows his struggle is futile but nonetheless tries to deceive his followers into thinking that victory is possible. I pointed out that, as a poet, as a dramatist, Milton had to make Satan a literary reality: he had to invest Satan with dramatic power. I explained, too, that Satan showed Milton's belief that evil was, and is, a potent, living power continuously at work in the world. My students argued with me until I was submerged in a state of weariness. I longed for the end of the teaching day and relaxation at my own pace.

Eventually I found respite as four o' clock approached. I told my students to go away and study what Satan actually says in the text. Look at his arguments. Judge them rigorously. Do they stand up to scrutiny or are they specious? I decided to go

149

straight to my car and get out of the place. As I threw some books on to the back seat of my car, I saw North making for the science labs. He could only have been making for Monty, there was no other reason for him to go there. I saw clearly that the initiative was always with him: whether in relation to Bernie or Monty, he made all the going. At the back of mind lingered the thought that it might be the same with me; but, I reminded myself, I was alert to that possibility.

I was about to get into the driving seat when Jenny called out. She was going to the common room and, when she saw me, came across and spoke.

'Tea? What do you think? You don't have to rush off, do you?'

'No. I just wanted to get out of this place. Why don't we go somewhere outside? What about Lacey's?' Lacey's was a café and bar on the edge of the centre of town.

'Fine. Let's go. I'll just dump my stuff and be with you in a moment.'

I stood with my car door open and waited. Jenny must have gone to the cloakroom. She would have wanted to repair her make-up and use the lavatory – it was characteristic of her always to freshen herself up before she set out anywhere.

North appeared out of the science building with Monty, North saw me and waved. I signalled back. Monty glanced towards me. They walked towards the sports centre.

Jenny soon emerged and joined me looking refreshed and as well turned out as she did first thing in the morning. We both got in the car and I drove into town, found a parking space close to Lacey's and fed the parking meter.

The late afternoon air was fresh. The warmth of the day was beginning to fade and the atmosphere was regaining the crispness of the morning as the temperature dropped. Jenny and I walked the thirty or so yards to Lacey's, pausing to look at the garden of Trinity which opened out to view through a set of wrought iron gates. The bust of Cardinal Newman stood at the far end of the vista, its stony eyes staring down at the long stretch of lawn which extended to the gates and the road. Behind the buildings and the bust, the sun was beginning its descent in the west. It was a beautiful, green and gold, calm, restful, sensuous scene. We appreciated it for its visual perfection and for the way it combined so beautifully the powers of man and nature. It was Oxford at its fabulous best.

Lacey's was not busy. Two or three tables were taken. There was plenty of room. We took a table by the window. I ordered a pot of Assam, Jenny preferred Earl Grey. We shared one round of sandwiches – Gentleman's Relish with wafer-thin slices of cucumber. It was a welcome contrast to the verbal cut and thrust of class and seminar.

'Did you see North with Monty?' I asked her.

'I did. I'm not sure what's going on there. But here's something interesting. I had a long talk with Bernie last night. She says she is going to disengage from North. She says she senses disaster if she doesn't. She thinks he's wonderful, and she certainly loves him, but she can see it's doomed – he will go away. She knows that he will have other lovers: she thinks he may have them now. Even if he gets into Oxford, she thinks she couldn't survive. If it happened later rather than sooner she thinks she would be so upset that everyone would get to know about them, Aitken wouldn't like it, and she would probably have to resign. So, she thinks it best to break off gradually, now. Easier said than done!'

'Well, that is news. I'll believe it when it happens. Has she calculated what North might think and do? I bet she hasn't. In her situation, people never do. North has his own ideas and his own strategy.' I voiced my doubts. I knew North and what Bernie said she might do would become insignificant in the face of what North decided. He was charming, charismatic, mesmerizing. He would have been amused at what I could see was a forward presumption on Bernie's part that she could end the affair. Her advocacy of the proposed course of action took no account of his combination of magnetism and determination and her total obsession with him which, for that moment, she chose not to acknowledge.

'Her plan will only succeed if North wants it to. Such is his power. Such is the power of all dominant lovers. He takes the initiatives. He is in control. She hasn't realized this yet. She thinks she is sensible and in control. She will soon find out that she is not. In fact, she suffers the dementia of love. This is going to be interesting. Ah, the *comédie humaine*. Such entertainment.'

My last remark did not exactly convey my mood. I was worried. I could see a great deal of trouble brewing. People were going to be upset, hurt. Once again, I wondered if I should talk to North as soon as possible; and yet, I knew the dangers of interfering. After all, what was I to say? I was not going to tell him what to do. Even if I thought I knew, I would not – on principle. A discussion, I supposed, was possible. I put that problem to the back of my mind.

'Bernie's such a sweetie,' Jenny said. 'I like her a lot. I don't want to see her hurt. She's got herself into an awful mess, if you ask me. Why don't you take North to one side and tell him what you think? He'll listen to you.'

She was right, of course. He would. Not that it would make any difference, because afterwards he would make up his own mind and go his own way. So, there were two factors: first, North would follow his own inclination come what may; second, I would not give specific advice anyway. What did intrigue me was how North's mind worked. I was extremely interested in knowing what he would think when Bernie started to distance herself. I resolved to watch and wait.

'I'll talk to him, of course, but he won't take any notice if he doesn't want to. He is confident of his power. Whatever Bernie says, I reckon she is at his mercy.'

'Perhaps I should talk to him at some stage. The older woman ... You know, that sort of thing. He might have ambitions along those lines. You remember that book of our youth, *In Praise of Older Women*? I might be able to exercise my fatal charm, entrance him, divert him.'

'Yes, well,' I commented, 'you can't be serious. You are not on a Red Cross mission. You and I know quite enough about these things not to become involved. You would be inviting the wrath of the gods. Keep your peace of mind.'

I was sure she would not do anything. She was too steady, too sensible, to enter the lists in any capacity. The war of love could no longer engage her. Her role, like mine, was that of adjudicator, diplomat. If either of us could help draw up a peace treaty, well and good. It had not reached that point yet.

Anyway, it was difficult enough for me to maintain my own peace of mind. It was not just Bernie I shared worries about with Jenny, it was North as well. I could never work out how vulnerable he was. He projected his wonderful presence for all to appreciate; I had never seen him depressed. The 'black dog' never seemed to sit with him as it often did with me. I envied him for that, but assumed that he must have low periods. It was something else I had to ask him about.

There was a nagging concern at the back of my mind about North and Monty. Where was that liaison going? It could not be long-term. North knew that, but how did Monty see it? What would happen if Monty wanted to end it? Would North be kind to him? North was the puppet-master, pulling the strings and taking part himself on behalf of some greater power – the god of love, a god of chaos. Who could know?

Jenny said she realized she had to stay out of it all, but that

153

she would keep an eye on Bernie. We chatted about a new film version of *Tosca* which had just been released and agreed we should go to see it. She had been in touch with one of our past students, now a fashionable stage and film director. She had met him by chance, walking in the High with his mother, whom he was visiting. They had arranged to have dinner one night at Sheekey's, the smart theatreland restaurant just off St Martin's Lane, near the director's office. She told me she was eagerly looking forward to it. She felt it would keep her up to scratch with London theatre news, boost her confidence and give her theatre-cred when she spoke to her students.

She told me of her family. I recognized in her sad and regretful accounts of the complications of family life, a general story that described the experiences of so many people I had known. She, too, had her moments of melancholy, but her abiding nature was buoyant: she always rose from the troughs quickly. Yet she served to remind me that my resolution to stay unattached was a wise move to preserve my equanimity, sanity and independence.

We finished our tea and walked back to my car. The bust of Newman was now in the long shadows cast by the setting sun, as it began to slide behind Trinity's buildings. I drove her a short distance to her garage where she was having a pair of new tyres fitted to her car, and then I returned to my flat. My cat jumped down from his lookout position in an ornamental pear tree to greet me with arched back, tail straight up in the air, and loud purring. I went to my study and sat at my desk.

After brooding for some time, I got up and poured myself a generous glass of Scotch. It was J & B, a whisky favoured by Graham Greene. It is a pale straw-coloured blend. Greene preferred it on the grounds that you could pour yourself a full tumbler yet, because of the lightness of colour, appear to be drinking whisky diluted with soda-water.

I returned to my desk, took a sip or two and, on impulse, decided to ring North. It was something I would not normally have done. I was reserved about ringing any of my students. My policy is always to let your students come to you. If they seek you out, bring their problems to you, prompt your response, then the communication is valuable, proved by the effort they have made. North was different. I had to ring him. I felt there was a painful urgency.

His mother answered. I greeted her and asked how she was. She responded positively and told me what she had been doing that day in a skittishly lively way. I liked her irrepressible energy. She was obviously someone good to know. I thought that when North went away I should cultivate her a little more. She would enliven my dull evenings. I considered it inappropriate now: it might offend North or, at least, alter in some way the relationship I had with him, possibly for the worse.

'Is North there, Francine? I saw him this afternoon to wave to, and I thought I should just speak to him if he's in. I was with Jenny and didn't have the opportunity to say anything.' I did not mention that he was with Monty.

'Yes, of course. I'll go get him.' She went from the phone and I could hear her call North. He answered in the background.

I had been going to suggest he might like to come round for a chat, but I was forestalled, pre-empted. He picked up the phone and said, 'Hi. I might call on you in a few minutes. Are you in? If you are, I'll wander round, if that's O.K.'

It was uncanny. It was as if he knew what I wanted.

'Of course, I'd love to see you. I was going to apologize for

155

not speaking this afternoon. But come round: that would be perfect.'

'OK. See you soon.'

'Give my love to your Ma, and I look forward,' I said, disguising the conflicting emotions of eagerness and anxiety I felt in my heart.

A quarter of an hour later he was in my study, sitting cross-legged on the floor.

'You're like a wizard,' he said. 'You sit here in your lair with your crazy cat familiar who stalks you and bothers you for attention. What spells do you weave? What have you in store for me? It's funny, I always feel you're watching me. Whatever I am doing, you are at the back of my mind. I hope you are Merlin, a force for good: I don't want to dabble with the darker powers.'

'Come on. I don't believe it. You go your own sweet way. I doubt very much that you pay any attention to me when you are going about your business, certainly not when you are with Bernie or Monty. You can't fool me.' I looked at him, and I had to look down. He was sitting on the floor: I was slightly above him. He looked up at me. His dark blue eyes sparkled but were nevertheless inscrutable. He sat there like a Buddha, completely at rest, calm, relaxed, dignified. He was most amazing. Never, in the whole of my tutoring career had I come upon anyone like him. He was both mysterious and mystifying. I continued, 'I'm no wizard. I wish I were. There's a lot I'd like to make happen.'

'What concerns you most at the moment?' he asked. 'You look a bit worried. Not worried exactly – perplexed, maybe just a bit stressed. What's wrong?'

He was inviting me to confide in him. Once again he was forestalling me. He had taken the initiative in this chess game of the emotions. I was annoyed with myself that I had apparently

156

betrayed my feelings. I knew that I was not stressed: that was not the right word for what I felt. It was true I was worried, and it was about him and his lovers. There was no doubt about that. I sensed that he knew it.

'Listen, my friend,' I said, 'one thing that does disturb me, is you and Bernie. I think she is in trouble. Let's face it, she can see there is no future in her affair with you. I think she would prefer to end it but probably doesn't know how.' I said this to North with no more evidence to back up my statement than Jenny's conversation with me. I readily believed what she said because anyone with any sense could see the stark reality of the situation: that her affair with North would end in tears. I went on, 'She hasn't the steel in her soul to finish with you. Everything else founders in the face of love. You could help her. Do it for her. Finish it off. You told me that you're in this business just for the pleasure. You could do it gently and find your entertainment with someone else.' I added unnecessarily, 'You've got Monty. He'll do merely for your pleasure.'

North looked hard at me and did not say anything. I prolonged the pause and then said, 'Look ... you know you don't have to take any notice of what I say. You know what I really think. And I don't give advice ... I just air views.'

The sparkle in his eyes changed, or so it seemed to me, momentarily to a glint or glitter. It was as though there was, somewhere deep down, sheer ice. The hard, cold, diamond facet of his mind reflected light back at me. It was only for the moment, but it disconcerted me. I did not want North to change towards me.

'Take no notice,' I said. 'It will all resolve itself. You asked about my worries, so, I've told you. Do what you like: I know you will anyway.'

He shifted his position, briefly stood, and then hunkered down, sitting on his heels. 'You don't have to worry, I've foreseen this problem. And you're right: she is not going to be able to do it by herself. I shall eventually have to help her. But not yet, I think. She enjoys me too much, and I, too, like it.'

I did not say so, but I immediately had reservations. That expression of undiluted hedonism unsettled me. It was satisfactory for North: he was entirely objective about the affair. Bernie, on the other hand, was totally involved. Any resolution to abandon North on her part was doomed to failure unless it had his complicity.

North shrugged himself out of his jacket. It was loose, black and extremely elegant. It slid to the floor. He then surprised me.

'I've bought Bernie a present – some underwear. I decided she's too suburban. So the other day in London, I went to b Store in the West End where my mother gets her stuff and bought her a set of Eley Kishimoto bikini beach-design kit. She'll love it and look really good in it.'

I had difficulty imagining Bernie in it: my mind would not stretch that far. Yet I was sure he was right: his taste was expert. He was already a connoisseur.

'It's about time we got her out of her M&S bras and pants. She's too good for that stuff.'

Various thoughts raced through my head. So, Francine shopped at places like b Store. And so, apparently, did North. Would his father approve of him spending his money on such gifts? Perhaps he put them on his mother's account. In which case, what did she make of that? Moreover, here was a mere youth telling me, his mentor, the kind of underwear his lover, one of his teachers and one of my colleagues, wore; that he disapproved and that he had bought her a present of expensive lingerie. North behaved like no other youth I knew. But that was it: North was different.

'The next thing you'll be telling me is that you've bought

new underwear for Monty. That brings me to him. How are you managing him?'

North was amused. 'It's an idea. He wears some rather dreary old boxers. Jess neglects him. I would give him some Hugo Boss briefs, but it would startle Jess and create problems. He'd look good in those. You don't have to worry about Monty. We both enjoy ourselves.'

North had no inhibitions. It was partly that which empowered him. You had to admire him for it. It gradually began to dawn on me that he used his frankness as a weapon, not against me, but against others. They had no idea that behind his openness was a hard, steely purpose. I began to see it.

'Is it your generous father who finances your lifestyle?' I asked.

'Yes. In a way you're right: he looks after me. There are other sources, but he makes sure I live properly. He doesn't want me constrained. He thinks I should get used to sophisticated society and learn to manage my own finances. In fact, he thinks I've done that. I now have the confidence of my father in his son. So, I don't lack much and he feels me to be an extension of himself. I'm very lucky. My mother is happy, too. She doesn't have to deal with the financial drain which I would otherwise be.'

I wondered what sort of a budget he operated on and what were the other sources he alluded to? Anyway, what he said explained his expensive clothes and his Tag Heuer wristwatch. I had once asked him about some sunglasses he was wearing. They had caught my eye because I had not seen any quite like them before: they were of extremely modern, contemporary design, fashioned in a light metal which looked like stainless steel. I had not been surprised when he told me that they were from Prada, a gift from his father.

It was remarkable that with all those fashionable accoutrements he did not look like a glitzy fashion plate. But he had a natural sense of style: they looked right on him. On other people they might have looked showy, ostentatious; on him they were worn of right, as if nothing else would do.

'What is it, again, your father does? He must be awfully wealthy.'

'Money, I suppose is what he does. He manages money. He buys and sells it. I don't fully understand his work but I know it is only to do with money. He is a sort of Mammon figure. Should I be ashamed of that? I don't know.'

He was touchingly unsure, or, at any rate, that was the impression he gave.

'I don't think you should worry. He is part of the economic society we live in. What he does, presumably, oils the wheels and makes the world go round.'

I told him he was lucky that he would not have to be short of cash when he was at university. Clearly he was not going to need to borrow money. His father would have that problem sorted out.

I now knew how he could afford to buy exclusive under-wear for Bernie. But would she not wonder how he managed it? Perhaps she would be content to receive the gift, engage in the erotic game, and ask no questions. Did Monty ever wonder about North's clothes? Or did he just think himself lucky that he enjoyed this youth's favours and attentions and ignore the awkward questions? I did not know, but it made no difference. North was himself. He was convincing. People took him as they found him and did not ask questions. It was only me, his sophist, his Apollonius, who wanted to know more.

He stayed with me for over an hour. He shifted back into his Buddha position and described an exhibition of painting and photography which he had seen at the Hayward Gallery on the South Bank. He talked about the failure, as he interpreted it, of *Paradise Regained*. He thought it lacked the atmosphere of dire and awful combat of the other poem; that it did not have the sense of terrible danger, of potent evil, of catastrophic consequences. Whenever I met North, virtually every time he mentioned *Paradise Lost*. It completely captured his imagination.

He suddenly said, 'When it comes to the act of sex, do you think Monty seduced me, or me him?'

I had not been expecting anything like that. I shifted upright in my chair and, startled, said, 'Good Lord! Why do you ask that?'

'I was just thinking of it from the point of view of moral philosophy. Should there be a culpable party? From whose point of view is it wrong?'

I did not feel comfortable on this ground. The discussion could go on all night. Not that I should have minded that. It would have been a delight to have North around for so long. The moral philosophical debate was a minefield. You had to define where you were coming from in the first place. For instance, if you were a Christian there were certain moral imperatives. Those would be the props for your argument. If you were a free thinker, then who was to care about culpability? I felt tired and disinclined to enter into that sort of discussion.

'North, it's too complicated. I can't argue at the moment. What's up, though? Do you feel guilty? Do you want me to comfort you in your anguish?'

Of course, I knew that was not the case. There was no sign of guilt on North. As always, he was in complete control. It was probably idle curiosity, a desire to understand how other people, who have distinct moral principles, think.

'No. But I wish you would talk. It soothes me. You relax me. That's why I like coming here. Well, it's not the only reason. I just like you. It's as simple as that.'

I was immensely pleased, and moved. Nobody else had

161

ever said anything like that to me before. It made me feel important, useful, appreciated.

'Reciprocated,' I said. 'I love having you here.'

It was quite some time later that I thought again about what he said, and it occurred to me that it was by design. He knew what effect it would have on me.

So, North thought Bernie too suburban. He was right: she liked going on walks – at her parents' home she kept a dog called Kirby; her view of the world turned inwards; and she was always inclined to look backwards. North surveyed the wide world, the universal. He did her good in that respect: he necessarily broadened her horizons.

Just before he left that evening, North mentioned that he was going to take Bernie to a gig, or a set, where there were going to be some well-known DJs playing. The following Saturday he proposed to go to Brixton, to the Telegraph, a fashionable pub amongst the cognoscenti of popular music. It was a well-publicized event. For weeks, apparently, hardboard notices had been put up all over Brixton advertising the evening. They had been attached to lamp-posts, traffic lights, any post or pillar that could play host to the placards. For four Saturdays beforehand, flyers had been handed out in the public parks, high-street shops and shopping centres. There had been a 'Free the Weed' rally, at which the publicists had turned up in force and handed out hundreds of leaflets. They read: 'Sofarockers, in association with DJ magazine. The Telegraph, Brixton'. The DJs were to be Slacker of Jukebox in the Sky, Ellis of Midset Recordings, Deez Ashford and Dario Marquez of Melonphunk, and two rarities: female DJs, Sharen Norden and Loll Martin. All this North told me. He showed me a flyer.

162

The emphasis was to be on funk and house music, and there was to be 'a set of techy underground grooves'. The DJs were out of the club stables Retox and Fabric.

It meant nothing to me. It was the sort of music, if you could call it that, which I could not listen to. North said it was a generational matter: I should listen and try to see what they were getting at. I loathed it. North was catholic in his musical tastes. He could handle the most progressive sounds produced in the pop music world and yet be utterly entranced by Bruckner or Brahms. He reckoned Bernie should experience the London scene.

'How do you know about Brixton?' I asked him.

'One of the girl DJs plays in Oxford. She tells me what is going on in the big wide world. She plays here sometimes at the Cellar and Thirst.'

I knew the names and where those venues were. I had never frequented them, but I had once been in Thirst. The Cellar was, as its name implies, an underground bar, in which, I am told, you will find an amiable mixture of Oxford townies and students. Thirst was a smarter bar with a huge, clear dancing space and a DJ booth at one end. The drinking area was lit by blue lights and the floor was always in semi-darkness and gloom until the strobes started up.

I wished him well. It was, of course, not my scene. He knew I was curious. Brixton, of all places, was extraordinarily cosmopolitan, multicultural. Some years back it had been host to several days of bitter race riots, but now it had been taken over by a breed of young people, disciples of new wave music who considered the colour of your skin irrelevant to any issue, social, political or religious.

'I'll report back,' North said. 'It might be a pivotal evening. I've got to decide what to do about Bernie. Anyway, I'm going to make her feel really good.'

It was soon after that North made his move to leave. It was close on eleven. I said to him that I was going to have a night-cap, a dram of Laphroaigh, that strangely medicinal malt whisky which tastes of seaweed and iodine. Its pungent aroma and tangy taste gives me an immediate lift: I imagine I am drinking some prescribed tonic. He declined; it was not for him. What was for me a tonic, he thought a poison. He took a sparkling mineral water, helped himself to ice from my fridge and drank it puritanically. That choice of drink struck me as a facet of his severe discipline. Unlike so many of my contemporaries, he knew when to drink alcohol and when not.

I liked the familiarity with which he helped himself to what was in my fridge. He seemed to assume what was mine was his. I had not asked him to take the ice: he assumed he could. He was welcome; that was true. He had an endearing, easy informality. He fitted in. There was no effort socially. He accepted me completely, as I did him.

At the door he embraced me quickly and went on his way. When he reached the footpath, he went in the opposite direction to his home where, I imagined, Francine would be waiting for him, perhaps worrying where he was. Almost certainly he was going to Bernie; but I could not be sure. Since he knew so much about the contemporary music scene and from what he had said about the female DJs, it crossed my mind that he must have other liaisons. As I was to discover, I was right to surmise as much: he had other lovers. Why did I not ask about them? He would have told me. There is no question about that. He held nothing back: he was not ashamed or inhibited. Yet I did not ask him then.

I lay in bed that night and thought that the writing was on the wall for Bernie. I half-watched a tawdry American thriller on the television, with the volume reduced to a whisper. It was a way I had of inducing sleep.

* * *

It was after that evening that things began to disintegrate. I heard from Jenny that there was trouble in Monty's household. Jess was becoming daily more and more suspicious. There had been several major rows. Jess was troubled, cranky, on edge. She was alternately pleased with her condition or extremely irritated by it. On the one hand, she saw the pregnancy as liberating: she was free to march with the band of real women who bore children. On the other, she felt herself confined, restricted; moreover her husband was not bound down, as she was, by the increasing weight in her body. She resented his absences and noted the increase in the number of times he made excuses to go out. All this she had told Jenny in a weepy, late-afternoon session, when Jenny had called round to lend her moral support for the rapidly approaching trial by birth that she was about to undergo.

Monty kept going out. He just had to pop out to the school. He needed to meet Jenny to discuss an outing. He had to discuss work with a student who was to take his exams in a few weeks time. He had to give some papers to Bernie which she needed for the following morning to finalize a sports visit to a national coaching centre. He just thought that he would nip out to the ATM in the wall of his bank. He never used to be like that. Jess said those habits had developed since she had become pregnant. Something was going on: she was convinced of it. Jenny tried to reassure her: it was quite natural that a man should become unsettled at this time. He would want to go out. She should not worry: he would find himself again. As soon as the baby was born, he would fall into line; indeed, he would want to be with her and the baby. She was not to fret. Jess was not convinced. She had heard, too, that he was often in the company of North. What was that boy like? She needed to know. He seemed rather strange, exotic, Jess thought. Jenny told her about North and said she had nothing to fear. She tried to put Jess's anxieties to rest.

In the end, Jenny told me, she had said to Jess that she would keep an eye on Monty, perhaps even have an old-fashioned word in his ear, and let Jess know if she discovered anything untoward in his behaviour.

'My dear Jenny, what did you think you were doing? What about Monty and Bernie? How did you propose to deal with that little problem?' I exclaimed, when she told me. I could not help smiling grimly. I did not see how Jenny could possibly help unless she became party to deceit and evasion. It was all becoming rapidly hopeless. There was no doubt in my mind that Jess was going to be hurt. I tried to explain to Jenny that she should maintain a distance from the domestic troubles of others. Monty was like a suicide bomber, except that he was not driven by one fanatical belief; but in the end he was bound, so far as I could see, to blow himself up and cause pain and distress to many others.

'Jenny, you are a married woman. You know about these things. Leave well alone. View from a distance.'

'I was a married woman,' she emphasized. 'No longer. I want Jess to be all right. I don't want her marriage to break up. It's awful when it does. Monty's a fool. She's so sweet. She shouldn't have to contend with this sort of thing. Why doesn't that enchanter North charm Bernie so much that she chucks Monty. It could be done discreetly.'

'That sort of thing is never discreet. Someone who knows always makes sure there is public scandal. Gossip, rumour, these make the world go round.' That was my opinion. Such stories filled the newspapers.

I never cease to marvel at the ability of people to delude

166

themselves. After all, there was Monty, a seemingly devout evangelical Christian, persuading himself that it was in order for him to have an affair with Bernie at the same time as being a dutiful husband. Now Jenny felt that she could, and should, help manipulate matters to make Jess more comfortable, when she knew from her own bitter experience that no one else can help. As I told her, you never know how the relationship between two other people works. What you decide on as an advisable course of action might well prove to be disastrous for the pair. Monty and Jess had to work out their own salvation.

North had said he would report back, and he did. On the Sunday afternoon after the Brixton gig, he rang me. I was reading the heavy Sunday newspapers, the review sections, books and arts. I had just read critiques of new art exhibitions at the Tate Modern and the Hayward. There was a brilliant retrospective of an American artist at the Hayward and some installation artist, recently out of the Royal Academy school, had made it to Tate Modern, blazing a trail of fame from one side of the Thames to the other. I was in the middle of reading a film review. Two French women directors had teamed up to make a violent, sexually explicit movie about women behaving as men more usually do: tough, cruel, callous. They seize the sexual initiative, do not take no as an answer, and rape if necessary. I describe the film as sexually explicit because the Frenchwomen disputed the term 'pornographic'. The reviewer, a man noted for his liberalism, found the film distasteful: the sex gratuitously stimulating and sleazy, the violence simply obnoxious. It was the sort of film I could never make up my mind about, whether to see it or not. How can you form a valid opinion if you do not see it? Yet it sounded like trash.

'It was some night,' he said. 'I feel wasted. Or at least I did. It's a bit better now. Are you busy? Can we talk?'

I felt I wanted to get out, away from my study. I was beginning to feel cramped, confined, always a prelude to acute uneasiness and even depression.

'Yes, let's. I need to get out for a bit. Why don't we meet at the north gate of the Parks, walk around a little and then have a drink in North Parade?' The Parade was a short, narrow street, both sides lined with shops of the bijou type, cafés, restaurants, bars and pubs. I added, 'We can go to the Red Café. It's not likely to be crowded.'

North agreed. The fresh air, he thought, would do him good, and the idea of the Red Café was agreeable. We met a quarter of an hour later. He seemed to me to have recovered: he was as composed as ever.

The sky was intermittently clouded, the temperature cool, but when the sun came out its warmth was noticeable. The walk was generally invigorating and made me feel much better than when I was cabined in my study. For all sorts of reasons, I was glad he had made me go out. The horizons were wider than if we had been sitting and talking in my flat.

'It was a hell of a fantastic evening, or, rather, night,' he said. 'The music was great. Stanton Warriors turned up as a guest set on the way to another venue. The punters went wild. There were times when you could hardly get on the floor. Bernie had never been to anything like it before. She loved it. She went crazy. And I'll tell you something, she had the Kishimoto pants and bra on. Don't ask me how I know.'

My imagination did not need much prompting. I did not believe that North would be slow off the mark. He would have made the most of his opportunities and Bernie would have been quick to respond.

'On the way back, about three in the morning, I told her.

I had decided the crunch had to come. I told her I had to stop our affair: that I didn't want to go on with the sexual stuff. It wasn't that I didn't enjoy it: she knew I did. She certainly enjoyed herself. I'm pretty good at bringing her on and keeping her going: she likes it. Anyway, I told her we had to stop because I was not going to be around for much longer: a few weeks, and I was off. I needed to concentrate on my work. It would be better for her to end it now.

'Funnily enough, she was not as upset as I supposed she might be. She agreed with me. She was slightly drunk, leant all over me, fondled and caressed me, and said she understood. That led to another assault on the fortress of love, as you might say; a long, sensual trip to climax. I love getting her there and then easing her down. She's good at it. And she looks after my interests very well. We enjoy ourselves.

'She saw the logic though. Finish now. Get it over with. She agreed. I'm just worried that her resolution won't stick. Then we could be in trouble. I shall make no move towards her. But there you are, the deed is done.'

I could scarcely believe what I was hearing. It was typical of North that he should adopt such an attitude: take an executive decision and stick to it. I admired his frankness: he held nothing back. I knew he would keep to his word. There would be no faltering on his part. Bernie I was not so sure about.

'It's extraordinary that she took it so well,' I commented. 'How did you leave her? She must be a bit distraught today.'

'We came back in Lee's car. He gave us a lift. I saw her back to her flat. We agreed to continue talking to each other, obviously; it would be difficult not to. It's just for a short time. She wanted me again, a last time perhaps. She was pretty ravenous. She unzipped me, but I didn't let her. I did bring her to ecstasy though. It was best that way.'

I could hardly credit what I was hearing. There was almost a calculated cruelty in his telling me this. He had been cold-blooded and clinical in that night's farewell, and I wondered if he knew the effect his detailed relation of events would have on me. Did he think I was indifferent to the description of his sexual exploits? Did he know that in some way he was titillating me? But his revelations, so intimate, did not change my view of him.

'That was it,' he concluded. 'I stroked her face, her hair. I kissed her: she kept on kissing me, reluctant to let me go, but in the end we parted. I made my way back home. My mother woke as I went in; but she was bleary-eyed and sleepy, relieved that I was back. I can't stop her worrying. I don't think I ever will. So, there we are, it's all over.'

I was not quite so certain as North. From his point of view, it was over. He would remain objective, and he had an inner steel that would sustain his resolve. I had seen it before. He would hold his position. Bernie was different – she was too emotionally involved. At times she might see matters clearly and logically, but for the most part she had been blinded by Cupid's arrow. North had led her into new areas of life. She had tasted fruit that she had only heard tell of. He had shown her new paths and she had followed them. The savours, the experiences, would, I suspected, be too alluring to surrender. Therefore, what would she do? Would she retire in terrible agony, internal torture and remorse? Would she grow, as the poet has it in another context, 'spectre-thin and die'? Or would she make a fuss, create embarrassing scenes? If anything, I thought the latter.

'What do you think she will do?' I asked North. I have mentioned before that I detected signs of extraordinary genius in North. Genius is difficult to be sure of; there are often false signs. There are plenty of faux geniuses around, but North convinced me of his authenticity early on. His clarity of vision amazed me. He replied, 'I think I can predict what she will do.

She'll try to retrieve me in a day or two. Then she will give up because I don't respond, and she will turn more and more to Monty. I don't mind that. Monty has to go in the end: I know that. It's a shame: I sort of love him. But that's life. So far as I'm concerned he's making his exit.'

North was ruthless. I had originally thought he was a romantic, but he was not: he was a ruthless realist. Later on, I was to realize he was more than that: he was something infinitely more dangerous.

'If she does that, she's going to make trouble in the Monty Ross household,' I commented. 'You could save him from that. Isn't there some other way you can handle this?'

'I've thought about it. There isn't. Can you think of some way to save Jess?'

I had the feeling that he was playing a tactical ball back into my court. He wanted me to return a winning shot or else play the ball and allow the game to develop. I had an intuition that I was being manipulated by a superior intelligence, but I dismissed it immediately: such an idea was not realistic. North was just a fascinating, unusual youth whom I liked very much. In a cold light he was just that.

I was sorry for Jess: I foresaw conflict and unhappiness. Were North to continue his relationships with both Bernie and Monty it was possible a crisis might be warded off, though when at last it came to a head it would probably be worse.

'I'll try to keep an eye on Jess and Monty. I'll do what I can, but it's not going to be much. Stay close to me North: I'll need you to talk to me. I feel tired at the thought of being involved in such a drama. You'll have to stay in the background and look after me.'

I said that only half-jokingly. I did not relish the idea of sorting out Monty's mess, and, anyway, North had not done with Monty yet. There were bound to be complications there.

By the time we had finished walking round the Parks, we must have covered a mile and a half. The Red Café was close by, a matter of 500 yards or so. We went there and North ordered Earl Grey tea. I settled for a Campari and soda, its pungently bitter taste reminding me of medicine from my childhood: thus, I convinced myself it was doing me good.

We sat for half an hour. I changed the subject. I was tired of other people's problems. We discussed the worsening situation in the Middle East. A friend of mine, a professor at the university, was an expert on the conflict between the Arab countries and Israel. He held a pessimistic view: the worst decision ever made for the region was the creation of the state of Israel after the Second World War; powerful nations creating a new nation state, *vi et armis*, would never work; in any case, Arabs and Israelis are all semitic – like battles like; fight Hamas but remember Irgun. North and I chewed over these matters. I recommended an article my friend the professor had written in the *New York Herald Tribune* and said that I would give North a photocopy of it. We talked about books I had seen reviewed in the latest literary journals. He was excellent, intelligent company. I could talk to him as though I had known him for thirty years. I forgot his age: his intelligence seemed ageless.

As the bells of Oxford's churches and colleges struck six, I said that I had better make a move back home. I wanted to send some e-mails: one to an old artist friend, another to an American, living in Los Angeles, I had known since my college days. Afterwards I was due to have dinner with the Aitkens.

North said that Francine was taking him and a female friend of hers, a librarian at the university library, out to dinner. He named a pleasant restaurant with a huge, airy, beautifully-lit conservatory in the Woodstock Road. He was looking forward to it; he was going to order a large steak. I wondered how the two women saw that remarkable boy. I knew that he would subtly take command. His natural charm would put him in charge of his mother. The aura of his personality would impose itself unobtrusively on the occasion and affect everyone there — Francine, her friend, the waiters.

He gave me his usual easy continental embrace and we left. He went towards his home and Francine. I walked quickly back to my flat and my computer. My artist friend had just completed a fine piece of figurative art, a self-portrait chosen for the national portrait painters' annual exhibition at the Mall Gallery. His picture was entitled *Popeye and Me*, and showed his grizzled self to the right foreground of the painting standing in front of a picture of Popeye, smoking pipe at an angle, in the left background. It was highly original: striking, pop-artish, sub-Warhol. I liked it and wanted to tell him. I composed my e-mail to him, fashioned some pertinent complimentary critical comments, and additionally told him that there was a reference to someone we both knew in an edition of Kingsley Amis's letters which was on special offer in Waterstone's, Piccadilly. Since both of us had liked the character concerned many years ago, and, surprisingly, so had Amis, I thought my friend would like to know and perhaps buy the book. I then wrote to my Californian friend and passed on some information I had found out about London literary agents who might handle a play she had written.

I poured myself a whisky and soda: long ago I had dismissed as superstition the injunction not to drink alone. Once I had found myself living on my own, there was no alternative. The prospect of dinner with the Aitkens in any case demanded a substantial rise in my blood-sugar level if I were going to survive the evening. A bracer was what was required.

I took a shower and smartened up. Just before I left, I went out into the garden and picked a rose for my buttonhole. There was a beautiful pink miniature, a Cecile Brunner, which kept flowering most of the summer and provided me with a supply of buds. I had discovered that as a plucked rose faded and died, so its scent grew more fragrant, which is why its petals go to make up pot-pourri. How different from the lily, which, as it decays and rots, smells vile and reeks of its corruption. Once a year I gave a commentary to my students on the symbolism of flowers. The school's emblem was the lily and I would remind them of Shakespeare's sonnet, 'They that have power to hurt, and will do none', and the closing couplet: 'For sweetest things turn sourest by their deeds:/ Lilies that fester smell far worse than weeds'. Recalling this, the image of North came to my mind and I thought I should bring his attention to the words. They were a warning. I wanted to tell him that he should think how he behaved, how he treated other people, that I did not want to see him tainted by corruption. The feeling was intense and I wore the Cecile Brunner to remind me of him.

I drove to the Aitkens. They lived in a wing of a monumental Victorian house, designed by AW Pugin, which belonged to the school. I parked on its terrace. This gave out on to a lawn, divided by a broad footpath and set with ornamental rose beds, which stretched down to the river. There, two brilliant-white chinoiserie bridges crossed two river tributaries to give access to an island cricket ground. Aitken lived in one of the most enviable houses in Oxford, central, private, possessing one of the best views in the city.

The dinner was fairly dreary. There were two other guests, a husband and wife, an academic couple from the University with interests in Spanish drama. Juanita, Aitken's wife, talked mostly to them. The husband had lived for three years in Madrid, so there was much nostalgia in the air. Juani, as she was called, enjoyed herself. I was not sure about Aitken. He found that he had to talk mostly to me, although he did make a valiant effort during the first course, a failed, leathery, soufflé, to engage with the wife. About half-way through the meal I decided to test Aitken again on Monty. I made the remark that the school was benefiting from a number of young talented teachers who were bound to go a long way in the profession. I asked how he thought Monty was progressing. He immediately lit up. His conversation became more animated. Jenny's analysis seemed to be proven. He extolled Monty: he was a very bright young man whose prospects were phenomenal; Aitken wished he could do more for him. I said I thought he had done Monty proud so far.

'I want him to do really well. I'd like to see him become the youngest head ever. I know he has it in him. I shall give him all my backing – I think he's well worth it. He has that wonderful combination of being popular and at the same time managing to exert an iron authority. There are not many people who can do that.'

'You've done a great deal for him already,' I commented. 'I hope he is grateful. I don't mean now, but in the future. He's a nice chap. He's one of the blessed. I agree: he should go far.'

There was no point in drawing attention to Monty's drawbacks, his weaknesses. It was not the place to expose Monty's mixed-up personal relationships, which ran the risk of bringing his world to ruins.

'How long before you think he should go for his own headship?' I asked Aitken.

'Perhaps even at the end of next year. He could start staking a claim. It will probably take him two or three tries, but I'll make damn sure he gets there. He's very good company and has tremendous loyalty.'

I thought to myself that there was something I could say

about the accuracy of that last statement. Perhaps I should have told him what was going on between Monty and Jess, Monty and Bernie, and even Monty and North. That dinner party was not the appropriate place, but, later, should I have taken Aitken to one side and told him what was really going on in his school? As a sort of *eminence grise* of the institution, maybe I should have done so. I did not. The game in which North was playing so large a part had to continue. To my mind that was certain. A natural resolution was necessary: it would work itself out.

Aitken could not stop talking about Monty once he had been introduced into the conversation. His obsession was clear. At one point, he said longingly that it would have been nice if Monty had been present. He regretted not asking him for dinner that evening. He knew that Jess would not have been able to be there, but she would not have minded Monty getting out. Monty was on his mind, there was no doubt about that. I smiled inwardly. I knew what Aitken's trouble was; and so did he, but he could not admit it.

We broke up at ten-thirty. I said my farewells and kissed Juani, with whom I had had a long talk over coffee. We had discussed her daughters. She was never happier than when she talked of her lovely daughters. I drove slowly home, taking in the glory of the ancient city, full of shadows, flood-lit towers and half-lit alleys.

My cat, my black familiar, greeted me by rubbing himself against my leg. He arched his back, miaowed complainingly and escorted me closely to my study, where, satisfied that I was staying, he curled up on my desk and went to sleep, purring heavily. I watched the news on television at eleven and retired to bed. I went to sleep, my mind filled with images of Bernie, North and, of all people, Francine. It occurred to me in an objective moment that I might fancy her. There was something about Francine which was curiously attractive; and then there was the fact that she was North's mother. What sort of union would that have been, Francine and me? I dismissed the conjecture: the image of G rose up to haunt me. I felt hugely tired and I must have fallen asleep within seconds. I slept deeply, not waking until a quarter to eight the following morning. I had not heard my alarm, which was always set for 6.30a.m., though I was usually wide awake before it went off. My lateness put me on quite the wrong footing for the rest of the day. I was uneasy, nervous, tense and irritable.

My mood was not enhanced by the weather: it was a terrible day. The rain came; the temperature dropped. I thought of the end of the world: it would surely be like this. It would grow cold; the atmosphere would become threatening; there would be rain, wind, thunder and lightning; it would become apocalyptic, cataclysmic; corpses would rise from their graves. The end of the world was nigh: that was what I felt like. The black dog was surely walking with me that morning. All was not right with the world: the Devil was abroad.

When eventually I arrived at the school, I was late. A group of my students had very wisely decided to do their own work. Some had dispersed to the library, others, no doubt, to have a smoke. I wearily sent out search parties to round them all up. They soon cheered me up. There is nothing like the presence of the young to bring you up to scratch. Their optimism, their enthusiasm, acted on me as a tonic and I was soon rehabilitated to my usual self. One or two of them had noted my depression and had decided to help rid me of it. We were discussing Keats's 'Ode to a Nightingale' and they talked non-stop: they were full of ideas and insisted that we all have to make the most of mortal beauty while we have time and space. The 'weariness, the fever, and the fret' in this world goes without saying. 'Darkling' we listen, but 'easeful death' should be avoided and delayed while we are able to hear the ecstatic voice of the nightingale, whose music is timeless: 'Thou wast not born for death, immortal Bird!'

By the middle of the morning I was feeling better. I spent lunch-time with an historian colleague, and at the end of the afternoon sought out Jenny. While she tidied her books and papers, I walked in the fresh air. The rain had stopped; the sun occasionally showed through the clouds, there was an invigorating, clean, freshness about the air. When I returned from the gardens, Jenny was ready and we walked into the city centre. She wanted to go to one of the big department stores to buy some Laura Mercier make-up for her daughter. It was a fruitless mission: the store did not stock the brand and told Jenny that nowhere in Oxford had it – she would have to go to London, to Harvey Nichols or Harrods. That was a disappointment, but I told Jenny that I would be in London later in the week and I would buy the make-up for her. We had some tea in a café bar, talked a great deal about Jenny's domestic life, and about Bernie. We then walked back to the school and our cars. As we approached Magdalen Bridge, that majestically impressive entrance to Oxford that the London road affords, we saw Monty and Bernie coming towards us. I cannot be sure, but it looked to me as though they were holding hands and, when Monty noticed us, he adeptly disengaged from Bernie's grasp. We stopped and spoke briefly: they were both on their way home. As soon as they had gone, I said to Jenny, 'I'm sure they were holding hands.'

'So am I. They were pretty quick to cover it up, but I don't think my eyes deceived me.'

'Exactly. It's rash of them to go around here like that. Very stupid. The publicity would be bad news. Aitken might see them. He wouldn't like it for all sorts of reasons. You should have a word in Bernie's ear.'

Jenny agreed and said she would look for an opportunity to do so.

It took me all of the first half of that week to re-establish my spiritual equilibrium. The nightmare scenario of Sunday night's sleep, my waking late and the unsatisfactory start to my teaching week demanded an unhurried recovery. Not that I did much teaching. I saw three different groups of students during the week. That was the arrangement I had come to, and it was that which enabled me to write. On the Thursday afternoon I went up to London by train. I was to have dinner with one of my first students, now an eminently successful lawyer, the senior partner of a famous city firm of solicitors. He had recently been acting for a politician, a disgraced former minister, who was being blackmailed and falsely accused of various sexual misdemeanours. The politician's wife was standing bravely by him; but then she herself was no stranger to that sort of scandal: a few years earlier she had had an affair with the then Defence Secretary and it had been blazed all through the news media. I was looking forward to the evening. We were to meet at his offices in Broad Street for champagne and canapés before dining at some French restaurant near St Bartholomew's.

On the way I stopped at Harvey Nichols and found the Laura Mercier make-up that Jenny wanted.

That Thursday night dinner proved the turning point for me and put me back on my proper course. I felt back in place, my mind relaxed and contemplative, my critical stance objective, and that night, when I caught the train back to Oxford, I considered again all the players in the game I had been watching so carefully over the last few months. I wondered how

179

North was proceeding and if Jenny had managed to talk to Bernie about her incautious behaviour with Monty.

The following day, I gave the Laura Mercier to Jenny and we arranged to meet in the early evening, as we often did, for an end of the week drink. I saw North in the afternoon. We stopped and talked. He had hailed me from a distance and said immediately that he had missed me during the week; had he not have been busy with his exam work and with escorting his mother on two evenings, once to the theatre and then to the opera, he would have been in touch. I explained that I had been recovering from a bad attack of gloomy despondency and it was probably better that he had kept out of the way.

'Rubbish,' he responded immediately. 'I should have come to see you. You should have told me. I know I could have raised your spirits. You ought to have told me. You know, too, that I could have helped. Don't suffer. Always, let me help.'

I was overwhelmed by his desire to help me and, even more, by his conviction that he could be effective. Yet that was North – he never doubted his own abilities. Of course, he was right. His presence alone, without anything said, would have made me feel better. I did know that. For some reason that I did not recognize, that I could not work out, I had suppressed my desire to see him. Deep down I had known that he could relieve me from my depression and yet I embargoed him. I blotted out his image. It was as if I felt that I had to suffer. It was a form of penance for some undefined, unspecified offence. It did not make sense, of course; but then, when the black dog is upon you, little does.

Jenny and I drove to a cocktail bar a little way from the centre of town but which was on our way home. She had been invited out to dinner that evening and I was going to a production of *Cosi fan Tutte*, given by the Welsh National Opera, at the local theatre. We were both in a relaxed mood. Jenny wanted a white wine, so I ordered a bottle of Bourgogne aligoté 'Domaine Belle-Croix', a fresh, dry wine that had been nicely chilled. My St James's vintner had recommended it to me once as the ideal wine for a dash of blackcurrant to make the traditional Burgundian kir, but I disliked polluting the pure wine and that aligoté on its own was perfect as an aperitif. The conversation soon worked round to Bernie.

'Did you get a chance to talk to Bernie?' I asked.

'Yes. I managed to tell her that I thought she should be careful when she's in public with Monty. I pointed out that if ever it became known that she was having an affair with Monty, the roof would cave in. Jess would almost certainly break down or walk out; and if that happened, Aitken would not keep Bernie on the payroll. She seemed rather low-spirited when we got on to this topic. She said that she really needed to rely on Monty more than usual at the moment.'

I knew the reason. North was disengaging; Bernie was turning more and more to Monty for consolation. Bernie was like Cressida, who, when she was unable to go on enjoying the delights of Troilus, turned more and more for comfort and support to Diomedes. Bernie was finding it very hard to resign herself to North's absence from the lovers' couch.

'If that is so, then she must be increasingly careful,' I said. 'I suppose, if I have the opportunity, I should say something to Monty. He might listen to me. His trouble is that he invests it all with an innocence that it hasn't, in fact, got. He has the remarkable ability of all good conjurors of creating illusions in which he actually believes. As the magician, he should remember it's all trickery.'

I knew as I said this that I would never talk to Monty about what he was doing with Bernie. It was simply not what I did. He was supposed to be a born-again Christian; I was not going to give him advice. With me, as I have said before, discussion is a different matter. If he volunteered a discussion about his love affairs, then I might join in; but not otherwise. The matter had to be left to Jenny. The Jenny/Bernie axis was crucial.

'I have this awful feeling that it will all end in tears,' Jenny said. 'I know Jess is in a terribly jittery state. I cannot see how she isn't going to find out.'

We concluded we could do no more and talked of other things. Jenny persistently asked me, in a half-jesting way, to introduce her to any eligible men I knew, some university professor perhaps, or someone in the newspaper world up in London. My stock answer was that I would if I knew of one; but I did not. None of my friends or acquaintances were available for an attractive divorcee like Jenny. I thought to myself that North might fit the bill: he could provide attention, care and, above all, sex. I considered that idea with malicious glee and, of course, at once dismissed it. Jenny was far too sensible. She would not consort with a teenager, and he was not the kind of lover she was looking for. She wanted someone mature, well off, who would give her security. The only person I could think of was me, but, as I have said, G was still in the background. I am sure, had I ever suggested it, that she would have loved to tie up with me; we understood each other and were comfortable in each other's company. There was nothing particularly exciting about it, but those relationships usually prove the most enduring.

We ate some Kalamata olives with our wine and then went our separate ways. At the opera, I saw, across a crowd of heads in the bar at the interval, Francine and North. They were with an older, rather regal woman, dressed in a formal black dress displaying a breast brooch which fired and sparkled to such an extent that it must have been fashioned with diamonds. She looked an expensive lady. She might have been Francine's mother. I wondered, and thought of forcing my way through the crowd and introducing myself. As I was about to do so, the interval bell sounded. So, instead, I made my way back to my seat, thinking I might meet them at the end. However, when the curtain went down and I had gone out into the foyer, I could not see them anywhere: I had missed them.

It turned out that I was right: it had been Francine's mother. Over that weekend, North rang me twice, the first time to check Sam's telephone number, which was ex-directory. North needed to talk to him about an exam that was to take place on the Monday morning. The second time he rang was on the Sunday evening when he fancied a break from his work. He wanted to walk round to my flat and talk for a little. That was fine by me.

I had eaten a sparse supper but, when he arrived, I offered him some cheese and fruit. I took out some Jarlsberg and Brie, some Italian salted biscuits, some grapes and kiwi fruit. There was still a half-bottle of Chablis left from my supper. I put it all on a small table in my study and we helped ourselves. I poured the wine and told North that a little would be medicinal for him; I would make coffee later. I told him I had seen him at the opera but could not fight my way through the crowds in time to talk to him; at the end, I could not find them. He said that he and Francine were with his grandmother who was over from America. She had been in London for the week and was staying with them for the weekend. She was flying back to New York on the morning of the next day. He would not stay too long as he would have to say his goodbyes that night.

North was presenting to me a new role: that of dutiful grandson. I had difficulty in collating the conscientious grandson with Monty's homosexual lover, the boy who wondered which one of them had been the seducer. I thought back to my own school days. There had never been anyone like North among my contemporaries. No one ever had adult lovers of either sex so far as I knew. There were occasional girlfriends; I knew of nothing more. Could North's behaviour be explained simply by the progressive attitudes of the intervening decades? Was it the sum of 'make love, not war' plus Andy Warhol and the whole liberation culture? There always lurked at the back of my mind a conviction that there was a more sinister explanation: North's influences were perhaps darker.

'I'm leaving Bernie alone,' he said. 'The only trouble is that she is spending more time with Monty and I'm not sure I want to share him with her. I don't want to give him up yet. I know I'll have to eventually, but I'm enjoying myself too much at the moment. I've made him do things he never thought himself capable of.'

I forbore to ask him what they were. I should have liked to have known the details but unless he was to tell me of his own volition, I calculated it would destroy our confidential mood. I preferred to use my imagination. In any case, he sometimes gave clues, sometimes was more or less forthcoming, and on a few occasions told me exactly what he and Monty did.

'You're pretty incorrigible,' I said. 'What happened last night? What were you doing? I hope you spent the night in your own bed. You make me envious. If only I were your age.'

I could not bring myself to condemn him. That was not my role. It would not have made any difference anyway. He had taken up his position.

'I did as a matter of fact. I saw Monty after he had returned from umpiring a cricket match. I knew what time they were finishing so I met him as he came up from the field. We went across to Café Coco and then, before he went home, I ... How shall I put it? I loved him and left him in his office. No one else was about. Then he went off home and I went out to dinner with my mother and grandma.'

'Where did you go?' I asked.

'To the Old Rectory. It was splendid. My grandma doesn't like to drink anything except champagne. I had their shank of lamb and masses of chips, British style, not those emaciated French fries. Yeah, it was good.'

I could imagine the scene. The Old Rectory had been a dilapidated, ancient wreck of a place, a teetotal lodging house, which was taken over and completely refurbished by someone I knew through a lawyer friend: it had long since ceased to be a rectory. It was now the best hotel in town, with a bar and extremely comfortable dining room. Quite a few people who lived in the north of the city frequented it regularly; some used it almost as a club. There would have been that elegant little party: Francine looking her best, the elegant grandmother, and the handsome North, two generations taking the third generation out to dinner. People who looked at him would have been intrigued, entranced, maybe, by North, but they would little have thought that he was more sophisticated in the sexual ways of the world than most men twice his age. You had to concede it to North, he could carry off those occasions. He had style.

'I envy you. It does sound—' I was about to say 'good', but a piece of hard, flaky, Italian biscuit went the wrong way down my gullet and I choked. I coughed violently, fought for breath, my eyes watered. Without hesitation, North was on his feet, stepping across to me and beating me firmly on the back. Then he made me put my head between my knees. The fit subsided and I started breathing properly again. North fetched a glass of water from the kitchen. I took a few sips and felt a little better. He patted my back firmly to make sure that I was not going to start coughing again, and then kept his hand resting on my right shoulder. It was extraordinary: he was like a revivalist healer. I felt, at once, immensely reassured and calmed. His gentle grasp had a warmth which seemed to flow through the whole of my being. He knew the effect he was having on me.

He took the glass of water from me and asked if I were all right.

'Yes. Thanks. I feel much better. You have an amazing gift for calming people. Thanks.'

'Not people,' he said. 'You, yes ... And a few others. Only those I choose.'

He had turned to look me full in the face to satisfy himself that I was recovered, and, as he spoke, I noticed again a deep, far away, glint in his eyes. It was peculiar, slightly disconcerting, and hinted of danger. There was the same hardness in it that I had seen in the light reflected from his grandmother's diamonds. I knew at that moment that there was something in North that I did not know or understand. I think he detected a trace of anxiety in me, because he quickly changed the subject; he was not going to expand on what he had said. He retrieved his glass of wine, raised it and toasted me.

'To your health. Come on, let's drink to it.' That was not a toast I was going to decline.

There it was: North was unique. If you knew him, talked with him, went around with him, it seemed a privilege. That is why Bernie and Monty were so in his thrall.

North was very abstemious: he sipped his wine and confined himself to no more than three quarters of a glass. He drank with it a small bottle of sparkling water. He said he did not want to wake up the following morning in any way befuddled.

We discussed travel; where he might go after his exams were finished. He wanted to visit Sicily, but before going there he thought he would return to Scotland where we had been nine months previously on a five-day 'arduous training' exercise. It had been enormous fun. We were a party of only ten people: our leader, an experienced mountaineer, eight students and me. We had stayed in the Cameron Barracks at Inverness, at that time the HQ of the Highland Regiment. They looked after us well and supplied us with equipment and expert advice. One battalion had just returned from a six-month tour, patrolling the border lands of Fermanagh and Armagh in Northern Ireland. They had stories to tell, and entertained us on two of the evenings we were there.

One particular day the weather was extremely bad – persistent rain, bitter cold – and when we had climbed above the snow line, the clouds enveloped us. It was exciting and dangerous. Visibility was no more than a yard and a half and we had to use our global positioning units to keep track of where we were.

North had seemed to be in his element. The more frightening the conditions became, the more North enjoyed himself. As others became silent and reserved, concerned for their safety, so he came to life. He radiated invincible confidence and glowed with energy. He stood with our mountaineer and, together, they led us on that expedition. It was remarkable; as though he was possessed.

One evening, as we returned to barracks from a trek into one of the great glens, we were about to pass Erchless Castle. We decided to stop and walk round this famed seat of the Chisholm clan. Opposite the building on the other side of the main road which eventually leads into Inverness, along the shore of Loch Ness, lies the burial ground of the Chisholms. We entered it through an old, rusted wrought-iron gate, passed through a screen of dark fir trees and were confronted by a vast burial mound. A track wound its way round and upwards to the top of the mound until a flat summit was reached. On this open platform of ground, above the tree-tops, stood the tombs and memorials of past Chisholm chieftains. It was an eerie, forbidding place. The sun, blood-orange, westered behind cloud and mountains. We stood in a heavy half-light above the dark shadows of the trees. A livening wind shook the branches and the coarse voices of crows intermittently sounded from within the woods. It was not the sort of place you would wish to be on your own for very long, but what struck me was that North was completely at one with the aura of the place. He relished the atmosphere of that sombre retreat full of ghosts and shades. I was relieved to reach the road again and I am sure the others, certainly those who possessed any sensitivity at all, shared my relief. North, on the other hand, was exhilarated.

I think it was that exhilaration that stayed with North. It was a feeling he wanted to regain. His memories of the Scottish expedition created for him a nostalgia that had intoxicated him to such an extent that he wanted to go back to those wild haunts and revisit those experiences. I suggested that he should go farther across to the west and perhaps visit the isles. The project appealed to him and he said he would study the map, plan a route, and discuss it with me.

We heard the Oxford bells strike ten. North said he had better go. He intended to sleep well that night, not that he was worried about the exam next day, but he wanted to be fresh for it, and afterwards, he said, he was hoping to meet Monty. He asked me if I was completely recovered from my choking fit. I was. He hugged me briefly and kissed my cheek. As I responded to this accolade, I noticed that his lips felt cold against my cheek and, when I kissed him, there was no warmth in his skin. It struck me as odd, since his hand on my shoulder earlier had imbued such warmth into me. I said, 'Are you OK. North? You seem a little chilled.'

'Yes. I'm fine. I know what you mean. It's something to do with my metabolism, I think. Towards the end of the day, my body temperature drops – not always, but sometimes. Feel my hands ... or my forehead.'

I did so. I took his hands in mine and felt his brow. They were icily cold. It was strange: he was most unusual.

'See you soon. Tomorrow, in fact. Take care.'

I walked with him to the pavement and saw him depart homewards.

A strange thing happened the following day. I was not accustomed to being the *intime* of Monty but he approached me after lunch and asked if we could find some time later in the day to have a quiet talk: there was something that he was worried about and he thought my experience could possibly help. It crossed my mind that I should establish a therapy practice, buy a chaise longue, sit behind it and explore the egos, super-egos and ids of my patients. I had read Freud, and in my literary studies understood the difference his theories had made to writing and, particularly, criticism in the twentieth century. I did not entirely go all the way with him about the brain being merely an appendage of the genitalia, but I had grown to know that there is something about our sexual drive that is absolutely fundamental to our state of mind. I agreed to meet Monty, in private as he wished, in his office after teaching had finished.

I duly went to Monty's department. His office door was closed. I knocked and he called out for me to enter. He had made himself a cup of tea and he asked me if I wanted one.

'Yes, please. Thanks.' I tried to assess quickly the mood he was in. He struck me as not being quite so surely in control as he usually was. There was certainly something bothering him. He dropped a tea-bag in a mug, poured on boiling water, and handed me a carton of milk so that I could add my own.

'Thanks for coming. I'm aware that we don't know each other all that well but I need someone to talk to, and Bernie said you would be the person. I can't talk to Aitken, as much as I like him, because it would be too official. I'm getting to know him better and one of these days perhaps he will be a real friend.'

Too true, I thought to myself. If what I think is so about Aitken, you could soon be very close to him. I said to him, 'Well, fire away. If I can help, I will, but I'm not sure I'll be much use.'

He then began to pour out an account of his domestic troubles, his religious conscience, his love for Bernie. The latter he misrepresented. He put the case that he was responding to her demands of him for her sake, whereas anyone who could see objectively knew at once he was satisfying his own inclinations. He made no mention of North. He told me that Bernie had become much more intense: she wanted to be with him more, she made greater demands. Of course she did: she was withdrawing from North; she concentrated on Monty. North was like a drug and Bernie's addiction would take a long time to break; meanwhile she was turning to Monty for company, consolation and satisfaction, sexually as much as anything else.

'I don't really object. I like it. She's a lovely girl and we suit each other. I mean, if you don't mind the confidence, sexually. There are terrible difficulties, though. Jess senses something is going on. She doesn't know quite what, but if I'm not careful she is going to find out. At the moment she is very vulnerable. She's going to give birth any time now. She'd be so upset if she knew. I don't want to hurt Bernie, but it's becoming dangerous.'

I stopped him, otherwise he would have gone on; his anxieties were flowing in a torrent.

'Hold on. What do you propose to do about it? Obviously the answer lies with you. You're a married man. You could put a stop to your affair with Bernie immediately. I suppose the question is, do you want to? You have to make that decision.'

That was about all I felt like saying. I have stated I never give advice to those I know, my friends, because I think it's the quickest way to lose them. Monty was not a close friend but, nevertheless, I still did not feel like committing myself to the role of counsellor. The ball had to be driven smartly back into Monty's court and, preferably, a return should be unplayable.

Monty put down his mug of tea and rested his hands in his lap. 'I know that; and I don't want you to tell me what to do. I'm sure you wouldn't anyway. You're too canny for that. I just need desperately to talk to someone. I would listen to what you think and then make up my own mind what to do.'

So, for half an hour or more, we discussed his situation. Bernie was obviously putting pressure on him, wanting to be with him more than before. She had turned up in his office at odd times during the day. He simply had to decide: it was either Jess, his family, and almost certainly his career; or it was Bernie. That was it. Bernie offered little more than sex, infatuation, obsession. When he was with her, her presence blinded him to reality. When she was not there, she was always on his mind. If he persisted in his relationship with her, he had to come to terms with the complications. If he dispelled her image from his mind, then he was free to continue with Jess and the imminent child. The issues were clear.

I spelled it out to him. Mine was the voice of common sense which took no account of the madness of love. And I did not mention that other major factor in the equation – North. He figured in both their lives as a major quantity, but neither would mention him to me.

Monty and I rehearsed alternatives. It occurred to me, although I dared not say it, that it would solve matters if North were to dominate Monty's desires and affections. Then Bernie would fade in importance. If Monty were serious about maintaining his marriage, it would be easier for him to keep the fact of his relationship with North from Jess; and even if she did find out, I thought it would not have been as serious as him having an affair with another woman. With North, she would presume that it was primarily sexual, physical, mechanical, with no, or few, deep emotional entanglements. Yet I was not in a position to make that clear to him: I could not compromise North. If Monty were to tell me about it, then I could discuss it.

At one point, during a pause in the conversation, when Monty was deep in thought, I wondered what that rather dull, ordinary office had borne witness to. I thought of North, who had told me of his meetings with Monty there: I remembered that North had 'loved him and left him' there. I had difficulty imagining the details of their physical encounters. I was inhibited by an instinctive distaste for what was, no doubt, the stark reality of their relationship: dishevelled underwear and sweaty bodies. I was more comfortable dealing with things on an intellectual plane.

By the time I left Monty's office, I had become more convinced that North was the key player in this particular phase of that game of love. He could control the game, its pace, development and eventual outcome. No one else could. The others were, in a sense, victims, part-players, who needed direction. North was the principal. Should I talk to him? I decided that if the opportunity presented itself, I would. I sought a natural lead-in to a discussion with North. I knew, of course, that he would talk about the difficulties: there was nothing that was off-bounds in our conversations. But I did not want to appear too direct or too concerned. I wanted North to feel that he should only act if he felt so inclined. I did not want him to think that he should do something just for me: that would be the wrong reason.

At least matters were now different between Monty and me. He trusted me, otherwise he would never have spoken to me in the way he had done. He regarded me as discreet and thought he might benefit from my experience. The change in our stance towards each other meant that in the future there were matters I could discuss which I would not have been able to broach before.

It appeared that I had become a chief diplomat in the delicate negotiations of amatory affairs.

A day or two passed. The next weekend showed on the horizon. I noticed, from a distance, that Bernie was to be seen increasingly in the company of Monty. Something desperately needed to be done. On the Friday of that week, I had walked to the school through the University Parks and part of the mediaeval city. It was a fine, sunny day, not a day to sit in a car. Around five o'clock, as I was walking back home, I stopped to watch the university cricket XI playing against Somerset. The university was batting and doing well: they had scored 150 runs for three wickets, and it looked as though the two undergraduates batting had settled in to a profitable partnership. I wandered slowly round the perimeter until I was standing next to the sight-screen at the north end. I could watch the bowler's arm. I enjoyed seeing the ball swing or break, moving to off or leg. I could judge the batsman's degree of concentration and, a fraction before he played a ball, predict for myself the stroke he would make. It was a restful, relaxing way to wind down after a day's exacting debate with clever, lively students. About fifty yards to my right there was someone I did not wish to meet. An old history don from my college, who frequently watched the cricket, was seated in a deckchair. During the summer, he habitually wore an MCC tie, as if he were making a statement about his own sporting prowess, which I knew to be minimal. I thought him a snob of the first order, disliked him and so steered clear. Added to that, he was not much good as an historian. Some years previously he had been caught out in his scholarship: he had produced what was supposed to be a definitive book but which he had based on a typescript of an original manuscript. A Harvard professor had discovered the fact, exposed him, and illustrated fundamental discrepancies between the typescript and the manuscript, which rendered the edition useless.

As the bowler produced a swinging Yorker which the University batsman blocked competently, I felt a hand on my back. North had come up unnoticed and was standing next to me. My spirits rose. It was good to see him. He too was walking back home.

'I saw you there,' he said. 'You're giving an expert eye to the bowling I suppose. But you seemed to be looking askance at someone over there. Don't you like them? Who is it?'

'It's the chap in the deckchair with the red and yellow MCC tie on,' I said. 'I don't take to him. I've known him for years. By the way, since when have you been using the word 'askance'? A bit archaic, isn't it?'

'I like it. I've got it from Milton, and Spenser before him. I don't think these good old words should die.'

'I agree. Keep it up. That's what I like about you, North. You have an eye and an ear for language. I'm going to miss talking to you when you're away.'

'Don't worry, I'm not going far,' he said, genuinely trying to calm what he interpreted as my fears.

Close to the pavilion there was a bar tent. I suggested we had a drink.

'That would be good.' North was enthusiastic and not in a hurry.

'Well, it will help me to relax on a Friday evening. The past week has been a bit of a strain.'

We talked about his exams and, holding our beers, made judicious comments on the cricket. The bar was serving a draught bitter or Stella Artois. It was appropriate to drink beer rather than anything else, so we had chosen the lager. It was refreshingly cool.

We walked a little way from the tent and took up an extended square-leg umpire's position on the boundary. After a short while, North sat down cross-legged on the ground. Fortunately, because of my practice of yoga, I could join him without much difficulty. I had been persuaded to learn yoga by a doctor friend and for about a year I attended classes, until I grew irritated by the teacher's mysticism and espousal of tantric sex. Since that time I practise intermittently, but enough to gain some lowering of my blood pressure and a measure of limb flexibility.

We sat half-facing each other and looking towards the cricket match. North sat straight backed, occasionally swaying with an easy suppleness. He remarked, 'I haven't been near Bernie all week. It's a hell of a change. I think she's OK. She's certainly on to Monty. I keep seeing them together about the school. Before I left just now, I saw Aitken talking to them outside the science buildings. Or rather, he was talking to Monty. I don't know why, if he feels like it – which he does – he doesn't just get on with it. I could tell him that Monty would enjoy it.'

'I'm sure you're right, but Aitken's a little green about these things. I'm not sure he would know what to do.'

'I could tell him. I know exactly what Monty likes.' North said this in what I reckoned was an intentionally provocative way.

He looked directly at me with those deep blue eyes. I was completely lost, almost enchanted by his spell. I thought of asking him if he were trying to seduce me; but I desisted because I felt I knew what his response, what his next tactical move, would be. He would have denied it or avoided a straight answer. He would probably have said something like, 'I value you too much. It would change everything. I'm not saying that I wouldn't like that sort of deal, but it would be so different and I want our friendship to last.'

His cleverness impressed me, and his comments about Monty gave me the opening I wanted.

'I think Monty is pretty worried by the increase in attention from Bernie. He's sailing into rocky waters so far as Jess is concerned. What can we do about it? It's necessary that you don't have her, which, of course, you easily could. We've discussed that. What's the answer?'

I mused. North contemplated.

He said, 'I suppose I could always take him over completely. Shut her out. I know I could captivate him exclusively. Was that what you wanted me to say?' He said it, not wryly, but with an effortless foreknowledge. He seemed to read my mind. I have said before that I admired his intelligence. This was an example of his vastly unusual maturity. He instinctively knew what I was leading to.

'It wasn't a million miles from my mind,' I confessed. 'The trouble is, I can't keep my thoughts from you. You seem to read them.'

'There's nothing strange about it, nothing supernatural. If you analyse the situation objectively, it's all obvious. But your mind does chime with mine. I like it. It makes me feel good. We are one of a sort.'

Again, I saw that awful glint in his eyes – just momentarily, but it was there, deep down. I felt for that instant as if I had been damned.

'Hold on, there are differences. In the matter of practising sex, you go far beyond what I have ever done. There are one or two definite differences.'

'Superficial,' he retorted, not crossly but speedily emphatic. 'Your mind and mine are fundamentally the same. What you or I might, or might not, have done is neither here nor there. Our minds are capable of the same things. That's what's important.'

I did not pursue that line of thought. I drained my glass. My left leg was stiffening from sitting in my yoga position. I got to my feet and stretched.

'Let's stroll round for a bit. Then I'd better make a move.'

'I'm the one who had better make a move,' he said quickly, with a smile. 'My move must affect the others. I'll see what I can do.'

We followed the boundary round, did one more circuit and then went towards one of the northern exits. Outside we parted; our ways diverged. He went towards his house and to Francine. I went home, back to my cat, my study and my meditations.

I wondered if Francine would be waiting for him. Would she have prepared a meal? Did she look after him as any other mother would? Or did he have to fend for himself? I assumed she looked after his clothes: washed and ironed them, that sort of thing. Or, perhaps they had someone who came in and did it all for them. The point was: I could not believe that they lived in an ordinary sort of way. Added to which, Francine was becoming, for me, a distinct curiosity. She had a little of North's exoticism. I wanted to know more about her. She was becoming more and more attractive.

There were other matters to attend to. I had some correspondence to catch up with, e-mails to write and phone calls to make. I rang my medical friend at Cornell. He had just published a seminal work on life in the womb: a book about how the development of the foetus is controlled in the months prior to the mother giving birth. He had successfully made the subject accessible to the general reader and a major publisher had agreed to produce his book. He stood to make money on the publishing deal. He was in his lab, as usual writing out some funding application. He complained that 80 per cent of his academic time as director of his research unit was taken up by filling in forms for grants and donations. I congratulated him on his book deal. He told me that he would be in England in the autumn. We agreed to meet for dinner in a Sinhalese restaurant just behind Buckingham Palace one evening when he was in London. I told him that I would be flying to the States in late October to lecture on CS Lewis. I enjoyed Cornell. I like its atmosphere, high up above Lake Cayuga, light, airy, free. There were nice people that I had met there. It was one of the places in America where I felt immediately at home.

So my weekend began. I meandered slowly through it. Nothing of note happened. It was quiet and leisurely. I had nothing specific to do. I spent most of the time at my desk, occasionally going for walks, and on that Sunday afternoon I drove into the Cotswolds, parked the car at Minster Lovell and walked in the Windrush valley. The ruins of the great manor house, standing in late afternoon light and shadow, reminded me of what it once was: a magnificent, grand house, majestically, proudly proclaiming itself and its owner on the bank of the river. I thought of those lines in Shakespeare's *Richard III*, 'The Cat, the Rat, and Lovell the dog,/ Ruled all England under the Hog.'

The hog was Richard's emblematic white boar and his symbol of power. Catesby, Ratcliffe and Lovell were his civil servants, promoted to virtually absolute power in their regions, who owed him everything. With Shakespeare's plays, you simply reduce the scale from kings to commoners and you have the man next door – or the one on the Clapham omnibus. Monty owed everything to Aitken. Aitken was Richard III to Monty's Lovell.

* * *

The following Wednesday afternoon was significantly awful for some of the players in that game of love. I was going towards my car to put a plastic carrier bag of papers on to the front passenger seat next to the driver's, when I saw Monty's car pull up. A very distraught, *enceinte* Jess braked abruptly, got awkwardly out, slammed the door and hurried to the science block. She was clearly in disarray. Her hair was untidy, flowing wildly. She shook her head back, set her mouth firmly in a grim scowl, and walked ploddingly fast away from her car. I tried to catch her eye but she was determined to reach her destination as quickly as possible. She was recognizing nobody. She was focused, single-minded, upset and angry.

I was not unduly worried. I thought Jess was in an understandable pre-birth crisis. I went to the seminar room where I did most of my teaching, tidied my desk, leafed through an edition of Philip Larkin's collected poems, and returned towards my car. I had almost reached it when I heard raised voices, then some hysterical shouting. The main door of the science block swung open and a livid, ranting Jess emerged, followed by Monty. I froze, not knowing quite what to do. Fortunately, there was no one else about except for a group of five or six small boys. They stood and looked amazed for a moment and then made themselves scarce.

Jess was shouting at Monty. She saw me but took no notice: nothing was going to alter her mood, her indignation, her tirade against her husband. Monty was protesting. I heard him say she had got it wrong. I heard Bernie's name. He said she was misinterpreting things. He asked her to calm down. That incensed her more. She stood her ground and shouted at him. He had betrayed her and her unborn child. For all his evangelical Christianity, he was a liar and fornicator. She would seek out Bernie and tear her to shreds. Who did she think she was? Was it her aim in life to break up families? Where was she? Jess was going to have it out with her now.

All this I could not help hearing. It was an appalling scene. Monty was beside himself, unable to stop Jess. I could see that she was nearing the point where she would collapse in exhaustion. Her storm and fury would burn itself out. What would happen then? I thought to myself. Fortunately, as Jess beat her fists against Monty's chest, Sam and Jenny appeared from the art centre. They halted, measured the situation, and Jenny whispered to Sam. He went back into the building and Jenny advanced towards Jess and Monty, just as Jess burst into uncontrollable tears and leant back against the bonnet of their car. Jess bent forward holding her stomach, sobbing pitifully. Monty appeared to be dumbstruck. Jenny went up to Jess and put her arm round her, gave her a kiss, told Monty to open the car's door, and sat Jess down on the edge of the front passenger seat. She stroked Jess's hair, gave her a Kleenex, and kept up a low murmur of consoling chatter. Jess calmed. I heard Jenny suggest to Monty that he should go home and prepare some tea for Jess. She would talk to Jess for a while and make sure she arrived back home safely: Jess was too close to parturition to risk any more emotional trauma.

At this point, I stepped in. They had all been aware of me in the background, but there had been no time to address me or bring me into the proceedings. I walked over to Monty.

'Come on Monty. Let me give you a lift home. Jenny will bring Jess. We'll get there well before them. I'll leave you to prepare for her.'

He seemed genuinely perplexed. 'I don't know what's happened. Jess exploded at me. She's very angry indeed. I'll have to keep out of Bernie's way. It's terrible. Jess mustn't upset herself. It's not good for her and certainly not good for the baby.'

I did not say so, but I thought what a fool he was. I remembered wise old Geoffrey Chaucer and his tales of courtly love, his 'Romance of the Rose', and multitude of other love poems: how love makes fools of us all. Love is the great magician, the infamous conjuror, who makes things seem not what they are, who creates illusions we believe to be true, who jests at our expense and, finally, laughs at our discomfiture. Love puts us through all emotions until we are exhausted and 'Fain would lie down', like Lord Rendall in one of Bishop Percy's ballads, 'and prefer to die.' Monty and Jess were both afflicted by the merciless god. I pondered how they could be rescued.

I dropped Monty outside his house. He thanked me, said he was pleased to talk to me, and went in disconsolately. I drove off back to my desk and my thoughts.

It must have been an hour or so later that the telephone rang and Jenny was on the other end of the line.

'Wow! That was some way to end a working day. You managed to get Monty back safe and sound. He was looking very sheepish when we got there. Jess was very weepy, but at least they are in the same house ... for the moment anyway.'

'Yes. I can't tell you how glad I was that you came along when you did: an angel of mercy. I think Jess might have gone through the roof of the science labs if you hadn't arrived. Look, why don't you come and have a dram, if you've nothing better to do?' I suggested. 'I certainly need one after that.'

'Good. I hoped you were going to say that. Anyway there are a few things I've found out and you ought to know. I'll be round in a quarter of an hour.'

In fact, she took a good half hour to arrive: some domestic detail to do with her daughter had intervened. By the time she stepped through my door I was eager for a drink.

'I'd normally offer you champagne, but how about something sharper? Let me make some dry Martinis.'

'That's a very good idea. One of yours will be a most welcome pick-me-up.'

I made them after the American fashion: two thirds gin, one third Martini Secco, ice and a couple of green olives. We stirred them with a teaspoon.

Settled with our Martinis, we reflected on the awful scene. I described how Monty was nonplussed by what had happened. He could not understand why Jess had suddenly fired up. She was like a fuse suddenly lit. She had fizzed away and her main charge had been about to go off. Why then? Why at that particular time? Monty could not work it out.

Jenny had an explanation. Having soothed Jess, they had talked for quite a long time. Jess had been in confiding mood and told Jenny how uneasy she had become over the past few weeks. Indeed, her anxieties and suspicions had increased over a few months. Monty never seemed satisfied to stay at home for very long; he was always going to some meeting, or he had to go to his office. It made no difference if it was an evening during the week or any time over a weekend: he would disappear for a couple of hours, then come home but never have very much to say. Jess felt their relationship was at an end. Their closeness had evaporated and she did not understand why. Then some odd things had happened.

Once, on an early evening during the week, he had said he had to go back into school to meet a student called North to discuss some exam project. He had not been gone twenty minutes before the phone rang. It turned out to be the student, North, wanting to ask Monty some question or other. He clearly was unaware of any arranged meeting at that time with Monty. When Monty returned, Jess had wanted to know what was going on. Monty said he had made a mistake, but since he was in the office he thought he might stay for a little and prepare some experiments for the following day. The trouble with that evasion was that a friend of Jess had seen Monty and Bernie coming out of the school about an hour before he had arrived home. Jess did not like it and was highly suspicious.

On another, earlier, occasion, the same friend had seen Monty with Bernie in a coffee bar, though Monty had told Jess that he was at a local science association meeting. Both of the incidents were the culmination of a string of events that left Jess deeply worried, agitated and disturbed. It was over the last few days, though, that Monty's excuses and absences had become too unbearable to put up with. Jess reckoned that Bernie was stealing Monty from her while she was pregnant and, as it were, otherwise occupied. She was furious. She did not care who knew about it, who saw her confusion and anger; she was determined to do something about it. So, she stormed down to the school where Jenny and I had, in some fashion, come to the rescue.

It crossed my mind that Jess was only partly on the right track. Certainly Bernie was in the picture and had been with Monty on many occasions, but over the past few days, if North were as good as his word, Monty's infidelities would more likely have been with him. North, I knew, would have been increasing the pressure on Monty, as he had said he would. That would have been why North had rung Monty at home.

The electrifying North would have been impossible for Monty to resist: excuses would have been made to Jess; Monty would have taken mindless risks – he would have stretched credibility to its, and Jess's, breaking point. I was sure that North featured in the picture in a big way, but I would have to check with him to know for sure.

Jenny was convinced that Jess and Monty's marriage was in serious trouble.

'I really don't see them surviving. Monty's a fool. He has made Jess resent him too much. She feels totally betrayed. All the suspicions she has harboured for so long seem to be realized.'

'The trouble with Monty,' I said, 'is that he doesn't seem to know what he wants. He has this new emancipated view of human behaviour. He has deluded himself into thinking that he can square it with his religion. He thinks that seeing Bernie doesn't matter: it isn't important. In fact, it does and it is. It's as though he's in a hall of mirrors where his vision of reality is totally distorted. At the same time he wants to keep his wife and embryo family.'

Monty was not anchored: he was buccaneering, freebooting. He felt that it was the right thing to do because his emotions directed him that way. It was the age-old problem of his heart telling his head what to do. If you like, it was an example of Freud's theories being played out. Monty's brain, his intellect, had to dominate his actions if his marriage was to survive, and it did not look as though it was likely to happen.

'Here we are pleasantly sipping our Martinis. I wonder what poor old Monty and Jess are doing now. Sitting in sullen silence or having a flaming row? I do find your flat relaxing. It's like a safe haven in a storm-tossed sea. You're lucky to be able to retreat here. When I think of my own place, too often in domestic turmoil, I can't tell you how much I envy your serenity here.'

She did not know the extent of the black moods that sometimes visited me. My island of calm in the tempestuous sea often seemed barren, bleak, forlorn. There were times when I ached for company, a familiar presence, a consoling look. I was not going to debate the issue; she was worried enough about Monty and Jess.

'Nothing is as good as it seems,' I reminded her. 'Look, I'm sure Monty and Jess are having a terrible time. We know how it goes. They'll sort it out.'

I refreshed our drinks, we listened to Beethoven's *Archduke* trio, Opus 97 and one or two other pieces. Then she left to prepare supper for her daughter. I spent the rest of the evening writing, watching the news on television, and reading Bulgakov's *The White Guard*.

The following day I was due at the school at eleven o'clock. I led a seminar on Keats's *Hyperion* and, at lunch-time, saw Monty sitting with some of the other scientists in the canteen, which I rarely frequented because the food was so mediocre. He looked white and drawn. After I had been there for about ten minutes, North went by his table, stopped and spoke to him. Monty immediately responded, the clouds lifted from his face, and he talked at length *sotto voce* leaning away from the table so that his companions could not hear. I imagined that an assignation had been made. I reflected that North's power was awful. He could make a difference to anyone, no matter how desperate the mood they were in. I resolved to speak to North. I wanted to know if he had increased the pressure on Monty, if he had been with him more, over the past few days, and if he knew what was happening between Monty and Jess.

I quickly finished what I regarded as an apology for a lunch and followed the direction that North had taken when he left the canteen. He had headed for the sports centre. Sure enough he was chatting to one of the girls on its administrative staff. She was the trained physiotherapist who also gave massages. Many users of the centre would exercise, use the steam room, take a massage, and finally go back to the steam room before a shower. I wondered whether North was arranging an appointment with her.

He was not. As I approached I heard him talking about the

latest film release, showing at one of the city's cinemas. It seemed that he was merely making a social call. It was typical of North: he cultivated a wide circle of people. All were mesmerized by his charm. It was as though he were tempting them. Some became lovers, but to most he rarely offered any further intimacy. I regarded myself as one of the immensely favoured few.

He sensed my approach, turned and greeted me.

'Hi. I didn't talk to you in the canteen. I wanted to see if I could meet Monty later on. Shall we get some coffee?' he suggested.

We went upstairs to a small refreshment bar that served the centre. It opened out on to a balcony and a roof terrace, where there were some potted shrubs and jasmine. I bought our coffees, a café latte for him and my usual espresso, and we went out to the terrace. I remembered the Terrazza dell'Infinito at Villa Cimbrone. There was no comparison. I yearned to be back there.

I said to North, 'Oh for the Cimbrone gardens, how I wish we were there.'

'Agreed. Some day we must return. It was god-like to look down on those coastal villages from Ravello's great eminence. I felt empowered. There was nothing to stop me doing what I liked.'

'It seems there is little here to stop you. What's happening between you and Monty? I get the impression you have supplanted Bernie or, at least, are in the process of doing so. You know, incidentally, about Jess? She is in a hell of a state.'

'Yes. I know. So is Monty. I am going to see him in his office at five. I've been with him quite a lot over the past few days. I'll try to make him feel better, give him a bit of consolation. The way to his soul is via his sexual appetite. I know how to satisfy that. The exquisite moment of rapture makes him forget the present.' He added after a brief pause, just pre-empting what I was going to say, 'The trouble is that after climax he sinks back into the inevitable *tristesse*. Still, we voluptuaries know what is most important, and that is joy for the moment, the Keatsian idea of the bursting grape. *Carpe diem.*'

I was no longer astounded by North's sophistication. He no longer held any surprises for me. He talked way beyond his years. He classed me with himself as a fellow voluptuary. I was not sure about that: I wondered if he knew something about me that I did not know about myself.

'Look, Monty is not going to avoid his sadness and depression. It's all there staring at him. It's Jess. She's the personification. I begin to think you should withdraw altogether. Leave well alone. Let them recover. What do you think?'

'I couldn't do that,' he said, eyes gleaming. 'My mission wouldn't be complete. I've given up Bernie. It's much better that Monty enjoys me. Jess won't connect him with me.'

'True: it's unlikely. But how will she know that Monty is not messing around with Bernie? I predict disaster. How do you see matters developing?' As I was saying that, I wondered what he meant by his 'mission'. I had not heard him talk like that before.

'You shouldn't worry so much. It will sort itself out. It's simple: either Jess will come to terms, or she'll give up Monty. Who knows? He might be happier as a free agent now that he knows he's bisexual. I'm not even sure he's bi. He might, in the end, prefer people like me.'

I was not sure about that remark. I said, 'Come on, North. No one else is like you.' Was I deluding myself? Was North all that unusual? Perhaps I, too, was mesmerized. I was not sure. Suddenly I was not clear about anything to do with this muddle of relationships. I knew that I was beginning to distrust my own feelings, my convictions. I stopped short. I could not lose faith in myself. I could not allow North to destroy that. I had to preserve my belief in my intellect.

He smiled at me. He was amazing. His teeth were perfectly even, immaculately and icily white.

'You mean he just prefers me?' he said.

That was it. The spell was broken; the moment of doubt had gone. My self-confidence returned. I thought, yet again, how unique North was. He possessed a power which, when exerted on other people, made him irresistible. The feeling of being immensely privileged to be his confidant returned.

I replied to his question, 'I simply don't know. Anyway, it doesn't matter. As you say, it will all work itself out.'

We were looking down on some all-weather tennis courts, where there was an exceptionally good game of doubles going on. The school's first pair was holding its own against a county coach and one of my colleagues. Some impressive shots were made, exciting and closely fought rallies played. A small crowd had gathered. It was turning into an exhibition match.

North said, 'There's beginning to be too many people around here. Let's walk.'

He was never good in a crowd. I had noticed that when we went on trips. He liked to steer away from the throng. He seemed to fear for his exclusiveness; it was as if he needed to protect and preserve it.

We left the sports centre and walked along a garden that bordered the access road to the centre's entrance. Thence we crossed the road and walked in the rose garden, at the end of which the Chinese bridges spanned the tributaries and gave access to the cricket field. The roses were extravagantly gorgeous. The very faint scent of them filled the air. *Quelques Fleurs*, I thought to myself: a Houbigant perfume. No wonder we try to imitate nature. We strive for a more permanent perfume than the one we are naturally given because we regret its transience. Human counterfeiters make sure the scent lasts longer, but not too long: the interests of commerce require the product to be replaced – a profit must be made. The counterfeits, by definition, lack authenticity. We never quite capture the true essence of the original when we manufacture these ersatz concoctions. North and I talked on. I got the impression that he had written off Bernie: he had enjoyed her, but he knew that she was only one of many beautiful women he was destined to encounter; she was not at a loss – she could fend for herself. I was sure that was what he thought.

Out of the old Victorian building at the top of the garden, Aitken appeared. He hailed us.

'Hello you two. Enjoying the garden and the sunshine? Glorious, isn't it?'

'Perfect,' I remarked. 'Are you busy?'

'I'm always busy. It's the nature of the job.'

North then surprised me: he took the initiative.

'I saw Mr Ross this morning, sir. He looked very stressed. Is he all right?'

I was stunned by this direct question. Of course North knew that Monty was not all right. What was he doing? I could not work it out. He was certainly putting Aitken on the spot. As he listened to North, Aitken's composure altered. He looked concerned.

'I don't know, North. I am sorry to hear that. I shall make it my business to find out.'

I was in no doubt he would. He would be beside himself with anxiety until he had talked to Monty and discovered what the matter was. For my part, I could not wait for Aitken to leave so that I could ask North what he was doing. There was no problem there: Aitken could not wait to get away. He wanted to track down Monty, no doubt to see if he could offer some comfort.

'Well, enjoy the garden. I must get on.' Aitken hurried off towards his office.

'You were pretty direct about Monty,' I said to North. 'What are you doing? Why have you put Aitken on to the trail? It might have been better if he were left in the dark over the domestic dispute. I'm sure he doesn't want to know about Jess.'

'It wasn't Jess I was thinking about; it was Monty. I think I can do something for him. Aitken comes alive when there's any mention of Monty. I'll try to get Monty to encourage Aitken in the amorous stakes. He might even seduce Aitken. I don't suppose he needs much tempting. Once he's there, Monty's made: Aitken would do anything for him and it would give Monty a hold over Aitken. What do you reckon?'

What I reckoned was that North was a cool, calculating operator. He had swiftly seen the possibilities of that proposed liaison and was on course to exploit it. Was he serious about the possibilities of blackmail? I doubted it; but, then, perhaps I was being naïve. He had a command of strategy I could not equal.

'Well, I'm not sure. So you think you can suggest – rather, persuade – Monty into an act of sexual seduction, man-to-man, as it were? How appalling. But you're probably right.'

'I don't think it will need much persuasion,' North said. 'Remember, nothing will happen unless the parties want it to. My role is to put ideas into minds. If the pair of them like the idea, they'll get on with it. If they don't, they won't.'

I knew he was right. I also knew that the bias was there. Jenny had been one of the first to see it. As the position stood then, Aitken would seek out Monty. North would plant a seed in Monty's imagination and desire. Who was going to reach Monty first, North or Aitken? That question had occurred to North. He said, 'I had better find Monty before Aitken does. I

210

should like to put a word in his ear first. I'll try to be in touch later.' He gave my arm a pat and walked away, obviously intent, but not in a hurry. That was another thing about North, he never seemed to be unduly hurried. He had a controlled, measured, laid-back demeanour, something else I admired him for.

I went about my business. It seemed to me that affairs were accelerating towards a resolution. I hoped it would happen soon. There were now players in the game who were extremely vulnerable: Jess, Monty, Bernie, and now, possibly, Aitken. I brooded about those people, but to little effect. I eventually went home, settled in my study, took some tea, read my Bulgakov and listened to music.

North had reached Monty before Aitken, and had arranged to meet him at five that evening. He rang me towards ten to tell me that he had laid the foundations of the proposed seduction. He said that it would be difficult for him in the future, knowing that he might be sharing Monty's 'bodily delights', as he put it, with Aitken; but it had not happened yet and maybe it never would. I was not convinced. I thought that if North put his mind to making something happen, it probably would.

North said he and Monty had spent a good hour in the office undisturbed; it had been most agreeable. Monty needed physical contact. He had responded greedily. They had tempted and teased each other: advancing, retreating, delaying, each taking the lead in turn. They had had a good time. I believed him. It seemed North was an accomplished young master of the sexual arts.

It had been after they had left the office and were in the pub, where they had gone for a drink to refresh and recuperate, that North brought up the subject of Aitken's infatuation. Monty had replied that he was aware the he was attractive to Aitken.

At that point, I told North to hold on. I could not easily digest the information he was giving me over the phone.

'Look, it's ten. I'd prefer to speak to you face to face. Can't we meet? Just for a short time.'

North said he would come round. His mother was dining in one of the colleges with a friend. She would be back about eleven. Anyway she would not worry about him. I could credit that: she must have been used to the ways of her precocious son. She would not worry about his whereabouts. Anyway, he said, he would leave her a note to say that he was talking with me at my place.

Within a few minutes he was with me. We decided to have a dram of malt whisky. He told me that in the pub Monty had drunk quite a lot. He had been receptive but not eager. He accepted the contention that Aitken wanted him; the question was: did Aitken understand his own impulses? To which the answer was: probably not. It was not in his realm of experience to recognize that he might be in love with Monty. It was therefore up to Monty to point it out and to show Aitken that he, Monty, was willing and ready to proceed with the physical aspect of what was haunting Aitken. North had emphasized the advantages for Monty, although I do not think he mentioned at that stage the blackmail option – he was too careful for that. I was sure that he would bring that issue into play at some suitable later date.

In spite of what had passed that afternoon, I found it hard to believe that North had gone so far. He had lost no time. He said that he was going to work on Monty over the following few days. It would be so easy for Monty: he had a ready, receptive partner waiting for him. It was up to him. North finished by telling me that he had made Monty promise that he would continue seeing him. North was not going to let him, so to speak, out of his hands.

North's calculation was considerable. He thought his strategy was bound to succeed.

'The thing about Monty, as much as I like him, is that he fancies himself. Once he is in, he's going to have to succeed. He will see himself as irresistible to Aitken and he will behave in a way that is certain to bring Aitken on. It's a winner.'

I was not so confident but I thought the chances great. We would wait and see.

At about ten to eleven, North said he would go home. I suggested I might take some fresh air before going to bed. I would walk with him just as far as his house. The streets were dark, full of shadows. Lights were on in upstairs rooms. There was a peculiar empathy between North's mind and mine. His thoughts ran along the same tracks as mine. He remarked that he often tried to imagine what was happening behind the windows of those lit rooms at that hour of night: what sort of sex was taking place? Who knew? Who ever knows? Only those taking part in the dance of love know. How many eightsome reels might there have been? How many solitary movements? How many prancing Gay Gordons? How many sultry, slow, sensual waltzes? Each to his own imagination, North commented. I preferred not to think of it. I thought of my cat, my study, the security of my half-lit room. Yet I felt better when I knew that there was company nearby, and over the past few months I had come more and more to rely on North's.

Within minutes we had arrived at North's house, and just as we did so, a cab drew up and Francine emerged, paid the driver and, showing no surprise at seeing the two of us, cheerily said hello. She was radiantly elegant in a figure-hugging black dress, formal but daringly décolleté, and she carried a rather bizarre handbag that reminded me of Lulu Guinness's floral creations. It stood out as a curiosity, an eccentricity, against her severe black clothes. I was rather embarrassed; being there with her son late at night. Most other mothers, I think, would have been guardedly concerned. Not Francine. She accepted what her son did, without question. She trusted the company he kept. I had no need to feel awkward. I recovered and kissed her on both cheeks. She really was a lovely woman. I could sense North's amused reading of my reaction to his mother's arrival. He was obviously conscious of my attraction to her; and, if he was, surely she was too. She did not show it. A woman of her sophistication and experience knew how to manage someone like me.

Francine wanted me to go in for a nightcap. I would have liked to, but thought it better to stay no longer. I made my excuses. North embraced me, which Francine seemed not to find unusual. She was, I suppose, confident of his judgment. I marvelled at the two of them. I envied their worldliness, confidence, stability and warmth. It was only as I walked slowly back home that I remembered a certain iciness of touch and that strangely ominous glint that was occasionally to be seen in North's eyes.


By the time the following weekend had come to an end, the disposition of the pieces on the chess board in this particular game of love had shifted irreversibly. On the Thursday of that week Jess had been taken into hospital with complications to do with the position of her baby. She had to be kept under close observation. Jenny was looking after her at that point. She had been visiting her regularly, offering her the advice of an experienced mother, and acting as a sounding board for Jess's anxieties and complaints and, especially, for her resentments against Monty. Jenny told me that she had tried to persuade Jess, without much conviction, that everything would be all right when the baby was born. As I commented to Jenny, it would probably make matters worse. The birth would certainly concentrate Jess's mind and, when she had gathered strength, she would make her decision. The likelihood was that she would throw Monty out. She struck me as the sort of girl who would pack Monty's bags, roughly and clumsily, and have them delivered to the Randolph Hotel, change the locks on the doors, and retain a divorce solicitor.

For the moment, Jess was off the board, out of play, the whole of her energy committed to her child. Jenny told me that Monty had made an attempt to visit Jess in hospital, had stayed for about twenty minutes but had received a frosty reception. Naturally, that had left him time to spare over that weekend. He spent it, according to North, with him and, with North's encouragement, in pursuit of Aitken. Both of Monty's weekend activities were successful.

North told me that their time together was leisurely and delightful. He had especially enjoyed being taken back to Monty's little terraced house, where he had persuaded Monty to take him into the marital bed. What did it matter? he had argued. Jess would be none the wiser. It had happened on the Sunday morning. North told me one or two details of their time together that I prefer to forget. I try to expunge what he told me: it is too disturbing – I begin to feel myself losing my hold on normal society and I become fearful of a form of sexual anarchy taking over my accustomed world. As Lear says, 'That way madness lies'. I cannot stand the pitch and roll of emotional turbulence. I desperately need the stability of calm seas and a humdrum voyage. I asked North if Monty had been to church.

'He managed to argue himself into a position of not needing to go. He said what with Jess in hospital, the elders, or whatever they call themselves, would forgive him. He then put his head on my shoulder and bit my ear. That was it. We were in bed immediately. It's extraordinary how these born-again Christians can justify almost anything.'

I agreed with him about the ability we all have to blind ourselves to reality and reflected on the weakness of human nature.

In the late afternoon of that Sunday Monty visited Aitken. They had already seen each other on the Saturday morning, when Monty, inspired by North, had organized a meeting ostensibly to discuss re-equipment of a laboratory. As expected, Aitken was intoxicated by Monty's company. In the afternoon sunshine they walked in the garden, crossed the chinoiserie bridges, and sat for nearly an hour on a low mound on top of which grew an old walnut tree. They admired the view of Oxford's towers, the constant noise of traffic suppressed by a lovely screen of poplars. North was in no doubt that Monty's seduction of Aitken was in hand.

The following Tuesday saw me in Paris. In terms of the game that was being played out, I was reluctant to leave the board, but I had to take some time away from the school in order to meet a publisher who was interested in buying the rights of one of my books for a French edition. My agent had set up the meeting. I had told Aitken that I needed the Tuesday and the Wednesday off. He had agreed. I mischievously thought he had more pressing matters on his mind. He would not worry about my absence. He knew, in any case, that he could rely on me to cover the little teaching that I did.

I told North I was going. He was very jealous. He would

have liked to have gone with me: Paris was one of his favourite cities. He had been several times with Francine, and once they had met his father there. He saw himself as a *promeneur* of the boulevards and habitué of the Latin Quarter. I caught an early flight to Charles de Gaulle and took a transit bus into the centre. There, I hired a taxi and went to my usual hotel, a beautifully restored art deco mansion in the Latin Quarter. It was famous for its role as HQ of the Allied liberating forces at the end of the Second World War. It stood just off the Rue Saint Jacques, was comfortable, hospitable, and was in walking distance of all the places I wanted to visit. There were good restaurants in the vicinity: famous ones like the Deux Magots, and smaller, less well-known ones too. A huge up-market Upim department store, with a superb delicatessen section, was no more than fifty yards away across a square.

I checked in, smartened myself up and decided to walk into the centre where I was to meet the publisher at three in his offices on the Boulevard Haussmann. I strolled through those magical streets of that fabled city and stopped at a café for my customary espresso, and a *craquelin* that served as my lunch.

The business that afternoon went well. I liked the publisher. We had previously spoken only on the phone. There were no snags. After a call to my agent, I signed a favourable contract. I realized I could have gone back to England that evening and I felt a moment's frustration at having to stay the night in the city. I had miscalculated my time. The game developing at home was doing so without me there. The annoyance did not last. Distance from the scene inevitably lessens the apparent urgency of a situation back at home. I decided to enjoy myself. I called in at the Musée d'Orsay, returned to my hotel, drank some champagne at the bar, and then went to one of the small restaurants I know, Le Petit

Verdot. I ordered a simple but delicious supper of slices of Morteau sausage with salad. The smoked sausage tasted authentically of fir and juniper. I followed that course with a generous slice of Pithviers cake. A bottle of white Bergerac, recommended by the proprietor, accompanied those dishes. I drank almost the whole bottle. I took black coffee as a digestif and then went by taxi to Le Bilbouquet in the Rue St-Benoit where an African-American jazz group was playing. I listened to them for an hour or so and returned to the 1920s interior of my hotel room. The concerns of Jess, Monty, Bernie and Aitken were far from my mind. I thought about North. He would have liked to hear the jazz. It had been classy and polished. He and his mother went to jazz concerts in Oxford that were, at best, mediocre. They would have relished Le Bilbouquet. I was sorry they were not sharing my experiences in Paris.

That night in bed, images of North and Francine haunted me. My mind seemed to tell me that I should do something about Francine. I should make sounder approaches to her. She might be an agreeable companion, not just for an evening, but maybe for life. Perhaps she might become more than just a companion. After all, North must surely have derived some of his sexuality from her. As for North, what my dreams were trying to reveal to me was more complicated and slightly threatening. The more I pondered what was happening back home, his influence was always the dominant and important one. It occurred to me that the others would not be having the difficulties they were now experiencing had North not intervened. Had he not become involved in the complicated game of love that was going on, little that was out of the ordinary would have happened. Certainly some of the more serious, damaging consequences would not be in the offing. North was an *eminence*, at once powerful and, it seemed to me from that distance, dangerous. He

218

was not there to dispel the impression. I knew that if he were I would have banished such thoughts. His confidence would have made everything seem all right; it would have made my misgivings evaporate. His being there would have delighted me to the exclusion of any other feeling.

I was more able to be objective in North's absence. In my hotel in the middle of Paris, miles away across the Channel, surrounded by masses of strangers, foreigners, what was going on at home took on a decidedly parochial aspect. It exercised my mind, though, and would not let me sleep for some time. In that state of half-sleep before deep sleep, I kept imagining North to be like one of the fallen angels his admired Milton describes. Perhaps, like Satan, he was essentially bad, though gloriously attractive to behold. I remembered that it was this sort of powerful evil that Milton particularly warned against. He showed it at work in Paradise Lost and preached against it elsewhere. In the fantasy world of my head, I saw North as a servant of Satan, another fallen angel, who would wreak havoc in the world to the confusion and damnation of ordinary mortals.

At about midnight, I woke suddenly and recalled what I had been thinking of North. The television, which I had left on without the sound turned up, was flickering away. My interpretation of North's machinations back at home seemed ridiculous to my conscious mind. I switched off the television and went back to a calm sleep.

In the morning, the weather was magnificent. The overcast skies of the day before had given way to sunshine. I felt invigorated, both mentally and physically. Breakfast was brought up to my room: strong black coffee, hot milk, croissants, butter and various *confitures*. I showered and dressed slowly, enjoying gulps of coffee as I went along. My flight back was at midday. I decided to visit the Upim store, then walk to the Place de la Madeleine and pick up the transit bus to the airport.

* * *

My car was in one of the overnight car parks at Heathrow. It was not long after landing, not more than an hour and a half, before I was back in Oxford and reassuring my cat that I had not vanished for ever. A distinctively written note on a roughly torn piece of A4 paper lay on my floor, where it had been pushed through the letter box. I knew the handwriting: it was North's, as elegant in design as himself. It was a cursive, italic script, adjusted in form for writing at speed, presented in jet-black ink. He said he was sorry to have missed me; he had expected me to be back by the time of his call; could I ring him when I arrived.

The note intrigued me. What did he want? What developments had there been? I put my overnight bag in my bedroom, poured a whisky and soda, sat down at my desk and rang him. Francine answered the phone.

'Francine. Is North there? I've been in Paris overnight and he's left a note asking me to ring him.'

'He's not. He's just gone out. He said that if you were to phone I was to say that he would ring as soon as he gets back. What were you doing in Paris? I'm envious.'

I explained my mission to Paris and told her how much I had enjoyed the visit. I described the evening of jazz and she was even more envious. She did not seem to want to bring the conversation to a close, and her tone was warmer in address to me than it had ever been before. At one point she started using the term 'sweeting' to me. She said, 'The next time you go, sweeting, let me know and take me with you. You shouldn't be in Paris on your own. You need a chaperone.' It was a term of endearment I had not heard used before. It was old-fashioned, and when she first used it, I wondered for a moment what she had said; but she used it again and it registered with me. I was rather moved and felt much closer to her. She enticed me to describe exactly where I had been in Paris. We must have been talking for some twenty minutes when she paused and called out to North, who had come back.

'North, my love, the phone for you.' She handed it over to him.

He knew it would be me. 'Ciao,' he said. 'Good to hear you.'

He told me that while I had been away, Bernie had stepped back into the picture. Since she knew that Jess was in hospital, she had decided to lay siege to Monty. Monty was resisting and she was making a fuss. Monty had told him that she had threatened to make a public scene unless he saw her. She said she could not go on. She was, according to North, mouthing all the old clichés that thwarted lovers use: her life was not worth living, she intended to follow him around, he had to take notice of her. If he did not meet her that evening, she was going to go to Jess in hospital and tell her outright that it was she that Monty really loved. Monty could visualize a humiliating scene in the hospital and was distraught. He did not know what to do. He had made an arrangement to see Aitken at seven. They were to have a drink, supposedly to discuss Monty's career. Monty had told Jess not to expect him at the hospital until at least nine o'clock. Jess had replied that she did not care whether he turned up or not: she could not be less interested.

'This is awful,' I said. 'What can we do? What do you think about it?'

It was extraordinary. There I was asking North for his views on this huge muddle that had come about largely because of him. The previous night's meditations in the hotel bedroom had confirmed my belief that North was, in large part, responsible for the ghastly problems that existed in our small world. And, yet, I could not believe he was a malignant influence.

221

'I don't know. I tried to get Monty just now, but I think he's already gone to see Aitken. I'll track him down later, when he leaves Aitken to go to the hospital. I'd better see how things are with him and at least give him some support.'

I wondered if I should mention that, from one point of view, it could be seen that North was responsible for a great deal of unhappiness. I did not. It was too cruel. After all, I did not like to think that he intended to cause so much misery, and I could not bear the thought of upsetting him. I had never seen him upset. I would not have liked it. Anyway I did not believe he was malicious.

On reflection, it was odd that I had never seen North in a downbeat mood. He had seen me dejected and depressed. He was always the same: balanced, cheerful, never morose or difficult. The only evidence of emotion was that occasional strange sparkle in his eyes. I could not convince myself that it was significant, or, indeed, even if it had really been there. Perhaps I had imagined it.

I said to North, 'I can't see what you can do. I reckon matters will have to resolve themselves. Maybe we should leave well alone. You know my philosophy: when in doubt, do nothing.'

'You may be right, but I can't just let Monty fester; he needs me. And what about his conquest of Aitken? Nothing's going to make any difference to that. It must be happening right now.'

I quoted Khayyam, 'The Moving Finger writes; and, having writ,/ Moves on.'

'Just so,' he said. 'Anyway, enough of this. You've got to tell me about Paris. I want all the details. When can we meet?'

'I think this evening's out. Some time tomorrow. Let's arrange something in the morning at the school.'

'Good. I like it,' North exclaimed. 'Hold on, my mother wants another word.'

Francine came to the phone. 'Why don't you come round for supper one night?' she said. 'It would be nice, certainly for me and, of course, for North too.'

'I'd love to. You wouldn't prefer to go out somewhere?'

'Darling, no. I'd have great pleasure in cooking for you.'

Again, she used an endearment. I felt flattered. She was beginning to exert the same power over me that North did. She made me feel particularly special. It was as though I were being admitted to a privileged coterie.

I put down the phone and settled back in my study chair, folded my hands in a praying position and reflected on my travels and experiences of those last two days. I thought hard about North, Monty, Bernie, Jess, Aitken and, particularly, Jenny. She was the person who, more than anyone, kept me firmly in touch with reality. When I thought of her in comparison with Francine, I thought how steady, nice and reliable she was: she was a sanctuary from all the idiocies, insubstantialities, superficialities, of the world. Francine did not reassure me in that way: she was exciting, slightly dangerous, definitely sexy and, because I did not know her well, unpredictable.

Later on, I made a light supper for myself and finished my Bulgakov novel. I had intended to watch the ten o'clock news on television, but dozed. I was woken by the shrill, insistent ringing of my telephone. I looked at the time. It had just turned eleven-fifteen. North spoke from the other end of the line, 'Are you still up?'

'I am. I rather reprehensibly dozed off. I'm pretty tired,' I replied.

'Can I see you in about five minutes time on my way back home?'

'Of course. What's happened? Are you OK?'

'I'm fine,' he said, 'but there's going to be trouble. I'll tell you in a minute.'

There was no possibility of my door being shut to North. Had he wanted to talk to me at three in the morning, I would have admitted him. That was my philosophy of friendship. Nothing would have altered that.

He arrived unruffled, but his eyes shone with glimmering excitement. He had intercepted Monty and walked with him to the hospital. Monty had made progress with Aitken. He had told North that towards the end of their meeting, which had to do more with Monty's domestic disaster than anything else, they had held each other. The otherwise efficient, discreet, objective administrator had become involved emotionally, and more important than that, physically. Monty told North that Aitken had thrilled to his touch.

When Monty and North reached the hospital, Jenny was leaving. They saw her coming out of the entrance. North had retired to the shadows behind a row of ambulances. Monty and Jenny spoke for a couple of minutes and Jenny left. Monty had waited in the vestibule for North to emerge from his cover as Jenny went towards the car park. Monty was apprehensive about the visit, but North had told him it had to be made, kissed him lightly on the cheek, said he would wait. Monty had gone to the lift for the second floor.

About a quarter of an hour later, a distraught and tearful Monty had returned to the vestibule. North said that he had been patiently sitting there reading an annotated edition of *Paradise Lost, Books IX and X*. He had been concentrating on Satan's address to his benighted followers in Pandemonium, those 'Thrones, Dominations, Princedoms, Vertues, Powers'. The Prince of Darkness, 'Their mighty Chief', dwelt on how he had brought mankind to ruin: 'Him by fraud I have seduc't From his Creator'. As North had been pondering those lines, Monty had reappeared.

Apparently Jess was being treated for an overdose of

aspirin. After Jenny had gone, Jess had swallowed about fifty aspirin capsules that she had in her bag. A passing nurse had noticed her looking fearfully white and very sleepy, mumbling to herself. Two aspirin packets lay on her bed; a plastic beaker was on its side near her pillow, the little water that remained draining into the bedding. She had been wheeled away and, presumably, was having her stomach pumped. North said he comforted Monty as best he could, but Monty was convinced that the desperate situation that had developed was his fault. North had consoled him: it was not Monty's fault; Jess was unstable. She had to come to terms with what the world is like. Life develops of its own volition. North had been firm. There had been no point in deluding Monty.

North was certainly not upset. He showed no perturbation, just excitement. I thought bleakly to myself that it was as if he knew matters were coming to a head. Jess had made a gesture, a welcoming wave towards death. I remarked to North that it could have been no more than that. Where was there a safer place to take too many aspirin than in a hospital ward? It was a demonstration, a dramatic statement of extreme discontent, unhappiness. I remembered Burton's *Anatomy of Melancholy*. Perhaps the purge Jess would be subjected to in hospital care would cure her of her sickness.

'Oh dear, where do we go from here?' I said.

'I don't know,' he replied. 'I gave poor old Monty what I could by way of spiritual and physical comfort. I was rather better at the physical. You should counsel him. You'd know what to say.'

I was not sure whether North was being ironical or not. I was about to pin him down on that but he continued.

'It does make things difficult for him. He's going to be in a hell of a state in the morning. I doubt that he'll sleep much. I told him to take time out tomorrow. He said he wouldn't know what to do with himself; he would have to go to work. Anyway, he and Aitken are planning something. Tomorrow evening they are supposed to be going to a science lecture. Monty is full of contradictions: he's not going to take his eye off Aitken, no matter what Jess is up to.'

I had offered North a drink when he came in. All he had wanted was a glass of water. I put a slice of lime and some ice in it. He finished it now and said he had better get back to Francine.

'Give her my love,' I said.

Again, I thought I saw that dangerous sharp glint in his eyes.

'Why don't you two get together? You suit each other. I should think the sex would be good and I'd like you for a step-father.'

I could not understand how he could talk about his mother in that way. It went completely against my upbringing: children did not concern themselves with their parents' sexuality. It was improper: a sin against the respect due to father and mother. It sounded as though he were trying to recruit me; but, I wondered, to what?

He gripped my left hand with his right, leant his head briefly on my shoulder, patted my back and went home. I went to bed, my head full of images of Jess gasping for life, and awoke later from a vivid dream, in which I had been having sex with Francine while North, half obscured in shadows, looked on.

The following day was decisive, cataclysmic, terrible. I woke early from a disturbed sleep. I rose, made a mug of tea, and sat, half-reclining, in bed, relaxing totally. At seven I listened to the weather forecast and the news. There were the usual tales of woe from Ireland and the Middle East, two areas of the world where the devil prospered in his work. A cheering item followed. It concerned an old student of mine who became a brilliant research scientist after he left me and, earlier this year, had been awarded the Nobel prize for medicine. His laboratory had just announced that his important seminal work on genetic engineering was diversifying and going to save thousands of lives every year, especially in developing countries. I rejoiced for him and the people he worked with. When he had received the prize, he had made a speech, saying that he regarded the prize to be for everybody who worked in his lab rather than just for himself.

Looking back now on the events of that day, I find them incredible. At the time, I was caught up in the momentum. There was no interval then to stop and think how absurd, in the first place, and how appalling, in the second, things were: they just happened and had to be accepted. Maybe the gods laughed at our mortal folly: no one else did.

I arrived at the school at exactly ten o'clock. As I entered the grounds, the numerous clocks of Oxford's towers were starting to chime. The signalling of the hour goes on eccentrically for some little time since the clocks are not synchronized. This bizarre hourly concatenation of bells is part of Oxford's charm. As the first chimes struck I thought of the parade commander of the Guards regiments who must time his procession's arrival on Horse Guards Parade precisely on the struck hour at Trooping the Colour. I looked in at my tiny office and went to my seminar room. I preferred its more spacious atmosphere and its aspect overlooking the trees and towers of the city.

I spent the rest of the morning discussing two of Shakespeare's plays, *Lear* and *Hamlet*. I tried to illustrate the awesome wealth of Shakespeare's language and his unparalleled gift for imagery. We considered the compassionate Lear during the storm scenes, '… Mine enemy's dog,/ Though he had bit me, should have stood that night/Against my fire.' We argued about the black and haunting *Hamlet* that finishes in a litter of corpses, '… This fell sergeant, death,/ Is strict in his arrest.'

It was not until lunch-time that I saw any of those caught up in the circumstances that had occupied so much of my thinking over the past days. Monty, hurrying from his lab to the canteen, looked worn and tired. A science colleague stopped him and said something. Monty responded agitatedly and went quickly on his way. I saw this from the window at the top of the building, where I was closing my books and putting my papers in my case. When I descended into the courtyard, Bernie went rushing by, totally preoccupied with her own thoughts, did not see me, and headed for the canteen. I left my bag in the library and headed towards the canteen for a light lunch. When I reached the sheltered veranda I heard shouting, and then some screaming.

I had no idea what was going on but I knew there was trouble. I had never heard anything like it before. There was often noise in abundance: you cannot have nearly a hundred students at a time eating together without a high level of noise. I kept myself calm and pushed the door open. The general din of the place was dying down, and as I entered there was complete silence from the students, leaving the hysterical sound of Bernie shrieking angrily at Monty. I immediately thought to myself, poor Monty: he has two women making demands on him now, Jess and Bernie, and he is not making a success of dealing with either of them. Monty stood aghast, every so often trying to stop her shouting, putting out his hand to touch or hold her. She hit him away angrily. She was in no mood for conciliation or compromise. Of course, all the students were looking on in hideous and embarrassed silence.

Bernie's shrieked complaints were perfectly audible for all the world to hear. She did not care. She called him liar, fool and hypocrite. She said he was a seducer, weak and spineless. She let rip completely.

Monty suddenly realized that she was not going to stop, and then he, too, lost control and shouted back at her. I noticed North standing in a small group of students: they had been lining up to collect their lunches. He was watching them both carefully. He had not seen me go in. He fixed his gaze on Monty as Monty shouted at Bernie that if anyone was a seducer, it was her: she had slept with her students. I remember thinking fleetingly that it was not technically correct to use the plural: she had slept with North; I did not think she had done so with anyone else.

At that moment, Aitken pushed past me. He went up to both of them, laid his hand on Monty's arm, spoke quietly to them both. They calmed down. Monty looked embarrassed and confused. Bernie was red in the face and still seething with anger. I was aware at the same time that North had disappeared. I looked round for him but he was no longer there. I calculated he had made a tactical retreat when he heard Monty accuse Bernie of sleeping with students. I reckoned he must have been upset.

Gradually the noise returned to the canteen as Aitken, Bernie and Monty left. When they had gone, there was uproar. I left immediately. I could deal neither with the noise nor with the inane speculation which was bound to be the subject of colleagues' conversation. I decided to forego lunch and walked towards the rose garden. I went down to the Chinese bridges and stood, leaning against the balustrade, looking down into the slow-flowing water. I was lost in thought about what was going to happen to Bernie and Monty when I felt a touch on my shoulder; and there was North.

'I followed you over here. I saw you leave the canteen. What an awful scene. What do you think will happen?'

'I've no idea. Bernie and Monty, I suppose, will be suspended. It's a disaster. It couldn't be more ghastly. Are you all right? For a moment I thought you were about to feature in the shouting match. It would have been so awful if Monty in his frenzy had named you as Bernie's lover.'

'Yes. In a way ...' he said. 'I could live with it though.'

That remark was extraordinary. He was calculated, icily cold about what had happened. He saw that the public row was awful, but was unmoved by it.

'You think you could have survived naming and shaming?'

'Of course. I'm a minor player on this stage, a Prufrockian 'attendant lord'. This doesn't really concern me.'

I was amazed. Anyone who could calmly quote Eliot after what had just happened certainly stood apart from the action. At the same time, I was not convinced.

'You must be upset about Monty. He must be suffering torments. He won't know where to turn.'

'Poor Monty. He's a fool; Bernie's right. He can't stand back from himself. He'll be all right, though: he's still got Aitken. It'll take a lot for Aitken to give him up. Aitken's never had anything like Monty before. The taste of honey. He'll want a lot more. In that respect Monty's safe.'

Yet again in my relationship with North, I marvelled at his perspicuity. I would not have expected it from one so young. Yet I recognized a hardness in him, a steeliness in his judgment. I experienced again that vision of the gods laughing at our folly, and I remembered a phrase of Graham Greene's about certain people being born with a splinter of ice in their hearts.

'You might be right. I can hardly bear to watch. All I know is that Aitken is going to want me to do more here if Bernie and, maybe, Monty are suspended. That is not appealing.'

'Don't do it then. He must sort it out. You must look after yourself. You must do what you want.'

This was typical North, and I couldn't work out if he was offering this advice out of loving care for me or whether he was simply advocating selfishness. I was beginning to suspect that with him it was a matter of principle to put yourself first all the time: looking after you own interests was always paramount. Here, perhaps, was another parallel with Milton's Satan: he, too, had his close friends and confidants, his recruits and his lieutenants; he was seen to be steadfastly loyal to them up to the point where his self-interest held complete sway and, then, even those closest to him became expendable. Hitler and Roehm also came to mind. I knew that if I expressed my reservations about his character to North, he would laugh it off. He would protest that it was nonsense, that he would never let me down, never betray me. I knew without doubt that he would say that. So I never brought the subject up with him.

We watched a pair of swans that, each year, nested on the bank close to one of the Chinese bridges as they escorted their cygnets slowly up-river, against the current. Then we strolled back over the bridges to the courtyard. There were one or two groups of students standing around in conversation, but, for the most part, no one would have known that there had been a major crisis in the school. I thought of Chaucer's *sursanure*, the wound that heals over on the surface but continues to fester at the core, slowly infecting the whole body. Often in mediaeval times, it was caused by a broken-off arrowhead. The school was suffering something akin to that. I imagined the root cause to be the sharp, barbed, point of one of Cupid's arrows.

North, unperturbed, handsome, a faint scent about him of one of his mother's perfumes, looked straight into my eyes and said he would make sure to see me later. I felt a powerful warmth in that look, but at the same time I experienced a great uneasiness. It was impossible to fathom the depths of those eyes. There was a contradiction there somewhere, because I had the sense that deep, deep down inside him there was an intense coldness.

I went to give a poetry class, a revision session for any of my students who cared to turn up. When I arrived, there was quite a number and it was clear their topic of conversation was the Bernie row. I brought them back to the reality of exams and literature. We lost ourselves in the realms of Keats.

At the end of the afternoon, as I was going to leave, I met Jenny. We talked about the terrible day, and she wondered what Aitken was going to do. She pointed out that the governing body of the school was having its termly meeting at six o'clock. It was fortunate, in a sense, because Aitken was going to have to make some fundamental decisions which would need the governors' agreement. We decided to go to Café Coco. I was certainly in need of a drink. I ordered a scotch and soda, Jenny had a Campari and soda. We sat and mused. Neither of us had much to say. We were disconsolate and a little depressed.

'Jess won't know about what happened this morning,' Jenny said. 'It's just as well: it would drive her over the edge again. What an awful mess.'

'If anyone is going to tell her, it should be Monty – if she can bring herself to listen to him. I think their marriage must be at the end of the line.'

We pondered in silence. Leaning back in my seat, I said to her, 'Have you noticed that there is one person who has had a hand in all these troubled affairs and that is North. I'm not saying anything more than that. I don't think it means anything; it's just a fact. It is curious, though. I suppose it just shows that there is something basically wrong when someone so young gets mixed up in adult relationships. I don't know. Perhaps I'm talking nonsense. But it is odd.'

There I was: saying, in fact, more than I intended to. That proved to me that I was more than usually worried. Jenny agreed that North's presence was a common factor. It was as though he were an uncontrollable force exerting itself on people.

It was a glorious early evening, a perfect June summer evening. It was right in the middle of the month, the thirteenth as it happened: I remember the date because it was the day I had to make a payment to my stockbroker. I had bought some shares in a company that had just been floated on the stock-market. It was the brainchild of another of my past students, who had been in touch with me and tipped it. I had done my own research and decided that it was a good bet. I suggested to Jenny that we walked through the rose garden, down on to the cricket field and round the perimeter before separating homewards. She thought that a good idea. I settled our bill and we set off.

The air was comfortably warm and filled with different fragrances. Their intensity increases as the air grows still in the evening and the temperature drops slightly. We walked slowly. Jenny told me what she planned to do for her summer holidays. She intended to travel to the south of France, stay in a house near Andorra belonging to some old friends, and take the occasional day trip into Spain. Both her son and her daughter would join her at different times during her three weeks there. She said I was welcome to drop in for a few days if I felt like it. It was very kind. I had nothing planned and it was quite possible that her offer could be fitted in with whatever I finished up doing.

We returned towards the bridges, past the ancient, thick-trunked walnut tree on the mound that stood within the boundary of the cricket field. If a batsman struck a ball that hit it, according to local rules, he scored four runs. We crossed the bridges, stopped to watch the family of swans settling down together on the bank, and stepped towards the Victorian building at the top of the rose garden. I suggested we walked through the house. I could see at an upstairs window of Aitken's domestic wing, one of his daughters looking out. I waved to her, and then Jenny did too.

As we approached, the chairman of the board of governors shouted hello. He had parked his five series BMW, the most powerful in the range, under some trees beyond the house's terrace. We waited while he caught up with us. We went inside, down a short corridor, and turned towards where the stairs descended from Aitken's apartment into a well. Coming in through the door that led out on to the road was North. He raised his hand in salute as he saw me in the half-light of the dim corridor, and automatically switched on the ground floor lights. There, shockingly, caught as in a camera shot, in the gloom of the stair well, were Monty and Aitken. Momentarily, I saw them in intimate embrace, kissing. The image is seared on my memory to this day; and yet my view of them in that close position was no more than a glimpse, because, immediately we were upon them and the lights flooded on, they drew apart. I was in no doubt, though, that Monty and Aitken had been in the deepest of kisses, so passionate that they were virtually oblivious to anything around them. It had been the kind of kiss I had only ever seen before between man and woman. Monty's hand had been under Aitken's jacket, holding him tight. Aitken's right hand caressed Monty's head. I can see, now, Monty's hair in Aitken's fingers. I was astonished: I had never seen anything like it. It was also immediately clear that the others had seen what I had seen. I had not imagined it.

The pair steadied themselves. The chairman, Jenny and I stood not knowing what to do or say. North had come to a halt a yard or two behind us. The chairman recovered first. He came to, said to Aitken and Monty that the three of them had better go to Aitken's study. Aitken went first, then Monty. The chairman turned to Jenny and me, signalled North to step forward, and told us not to mention what we had seen to anyone at all. He then asked me to go to the room where his meeting was about to commence and tell the other governors that he would be a little late: the deputy chairman should take over. He followed Aitken and Monty upstairs.

Jenny, North and I went into the courtyard. I left them there, Jenny rather stunned, North calm and composed. He had an air of acceptance about him. What we had witnessed had happened: that was all there was to it. I said I would return to them straightaway.

I found the deputy chairman, told him of the delay, and the governors stood around drinking sherry, quite happily waiting. There was a buzz of animated conversation. I imagined what the atmosphere would be like in ten minutes time.

Jenny had recovered her composure by the time I walked back to her and North. We discussed what might happen next. I was certain that both Aitken and Monty would have to resign: there could be no way round that. The chairman was not going to risk leaving Aitken in post. Even though only four of us had borne witness to the flagrant indiscretion, the chairman, a bullish businessman and man of the world, would understand directly that there could be no second chances. It could not be left to trust that it would not happen again. Should Aitken and Monty wish to fly their colours again, it would be elsewhere. They would have to go. Jenny was more compassionate: she lacked any political sense. North agreed with me. In a matter-of-fact tone, he said it was a shame for the two of them, but it was obvious that they would have to step down.

I said to North, 'I reckon you'd better stay out of the way for the moment. You'd better go home. This is simply terrible. I can't believe it.'

'Yes, you're right. I'd better keep out of the way. I'll give you a ring a little later. What are you going to do?'

'I'll go home too,' I replied. 'I need to think quietly about all this. The implications are awful. There is no way Aitken can survive. What will happen to the school? I don't know.'

North said, 'It will either collapse in chaos and confusion or it will stumble briefly and just carry on.' He showed no emotion as he spoke but there was some degree of relish in those words. He was right; of course, and it was more likely that it would do the latter.

North turned to go. There was no farewell hug. I suddenly felt great compassion for him, caught up in all this turmoil. He said, 'I'll talk to you later. You'll be there, won't you?'

There was just a trace of anxiety in his voice. It was the first time I had ever detected that in him. On the other hand, he could simply have been pinning me down. I reassured him, 'Yes, I'll be there.' He went away.

I walked with Jenny to her car, in silence. We saw, across the courtyard, the chairman hurrying to the meeting. He had a strong, determined face under gently silvering hair. He was like a good politician, firm, unwavering, full of his own self-esteem. He was about to go before the rest of the governors and exercise unequivocal leadership.

I opened the door of Jenny's car for her and we stood talking for a while. Jenny could not understand how Aitken and Monty could have been so foolish as to risk behaving as they did on site, in a place that was only semi-private. I explained that love and passion know no bounds: I reminded her that love is blind; it certainly brings with it an inability to see things as they really are. Thus does love make fools of us all unless we are wary, constantly vigilant.

I replayed in my mind the scene, clear and bright, as North had switched on the light. It suddenly occurred to me that there was something strange about it. It was North's presence at that particular time. Why had he appeared when he had? What was he doing there? I could think of no reason why he should have been in the building at that time. No doubt, if I asked him, he would have produced a plausible explanation: he had seen us in the rose garden and was coming to see me because he wanted to talk to me – something like that. I would, of course, have believed him. And yet, there was a nagging doubt in my mind, a suspicion that he was there for some other reason that I would never know. I said to Jenny, 'Don't you think it odd that North turned up when he did? I was thinking that he's always there in the background when something terrible happens. When you think of it, he was there when Bernie had hysterics in the canteen. Now, he is involved again. I don't mean involved, except in the widest sense, but there he was, instrumental in a way in Aitken's and Monty's downfall. There's no denying that.'

Jenny agreed. It was odd, but she did not give the matter any weight.

'Well, there you are,' I said. 'I can't explain it, but he does seem to be present at most disasters.'

'I shan't be doing any work tonight,' Jenny said. 'I'm going to go home and totally relax. Or, at least, try to. It's been far too much.'

I took Jenny's bag as she got in her car, then gave it to her as she settled in to the driving seat. I grasped her hand briefly and she drove off home.

My journey home was a daze. I operated on autopilot. My mind was occupied solely with thoughts of what had happened and what was going to happen. I barely remember the drive home, so absorbed was I in my thoughts about the key players in the love game that seemed to be nearing a destructive end. Bernie, Monty, Aitken, even Jess, all seemed to have taken leave of their senses. Philosophically I reflected that it was to be expected: love is madness, madness love. I remembered what one of Dickens's daughters had said when he became besotted with Ellen Ternan, 'It was as if my father had suddenly gone mad'. Just so.

My cat crouched on my doorstep. As I approached, he raised himself, stretched, arched his back and pointed his tail straight up in the air. Silhouetted against the white door, he resembled the archetypal witch's cat. We went in. I had a bottle of Krug in the fridge. It was no time for celebration, but I reasoned that a glass or two would give me a lift. I eased the cork and poured a generous amount into a *flute*. I played a CD of Albinoni's Oboe Concerti, Opus 9. Nothing, neither the champagne nor the music, calmed my soul. Towards eight o'clock I ate some anchovy fillets and brown bread with some asparagus spears I seethed in a saucepan. The salty sharpness of the anchovies went well with the champagne.

About nine, Jenny rang. She had bad news. Bernie's flatmate had grown increasingly worried during the afternoon, following a call from Bernie on her mobile. She had returned to the flat to find Bernie in a completely paranoid state and so had rung Bernie's mother, who had driven down immediately from near Stratford. On her mother's arrival, Bernie had collapsed completely. The GP had been called and, in the end, Bernie had been temporarily admitted into the local psychiatric hospital. Bernie's mother was still there with her. I thought things could not get much worse.

Jenny and I tried desperately to be cheerful and optimistic, but each of us knew that the other was simply putting on a brave face.

Soon after I had spoken with Jenny, North rang, as he had said he would. I told him about Bernie, but he already knew. He had been in touch with Monty. Monty had told him

(Bernie's flatmate had earlier phoned Monty with the news). Monty had also said that both he and Aitken were suspended; Aitken's deputy had taken over. The chairman had told Monty not to go near the school. Monty told North that he was packing some of his belongings and was going to Cambridge to stay with some friends. He did not know what was going to happen in the immediate or in the long-term future.

There was an unfamiliar edge to North's voice. I could not work out whether it was nervousness or a new reserve that he had adopted. I asked him if he was all right. He recovered himself. He must have realized that he was showing signs of worry or disturbance which were obvious to me and he did not want to do that. He said he was fine.

'I'm going to go for a walk,' he said. 'Why don't you join me? It would do us good.' He took the lead again. It was the old North.

'I'm not sure,' I replied. 'Where will you make for? I might catch up with you.'

'OK. That's a good idea. I'll be in Radcliffe Square by St Mary's between ten o'clock and ten past. Come on. Do come. I want to see you.'

Again North was consciously and purposely seducing me to his will; he knew I would not refuse him. I would have responded to such a request from anyone I knew well and he knew it. He knew I would go to him.

'Yes. If I go out, I'll meet you. Otherwise ring me in the morning before you set out.'

'Fine; but I want to see you later on.'

Left to myself, I could not think. My mind, in turmoil, had lost its capacity to make sense of anything. I began to see the handsome, beautiful North as a dark, malign figure, someone who had played a constructive part in several downfalls and was always present when the crisis came. There was hardly any denying that. He seemed to have directed and choreographed catastrophes. Jess was recovering from a suicide attempt; Bernie was in a mental hospital; Aitken and Monty had been suspended. Yet I still could not seriously believe he had intended to be such a bad, destructive influence. I dismissed ideas of the supernatural, they were not for me. I was not in any way superstitious, and the paranormal was, for me, mumbo-jumbo. I decided I had better go for a walk. I could meet North. I could talk to him, ask him what he was thinking about those tragedies.

I left the house about ten past nine and returned around eleven. Oxford's slow bells sounded as I was closing my door. I had not met North. I had been in a terrible state: confusion, indecision, too many thoughts rushing through my mind. I walked to clear my thoughts. I hoped the walk would be a means of expurgation. North, I knew, would not mind me failing to meet him: he would understand when I told him my state of mind. In the meantime, he would think I had decided to stay in. I told myself I would see him the following morning.

Even now, I am not sure where I went that night. I know I set out towards the town centre. I walked into the Woodstock Road, and I remember passing the Oratorian church of St Aloysius. Then it is a blank. I have always said that my best thinking is done when I am alone and on one of my long walks, and on this occasion my brain was in overdrive. As I walked, matters sorted themselves out, issues became clearer. I understood things – causes, implications, outcomes – that had been obscure before. I returned home thinking that decisive action was necessary. Somewhere and at some time on that walk, I knew that I had made a decision about the need for drastic measures. The trouble was that, rather like a dream that cannot be recalled on waking, I could not, as I sat down in my study, remember where I had been or what I had decided. My cat lay like a sphinx on my desk and purred loudly. I stroked his head and tried to remember what action it was that I had decided to take.

I rose from my chair, paced round my room, poured a dram of whisky for a nightcap. I would not worry: I was in a mental cul-de-sac. I would simply go to bed, settle and sleep. In the morning I would remember what I had thought I should do.

At about ten past midnight I went into my bedroom and drew back the duvet on my bed. I needed to sleep: I could no longer focus my mind – it flitted between one thought and another non-stop, a flow of free-association images racing along, like the closing pages of Joyce's *Ulysses*.

As I went into the bathroom to wash and to clean my teeth, the doorbell rang. Immediately, I thought that it would be North. He would have been unable to sleep, and, most probably after talking to his mother, he would have walked round to see me. He would have known that I was likely still to be up. He would be able to see if my lights were on; he would want to know why I had not met him in Radcliffe Square.

I put down my toothbrush, went to the door and opened it, expecting to see North standing there with his habitual, faint smile of greeting. What I saw was a man, aged about thirty in a rather worn suit, and a policeman in uniform. They wanted to talk to me. Mystified, I asked them in.

The man in the suit introduced himself as a CID detective and showed me his identification. He said that he understood that I knew North and that North had been used to seeing me often. I told him that was so and, naturally, asked why he wanted me to verify that information. And then he told me ... North was dead.

I was utterly shocked. I froze. For a short time I could not speak, perhaps for as long as two or three minutes. The detective told me to sit down and I did so, on a sofa. Immediately, I felt awkward, uncomfortable, handicapped. I stood up again. I said I could not believe it. Was he sure? How did he know? North, dead? I made one of those idiotic statements that are uttered on such occasions, that it could not be right because I had spoken to him on the telephone earlier in the evening. We always choose to forget that *Pallida mors* does not have to give notice and makes no distinction when he kicks down the doors of hovels and palaces. The detective repeated that it was true. North had died, probably some time between ten and eleven o'clock.

'How did he die?' I asked. 'Where was he?'

'He fell. It appears that he somehow got to the top of Magdalen Tower. He fell from the top to the small quad below, where there are sculptures.'

'What was he doing there?' I could not think of anything else to say. Again, it was a stupid question. Why should the detective have been able to answer that? I added, 'When he rang me, he suggested we meet. I might have been able to stop him. I could have talked to him.' I was close to tears. I could feel my eyes watering.

The detective said, 'We think so far, that it's a case of suicide. You think so too, sir. Why do you think that?'

It was then that I could not stop the tears. I had difficulty seeing properly. I said, 'I don't necessarily; but my first thought is that it must be. Or maybe it was accidental. I don't think anyone would want to push him.' I paused. 'I simply don't know.'

I sat down again and wiped my eyes with my handkerchief. The detective said, 'It was his mother who wanted us to come and tell you. She said you should know straight away as a close friend of the family.' I was very moved and even more saddened. Francine saw me as a close friend of North and, evidently, of her too. I was not too upset to see that what she had

242

said to the police did not add up: I was not a close friend of hers.

'Thank you,' I said. 'I cannot take it in. Can I see him? I cannot bear the thought of never seeing him again. He was so extraordinary, so original.'

'I don't think you'll be allowed, sir. He was too badly injured to be presentable. They haven't even allowed his mother to see him.'

'I must see Francine – that's his mother – as soon as possible. She must be completely distraught. Where is she now?'

'She's with a policewoman at the moment, sir. A friend of hers is driving up from London to be with her. The policewoman will stay until she arrives. If I were you, sir, I'd see her in the morning. She'll need a lot of support.'

'How simply awful,' I said, half to myself. 'I'll see her first thing.'

'We'll let you get to bed, sir. We'll have to interview you again, and I'll have to take a statement. We'll need to know where you were between about nine and eleven, but that can wait until tomorrow. Try to get some sleep, sir. I know it'll be difficult.'

I let them out and returned to my study.

I pictured North's badly damaged body. I had once before seen a corpse that had fallen from a great height. It had been in Cyprus during my military service. Someone we knew to be an EOKA terrorist had been found in Nicosia at the foot of a tall apartment block. He had been defenestrated. His remains were a complete mess, a split and bloodied bag of broken bones. His face was unrecognizable. How could North have ended like that. I paced around my study, completely dazed, hardly able to see through my tears.

The natural instinct is to convince yourself that the tragedy never happened. Yet I could not deny to myself that the policemen had been there minutes before. It was a fact. The policemen's presence had been no hoax. It did not stop my ringing Jenny. I could not think of anyone else to talk to. Somehow I felt that I could not speak to Francine: it would have been too awful. I did not know if Jenny had heard the news; but she had. The college secretary, a friend of hers, had been in touch and told her of the terrible accident: she had wanted to know what the victim, that strange boy, was like. Jenny was too shocked to tell her.

Jenny had thought about ringing me but had decided to wait until the morning. It helped me to talk to Jenny. She was someone I could be completely open with; she appreciated the depth of my grief. We reflected on the chaos that surrounded North: at least all that was going to stop. It was a cold, dispassionate way of looking at his life, his presence, his involvement in our lives, but it was true. He had become central to the way I led my life; but he was no longer there. I could not delude myself that his death was not true: Jenny had confirmed what the police had told me.

We agreed to meet in the morning. I returned to pacing my rooms. In my imagination, I saw clearly the small quad between the tower and the lodge. It had recently been turned into a sculpture garden, beautifully laid out, full of light and deep shadows created by the huge flood lamps that illuminated the tower. There were some topiaried shrubs in pots scattered among the sculptures. I saw with relentless clarity North's corpse lying beneath the famous statue of the risen Christ and Mary Magdalen by David Wynne, Christ's hands uplifted above his head in a forgiving but triumphal prayer-like gesture. His figurative style partly mimics the emaciated presentations of Giacometti: tall, thin, elegant. I saw North lying shattered beneath the arms of Wynne's Jesus and Mary.

I sat at my desk and, in a sudden, lucid flash of inspiration

I saw what it all meant. My fanciful imagination gave me an interpretation, an explanation. North was the fallen angel, still angelic but evil. His influence had, in my final, crazy analysis, been malign. Now at the end, he was twice-fallen: the great tower had facilitated his second fall. Wynne's sublime statue, symbolizing the victory of the living redeemer Christ over mankind's sins, looked down in compassion and forgiveness on God the Father's beautiful but corrupted angel.

My cat, my familiar, jumped on to my desk, arched its back and then rubbed itself against my arm. My elbows were on the desk-top, my head in my hands. He pushed insistently against my arm. His demand for attention brought me back to myself, and I dismissed as fantasy what I had just been thinking. Such thoughts had little to do with reality.

I went to bed.

I had a disturbed night, haunted by vivid dreams. Although I had discounted my wild theories of North and the Devil, I dreamed of North as a latter-day embodiment of Satan, the fallen Lucifer. I awoke, tried to rationalize my thoughts, went back to sleep and dreamed again. I was possessed. North featured on the cinema screen of my mind as the damaged archangel. God's inevitable, certain justice had caught up with him in the small quad of the College.

When I finally woke up again and decided that I should get up because there was no point in lying there suffering mental torment, I thought of the Psalmist's words: 'Let a sudden destruction come upon him unawares, and his net, that he hath laid privily, catch himself: that he may fall into his own mischief.' North's fate fitted with his sentiment. North was gone: he was dead. The sun flooded in through my study window.

I would never see North again. I could not even see him dead. I was overcome by an infinite sadness; I sighed to the very depths of my soul.

What had happened to him in those lonely moments when he stood at the top of that tower? If he had thrown himself over, what had he been thinking? Did he give a thought to me? Did he think of Francine? What desolation of spirit must he have felt?

I knew that the police would wonder how he gained entrance to the College, but the students had ways of getting in. The tower might have been left unlocked, but, in any case, some students no doubt possessed a key to the door, counterfeited for some celebratory reason or another and handed down from one generation of students to the next. The fact of North's presence in the tower was not problematic: the police would discover in no time at all how he managed to get himself there. Yet I still could not convince myself, as I made some strong coffee, that he would have committed suicide. North was too confident of himself. He was always in control. If anyone knew him, I did. He confided in me. He could not have killed himself. In which case, someone had decided that the world would be better off without him. Someone had taken him to the top of that tower and effected his fall. He was a great romantic: perhaps he had suggested to someone he had met that night that they go to the tower and look down on sleepy Oxford. Did he have a romantic tryst that went wrong? Did his lover, at the end of a close embrace, push him over the parapet? Had that lover lured him, like some mafioso, to the top and, having lulled him into a benign state, administered the *coup de grâce*?

As I sipped my black coffee, the temples of my head throbbed. I remembered the last thing I had said to North on the previous evening: I told him to ring me before he set out in the morning, if we had not managed to meet the night before.

He had replied, the last words I had heard him utter, 'Fine; but I want to see you later on.' I wanted him to ring me now. I was desolated. He would never be with me again. Now, he could not ring; he was dead. I thought of the last time I saw him alive. It was difficult; there was a blank in my memory where the image should have been: I could not pin the occasion down.

What did endure was the sensation of his embrace, the power and competence he transmitted, and the memory of those deep, dark blue eyes. What lived on to disturb me was the glittering, diamond-hardness that I had sometimes glimpsed in those eyes. The hidden secret of North's soul I would never know.

Visit **www.panmacmillan.com** to read more about all our books and to buy them. You will also find features, author interviews and news of any author events, and you can sign up for e-newsletters so that you're always first to hear about our new releases.

# www.panmacmillan.com

GIFT SELECTOR
YOUR ACCOUNT
WISH LIST
WAITING LIST

HOME | ABOUT US | IMPRINTS | TRADE/MEDIA | CONTACT US | ADVANCED SEARCH | SEARCH | GO

BOOK CATEGORIES | WHAT'S NEW | AUTHORS/ILLUSTRATORS | BESTSELLERS | READING GROUPS

**Coming Soon...**

**Reading Groups**

**Competitions**
Feeling Lucky?

**Extracts**
Sneak Previews

**Interviews**

**Events**
Meet Our Stars

**Reviews**
What The Critics Say

**News & Awards**

**Editor's Choice**
What We're Reading